SIMON JACOBS

Palaces

a novel

Two Dollar Radio
Books too loud to Ignore

Two Dollar Radio
Books too loud to Ignore

WHO WE ARE Two Dollar Radio is a family-run outfit dedicated to reaffirming the cultural and artistic spirit of the publishing industry. We aim to do this by presenting bold works of literary merit, each book, individually and collectively, providing a sonic progression that we believe to be too loud to ignore.

TWODOLLARRADIO.com

Proudly based in
Columbus
OHIO

 @TwoDollarRadio

@TwoDollarRadio

/TwoDollarRadio

All Rights Reserved   COPYRIGHT→ © 2018 BY SIMON JACOBS

ISBN→ 978-1-937512-67-5   Library of Congress Control Number available upon request.

SOME RECOMMENDED LOCATIONS FOR READING *PALACES*: Alone in a borrowed bed; your friend's basement; the free verse section in Patti Smith's cover of "Smells Like Teen Spirit," repeated ad infinitum; an empty beach after dark; pretty much anywhere because books are portable and the perfect technology!

AUTHOR PHOTOGRAPH→
Courtesy of the author

COVER DESIGN→
by Two Dollar Radio

For John Baren, wherever you are

Palaces

"And who are *these?*" said the Queen, pointing to the three gardeners who were lying round the rose-tree; for, you see, as they were lying on their faces, and the pattern on their backs was the same as the rest of the pack, she could not tell whether they were gardeners, or soldiers, or courtiers, or three of her own children.

—Lewis Carroll

I.
RICHMOND, INDIANA

THE VERGE OF DECEMBER: OUT BACK, AFTER THE show, a late-high school kid native to this town with his ears stretched to the size of clementines, Casey, shrieks and skips back and forth in the middle distance, just slowly and deliberately enough to let each firecracker hit him.

Beyond, skies like you don't see except in the middle of flat states like Indiana, where the only visible landscape—here, the tops of distant pine trees—is too far back to seem like real life, to be taken seriously, and this kid flickering up from below, a giggling blot on the horizon.

A buddy of yours, I think the frenetic banjo player, offers me a firecracker in the spirit of camaraderie, of inviting a stranger into their midst. "John, right?" he says. I don't like that he knows my name, that he got it from elsewhere. I hold the firecracker in my hands like a priceless flute.

"Y'all just pull it," he says. The Southern accent is fake.

Instead, I pass it off to you, unfamiliar at this point but standing incidentally beside me, a presence I haven't fully processed yet, and shove my hands into my pockets. You take it like a favor and, with a practiced hand, fire away.

It cracks out of your fingers and hits Casey's bright red leather jacket in a splash of tiny sparks—he yelps and stumbles to the side, the frosted grass crunching beneath his feet. Someone calls out: "Make him dance!"

We watch the display of loud, harmless explosions as your friends let loose, all the ostensible rage and frenzy from an hour before now dispersed into something that seems almost quaint and wholesome, edging on nostalgia. I stand stock-still and feel sweat trickling down my sides, starting and starting.

From that night on, we never stopped running.

II.
MANHATTOSI

A YEAR AND A HALF LATER, IN A CITY TO THE
northeast, you catch me easing out the entrance of the museum with my arms wrapped around a human-sized, 17th-century
Japanese vase painted in pink and white flowers. It's early summer and the heat is already trippy and oppressive; we're awash in
sweat and the new thrill of finally having a home base to return
to, a domestic excuse for acquiring this artifact.

I'm about to topple from the weight, but suddenly you're on
the stone steps in front of me, skimming your hands over the
glossy surface and running through your knowledge of lotus
petals and cherry blossoms, the most symbolic of all flowers. I'm staring at the blackening tips of your fingernails, your
scalp—the feathery ridge in the center, its tips barely clinging to
color, the uneven fuzziness creeping in around it—and thinking
about haircuts, about matters of personal hygiene, about show-
ering using a sink.

"This vase is super heady," you say. You point to a cherry
blossom. "Transience"—dragging your finger along a painted
whorl toward a lotus—"to resurrection."

I tell you, distractedly, in the manner of filling conversational
space, that the pattern of flowers reminds me of a fourteen-
year-old's idea for a sleeve tattoo, and it takes a second for me
to remember that's basically the design your brother who died in

Iraq a year ago had on his arm, and that I'd picked this vase out, specifically, as a sort of memorial to him. I'd stood examining it in the empty gallery, certain that it reminded me of someone close to you, of death experienced at a distance. I remembered, and then promptly forgot.

To divert you from my blunder, I motion with my foot at a passing fashion disaster on the sidewalk, a skulking guy with a massive hiker's backpack and crooked horizontal stripes shaved across his head, whose remaining hair looks like "the world's worst corn maze." It's enough, and your reaction is bigger than I expect—a full-bodied, guttural laugh and half-collapse, you actually slap your knee, while the vase slips beneath my sweaty fingers—such that it, too, feels like overcompensating to fill polluted space. The man rounds the corner with his spoils, and we negotiate the remaining stairs with ours.

It takes over two hours to get the vase back to our building, and a superhuman effort to haul it from the basement to the third floor, the sounds of our struggle magnified through the stairwell and across the spaces between neighboring buildings, but the whole way no one says anything to us, no one asks about its provenance. That night, when we always pose the most sensitive questions, when we're wrapped in our individual sleeping bags on the dusty floor like two little cocoons in the big big city, staring up at the crumbling ceiling cast by borrowed light through the empty windows, you ask if I took the vase—out of everything else available and still intact—because it reminded me of something.

It's the perfect time to mention your brother or, more broadly, willpower itself—the reason we're lying on this floor, the way we arrived here in the city—to bring up what we're both denying. Instead, I reach over and brush a swoop of stray hawk from your forehead and say something about our derelict space needing an "aspect of Japan," but it's a non-sequitur like my Mia Farrow tattoo is a non-sequitur—thematically distinct from the objects around it. I say pointlessly, reiterating, though I've never been there, "It reminds me of Japan." I say nothing about your hair.

*

Our last year in college, just after we moved together as a couple into the only apartment for which we ever paid rent, back in Richmond, on our first night we sat face-to-face on the second-hand couch and screamed at each other, the taped-up boxes and garbage bags and implements of our moving arrayed around us: no words, just long, sustained howls, repeated at different pitches and escalating volume until we both went hoarse. Your voice gave first—before our new neighbors started banging on the wall—but not by much. Like many of the gestures we made during that time, it recalled an animal claim about ownership, served as a marker of something (a living situation, a pair-bond) that we thought of as potentially permanent, despite the month-to-month lease and translucent white paint on the walls that hid no history, all of seven months between us and rival human life on every side. When I decided where to position the Japanese vase (which ended up being directly in the center of the living room, or what had once been the living room), you eyed it from the doorway to the stairwell like the presence of any furniture at all was an imposition, then took a running start and slammed into it just to prove the vase wouldn't topple, that it could take the weight we gave it.

In this new space, our aspiration is to the appearance of abandonment. To the police, the urban adventurer, anyone else who ignored the weathered surveillance placards and bolted door and made their way to the third floor of this building, the vase would register as a solitary, unwieldy piece of decoration left behind by the previous occupants when they moved on, a token bit of randomness, like the single pristine stuffed animal unearthed from a demolished office complex, a sign that some-one had once cared. It wouldn't betray us.

I'd looked forward to the anonymity of the city, its famous capacity for disappearance. The size really was beyond belief, and in the macro sense, true, I could die virtually without impact, but the promise felt unfulfilled—I hadn't been able to vanish in the way that I wanted. The first time I rode the subway alone I'd felt noted and itemized, broken into parts; whenever I raised my eyes above my lap I'd seen the man across from me staring beneath his cap, and I sat there caught in a confused mess of acknowledgment, reading menace everywhere, wondering what the problem was, if I exhibited some kind of aberrance I didn't recognize or had unknowingly breached a fundamental social contract between us, between me and this stranger, these strang-ers. I felt a tingling sensation pass from one extremity to the next, as if awaiting sudden blood flow, for a visible wound to re-open. I grew all at once more uncomfortable than I had with any cop. I crossed and uncrossed my legs. I watched his shoe—more of a workboot—but couldn't raise myself any higher. He got off the train at the same stop I did, and I dawdled until he moved off ahead. A part of it was obvious and all too familiar—we'd been fashioning ourselves to look like outcasts since long before we knew each other—but this was supposed to be different.

There was something between us and the city that didn't take. The facade of urban life was crumbling by the time we arrived, certain institutions had broken open for the taking, and as soon as we stepped off the bus, briefed in nothing, your empty car sitting in a lot X states away, we knew there was no way we were going to live according to someone else's formula. The vase, an ancient object from a past entirely separate to ours, was as good a marker as a door. We entered and exited at will.

I'm someplace downtown, far from home, when I'm turned out again, sent blinking into the sunlight like someone who's never seen it. I'm still learning to recognize the places that are patrolled versus those that are now left empty, but this one I entered on purpose, because the building positively bled luxury—stone beasts out front, deco columns into infinity, factory-level air conditioning you could feel from the street whenever the motion-activated doors slid open—and I was curious to see how deep I could go. In fact, I hadn't even crossed to the bone-colored elevator bay when someone was following me, was communicating via earpiece, was putting his hand on my arm and leading me back to the street.

The stifling summer air hits me full-force, and a feverish dizziness rushes through my body at the sudden temperature shift. Behind me, the guard returns invisibly to his post. Before me, the rest of the day uncoils, filled with unspecified activity. We've been in the city for just over a month, the apartment for the last two weeks, and I still have no idea where anything is relative to anything else. I consider retreating to our building and waiting for you, but when I linger there for too long by myself the disrepair and lack of functionality starts to eat at me, as does my inability to address it, and our situation dissolves into an unstable mess of contradictory, half-assed morals, something we wrote too large too quickly, a '90s squatter myth we were doing wrong. Our departure has felt like a given since before we arrived, since I reached into my backpack on the bus and realized I'd never owned a pocketknife.

A sickening wind blows across the city, and with it the unmistakable smell of baking garbage. The sidewalk is swarming. I watch the people dividing into pairs. A wasted kid in baggy tan clothes activates as a handsomely dressed young woman carrying black paper bags nears him. She pauses when he speaks to her and looks confused, tilting her head minutely, politely forward, like she can't quite make out what he's saying. I walk past them. After a minute she cuts him off and takes a few steps away in the other direction; he follows. She speeds up a little, quivering on her thick heels, and he matches her pace, continuing to talk while blocking her off, reaching one hand in front of her like, *You haven't decided where you're going.* I will them to separate, for the crowd to funnel in and redistribute them far apart, but they're quickly lost in the traffic. I imagine how much our circumstances would have to change for us to switch positions, me with this kid, this woman.

Along the sidewalk, a placid stream of milky-colored water stagnates in the gutter—the summer must be the worst season. I pass a high-end lingerie store advertising scandalous underwear. A bare mattress lies discarded on the side of the street. I consider it theoretically, as a fixture in someone's home somewhere in the past, sustaining their impact daily, now lobbed out among the populace. I'm amazed by how instantaneously everything can turn to funhouse-like squalor. I could close my eyes, open them, and everything would be different.

A spanging couple is camped under an awning with a sleeping dog and a cardboard sign offering hugs. The dog looks like a prop. I raise my hand to my face as I walk past, really my stretched earlobe, our visual match. I can't tell if they acknowledge me.

When they're out of sight, I close my eyes, and take eight steps in the dark. The experience is extremely disorienting, but in a pleasantly weightless way, especially when I don't immediately collide with anyone. It's liberating to think that, if I make myself willfully blind, people will make the effort to steer clear. I open my eyes, and voila, it's you, ten feet ahead, walking with your back to me.

You're dressed in the type of outfit I haven't seen since the months just after we met, clothes I didn't even realize you'd brought to the city: Converse, skinny jeans, a studded belt, and patched leather jacket (ridiculous in the heat), hair combed off to one side, glared by the shaved parts in the sun (mohawk at rest). It strikes me as gratuitous, this ensemble and its impeccable presentation, like a tailored denial of where I thought we stood, of the austerity to which we aspired. A kernel of resentment forms. A cop passes by my left shoulder, spares you a long look. I wonder why you chose today to trot it out—that's the phrase I use in my head, "trot it out," like goods on display—and from this distance, the whole of you, your posture looks different: I notice the way you take each step with just an instant of deliberation, a crackling bounce, as if the shoes are brand new and you're still settling into them, as if this is the first day out in your new disguise. It's strange to assess under these conditions, like you're the subject of some basic surveillance, like I'm just one among the many, but, apart and unnoticed, this is what I do. Perversely, I feel like I'm the one being checked up on, like I couldn't be trusted to take this neighborhood on my own, to reliably pass on the data. I follow you at a distance; I get caught up in it, crouch a little like the caricature of a detective, turn it into a game between me and your obliviousness to my presence.

It's unclear how long I keep following after I realize the woman ahead isn't you. Surely, we draw parallel long after I understand that the bearing, the accessories aren't yours at all. I pick up my pace on the sidewalk, crossing against a light ahead of her, now making directly for the subway but without a specific destination in mind. Just in front of me, a couple approximately our age walks holding hands. As I pass them, I lightly squeeze her free hand and then let it go—a glancing touch, noticeable but unmentioned. It's a small betrayal, an act of revenge for your absence, for my own misplaced recognition.

Underground, the train is packed enough that I'm still sweating like crazy, despite the air conditioning. I collapse into an empty space on the bench. The people to either side of me shift, and I worry that I'm starting to get that smell, the smell of days spent sweating through the same clothes. At the next stop, the center of the car clears out and I notice that the family sitting across from me—an entire family! mother, father, little boy and girl—are wearing surgical face masks, and all I can think to myself is *Finally*.

Three stops later—the family gone now, the car emptying—the train stalls at the station. The doors hang open. After a few minutes, I notice there's commotion in the car behind us. I hear shouting. I look through the window behind me and see people spilling out of the train onto the platform. The conductor comes on over the speakers: "Ladies and gentlemen, we apologize for the delay. A child has been left on the train."

I stand abruptly and exit the car, an odd ache in my chest. I walk up the platform beside the train, past a ring of onlookers and transit officials with their hands at their hips, clustered around this narrative of abandonment, guilt passing from face to face as the responsibility is shifted from one person to the next, as their humanity is tested. I'm surprised to find myself walking again beside the woman from the street above, who looks like old you. Other than the concerned crowd at one end, the station isn't busy, and I walk approximately behind her for most of the length of the train, still paused. Inside, at every car, every open door, there's a man standing: one by one, I watch each of them turn their heads to watch her, as if connected on a series of tripwires or pulled by something beyond their control, each taking a piece. The doors slide closed at last, and a final face rotates in the window, observing from a tank. The train barrels out of the station. Far behind me, the gathered crowd disperses, nothing at its center. I imagine the tunnel filled with water, the eyes drowned and blank. We walk up the stairs, the tiled walls punctuated with posters of missing people.

A mild panic of disorientation takes me at the corner on the street above, having exited at a stop I don't recognize, the traffic insistent in all four directions. The past version of you moves off with authority, and for a second—for the moment where I see just the top of her hair in the crowd—an old impulse nudges me to intervene. She disappears, and my recognition spreads to the rest of the street, skewed younger, toward my generation. Shifting from one face to another, I make inadvertent eye contact with a blonde girl, broadly familiar. I break it; the way I let my eyes fall to the ground, skittering over her body, makes it feel as though I've regressed by years, like I'll have to start all the way over, to re-teach myself how not to make these judgments. I blur my eyes until they—her and everyone—become teeming, indistinct shapes, straining as hard as possible to black out my gaze.

When I described my first subway encounter to you later, the staring man, you looked at me incredulously, like I knew nothing: these experiences had been your whole life. "What decade do you live in? Are you an ascetic?" you said. "It's a body. We're all being watched. Have you ever considered the use of lipstick? It's basically a bullseye for your cock." It was declarations like these—combative, associatively broad but unequivocal—that had drawn us together, had tonally linked us, and around us had built a wall against the world.

Three hours after someone's child disappears underground we reconnoiter at the apartment, new and disparate parts of the city poorly configured in our heads: today, you've been to the west, to slaughterhouses converted in recent decades to boutiques and gourmet dining. We fuck against the vase, our hands on its sides like a third party, a coolant wherever we touch it. Your breath fogs up the porcelain. I watch your fingers clench on its surface, tensing and unbending, the wrinkles flexed open at each joint, like bright wounds among the encroaching dirt gray. I've been to the library downtown, making use of the public bathrooms and reading up on the vase's origins and those of its kind, trying to put together what I didn't take from the plaque on the gallery wall. I whisper "Satsuma" in your ear, like an exhalation, a new word that's not your name but is actually a Japanese pottery style tailor-made for export, for Western consumption. The vase is probably not as old as I originally thought. In the end, the ways we each spend our days reduce down to the same thing, making maps of places we'll never visit again; a product of Japan is the same as a product of America. You wear the dirt like it's something you earned, but we didn't fall into this, we didn't end up here by accident. We jumped.

*

Our first week in the apartment, before we turn off our phones and find the vase, you read online—a link to the Richmond newspaper via a wayward text from someone you haven't heard from in a year—that Casey, the grinning, perpetually buzzed, hoop-eared kid from the old crowd, the kid we'd shot fireworks at the night we met, has died in a car wreck. The article is non-committal, but the shape of the thing is obvious: he and a friend, whose name you don't recognize, in a parent's borrowed car on eastbound 70 and fully blazed, sailed obliviously off the road and across the grassy divide between highway lanes, directly into oncoming traffic. Needless to say, both of them were creamed. There's a picture of each accompanying the article, an old high school yearbook photo from a familiar era: Casey, with his four-bar Black Flag cap and his preposterous ears, smiling as always over a neutral-cloudy backdrop. He was nineteen. It's hard to pinpoint the last time you'd seen him on purpose, though until a month ago, until we left, you'd both been in the same town your whole lives.

There's an immediate flurry of activity as you start texting people back, finally, after months of unanswered silence, in the wake of this tragedy re-establishing lines of communication previously cut or abandoned with a place we decided we would never return to, relationships that had ended long before we came here, before we met, even. You double over your phone and type ceaselessly into the screen, your multi-armed condolences and empathy reaching across borders and back into Richmond. The pattern, the technique of your virtual reappearance is familiar, and I watch you resurrect yourself, piece by piece, word by word, assuming the position of someone who left—as a lot of people left—but always remained connected, who has been a part of it all along. Every so often you speak a name, share a marginal anecdote like an incantation; the room, briefly, is populated with another.

An hour or two later—a time I'm meant to believe you've spent deliberating, that you hadn't made your decision the instant you saw the name in the *Palladium-Item* article—you look up from your spot against the wall and tell me: "I want to go back for the funeral."

"Back to Indiana?"

"Yes."

"Why?"

"I think I should be there."

"For who?"

"Are you kidding? He called me Mom, John. We've known each other since middle school."

I answer immediately, I go broad where I shouldn't. "This isn't something you want to be a part of," I say.

"They're my friends."

"You're not the grieving parent, Joey."

"Fuck you—I don't have to justify my relationships to you."

You don't, but nonetheless I'm moralizing before I know it, some stupid manifesto based on the train, an unrelated, arbitrary tragedy from those shared college years, which had already crystallized before we met my junior year. In the days immediately after that accident—equally fatal and conceptually the same, kids in the path of a speeding object—the tiny campus was reduced to fearful paralysis with the loss of two of its students. A girl told me how horrible she felt for "not crying enough"—one of the girls who'd died had lived in her co-op and been familiar to her, they had shared a kitchen. Eventually, this not-weeping girl would join the caravan of mourners to attend the funeral in the other girl's hometown, three hundred miles away. I was skeptical of the instantly formed grief, of her commitment to its totality. I remember thinking at the time that I felt too young for my life to be defined by significant deaths, and at the same moment that I couldn't have picked from a small crowd the faces of the two people killed.

"You can't just suddenly care again," I say now, equal in my resolve, deep in my moral hole, a code I've decided heedlessly to cling to, about consistency and friendship, like Casey's death was a ploy to coax us back. "You don't get reattached just because there's a disaster or someone dies. We said we wouldn't be those kinds of people. You don't reappear at a fucking funeral."

You motion at the empty vacant room around us, which for an indefinite amount of time before we arrived was explicitly ignored, condemned. "And that's why it's just the two of us?"

The silence through the empty doorway turns our domestic space into something else. There are times when I can't remember how long I've been this way, this absolute. Occasionally it's felt like we were locked in an unspoken battle for who could be more extreme, who could experience abjection most completely, but now I am the extreme one, the one pledging isolation—out of what, jealousy? spite?—and I answer, without really responding, "We left to get away from all that shit."

Your phone vibrates again. "I've always cared. I didn't leave because I stopped caring."

"Then why did you leave?"

You flick your finger down the screen of your phone, shooting one of your text conversations back in time. I'm distracted by this gesture—maybe that we're still grabbing internet from somewhere in this derelict building, that the technologies seem mismatched—and I only hear your answer, or think I hear your answer, quiet, a second after it clears the air: "For fucking you!"

It catches me, because I'm already losing track of how this argument began and the part I'm playing in it, the scope of our conversation escalating with every word, and because this idea, that I was the reason for our departure, that I instigated it, this is nothing that I've ever considered or conceptualized, such that I feel it's been slipped into the discussion like venom to disorient me, a trick you've been saving, subtly deployed.

And so my next point is even more opaque, when I feel that I've absolutely lost control of what I'm saying, having swerved from a line of reasoning grounded in actual life into pure abstraction. "I thought we"—the phone vibrates again, on the table whose origins, too, are unclear (no, the floor, on the floor, vibrating beneath me), and my eyes flick toward it, the proof I seek—"I thought we agreed on these things."

These things—by turns, everything becomes more and more vague. I feel myself, in my embodied half of the conversation, growing more horrible with every passing moment, becoming this monstrous, unanswerable thing. Your brother flickers back into my consciousness as an entity I should be aware of, that I should be cautious to remember when I speak.

"I'm still connected with the people there," you say, "whether it's against your fucking moral imperatives or not."

"Still connected? Are you gonna stop by your parents' too, then? Tell them where you've been since the last funeral you dropped in on?"

You let out a startled breath, as if from a blow. I feel evil. I knit my fingers together and flex them, struggling to find something to say next, to soften what I've said. My dry hands slide audibly in and out of each other, and I try to transmit the demonstrative angst of this sound over to your dark corner of the room while, to others, you re-solidify from afar. They poise for your reappearance.

Reading this memory after the fact, our bodies are difficult to orient—their relative positions, in what room of the apartment—because there's no furniture to base them around, just walls at intervals. In my memory, I'm sitting on the couch and you're in a chair by the window, though there wasn't a couch or reasonable chair left in the whole building. The light, the tonal makeup of the room built into the memory—they're all familiar elements, but not from the city. In the memory, it's as if we're in the apartment in Indiana, a different living space, as if we've made this decision already, to not engage, and this is a conversation we've had many times before.

The funeral comes and goes. We stay in the city, but I'm convinced that it has nothing to do with me—if you really wanted to go back, there's nothing I could do to stop you. Neither of us says anything, but within the same night that we hear of Casey's death, you stop texting people back, and once again, disappear. A while after that, we ditch our cellphones for good—it's not directed, we just do it, the way you sometimes abandon a habit. We take the vase. A son is lowered into the ground.

*

Like Casey, your brother is dead. He's been dead for over a year, but I often forget this, randomly, at terrible times. He died, or was killed, in the worst possible way, too, as a soldier in Iraq, years after combat ended, in a freak transport accident. The first time that I notably forgot—four months after the funeral, which I'd attended—when I asked if he was taking any leave to come back to the States for the holidays (feeling, at the time, vaguely proud that I'd remembered he was serving overseas, that you had a brother at all), you didn't seem to mind, and told me that if it were my own brother who'd died I would probably care more, which seemed harsh but, ultimately, true. As an only child, the absence of a sibling in my development was passive, innate, while yours had happened upon you after growing into it the opposite way. The worst time, however, was at a house party six months after that, the semester we graduated and did death-drive things like go to house parties, when some kid I didn't recognize saw your hair (spiked high at that point, like mine, or mine like yours—visually, it was more obvious than anything that we were partners) and tried to strike up an awkward conversation while I was standing nearby. "Do you have any brothers or sisters?" he asked, as his fourth question.

"I had a brother," you said.

"Had? What happened to him?"

"He died."

There's nothing I can say in my defense: he'd died during the time that we'd known each other, and I'd been sitting right there when your mother called to give you the news. Still, maybe there was something in your delivery, or maybe I was proximity-drunk or just too dissociated at that point to care about anything, but I actually laughed, as if it was a joke you used frequently to end conversations you didn't want to have. The kid looked over at me because he obviously believed this to be the case, that this kind of dialogue happened often enough to be considered classic: this was how the lie spread.

You stormed out—difficult to pull off given how packed the room was—while holding your middle finger up above the crowd, which made it obvious.

By the time I saw you again a week and a half later, I'd done something else irreversible: this time, the frightening blue head of Yama, the Hindu god of death, to join the collection of famous faces on my leg. You didn't notice until it had healed enough for me to blur the timeline.

Later on, at another party where neither of us were drinking, just before we left for good, I casually introduced you to someone as my wife, equally without thinking, at a college party for fuck's sake, but as if I'd been doing so for years, and in some way, by this forgetting where things stood, these two gestures—the gone brother, the taking of one family for the other—were the same reversal of history.

*

We go to a show, one show. It's farther downtown, at one of those venues that claim the origins of punk in this city, a place that by virtue of the pedigree graffitied onto the basement walls is supposedly different than the others, than its regional variants like the Hoosier Dome or Villa Scum in Indiana. It isn't any different. From the instant we descend the stairs, it's copies of people we've known before—Crass vests, hairstyles like wilting plants, street kids and their giant backpacks, someone's dog, figures huddled in the corner, smell of yeast and rot; every once in a while, a spiked leather jacket out of 1977. As we walk in, I tilt my head toward the crowd abutting the stage, maybe sixty strong, all frantic movement. The show is two or three bands in. I shout at you: "Do you see the poison?"

"I see it."

I always keep a wall to one side of me, and at first we hang back in the corner, straddling the line of backpacks shoved against the wall, but there's a particular hum to the atmosphere tonight, a frictive pull to the center, and when the next band comes on we're drawn forward, and are quickly separated. The room is densely packed enough for me to lose sight of you almost instantly, and the narrow walls cause all sound to bend inward, filling the air above us and quaking the bodies below, making of everyone rooted to the ground a bell, a conduit for vibration. The music is indiscriminate noise—I have the sense that the band onstage isn't actually playing their instruments, but just thwacking at them beneath some louder, all-encompassing sound. Unhooked from that sensory anchor, the experience suddenly feels alien from what I remember: a scrum of bodies pressed together, compacted but still full of frantic movement, digging into me at every angle, ceaseless contact like always, but this time it feels purposeful rather than casual, I feel surrounded, like the blows are directed specifically against me, shoulders, elbows, heads, and hands, a mix of camaraderie and revenge. The air is thick, particulate warmth; it coats my skin like a spray. I am insanely hot. I feel a pair of hands—an actual pair of hands, with serious fingernails, the act of identifying them is strangely enraging—push me forward. I stagger in the crush, an elbow hits me squarely in the ear, and my head rockets to one side—my falling body clears a few feet of space, I leave an afterimage of me behind. As I steady myself—which I have to do by using someone's naked shoulder as an anchor (the flesh is warm and sweaty beneath, like it's just come from a shower)—my left ear is ringing like the filmic equivalent of bad news. I turn to find you, but it's impossible in the flurry of movement and the physical smell and the smoke and the awful lights, which have started, or have always been, or merely appear to be strobing. My arm is still stretched out in front of me, hasn't been there for more than a few seconds, but as I draw my hand back from the human shoulder, with the ringing, I have consciously forgotten that I put it there, that it's even my arm at all rather than some hackable limb in a forest that's standing in my way, and from there, everything goes to shit.

It was another show like this on a different scale, watching from the middle distance and shouting along, to which I traced back the planting of this idea: that we could leave Indiana, Ohio—not just leave, but sever completely, our world and everything in it replaced with something new and unfamiliar, people without history, without our history. This show was later on, outside Richmond (after the Richmond scene had splintered apart), somewhere indisputably Business where you could buy tickets online; the band didn't matter. Initially I'd thought it was us both mishearing the lyrics, shouting the wrong thing at the same time, until I realized that in fact we were addressing each other through the noise, screaming from opposite ends of the couch: we were claiming space, we were testing how loud we could be without assigning the words meaning. We didn't know the lyrics but pretended we did, and our worst assumption was that they mattered at all. The music, or the energy behind it, or the fact that this kind of sound existed, however it was brought into being, this was the primal motivation: one of us was suggesting something, and the other was agreeing, the other agreeing. We were already making plans. We'd been together ten months at that point.

A pit breaks open in the front of the crowd, close to where I've moved up, its circumference dictated by about twenty people slamming into each other and repelling, a radius constantly re-defined, its outliers shoved away from the stage, forming an arced human barricade. I'm hit with a sudden swoop of nausea, sharp and overwhelming, as if I've just inhaled something foul. My vision pitches to the left like a mishandled reel of film, jumping abruptly forward, unaccountably shifting its elements. A guy at the center of the pit, naked except for his oversized sneakers and comically tall, like someone took his torso and just stretched it as far as they could, windmills across the open space thrashing people out of the way like he's felling trees. His face reads like an anthropomorphized slur, cartoonishly real. To my right, someone slips and goes down, and I don't see them pulled back up. I shove my fists into my pockets—which is how I always stabilize in moments like this—reassuring myself that there's nothing in them, nothing at all, but this negatively affects my balance, and when I'm hit again I do fall forward (everyone falls forward) and my face cracks into someone else's shoulder. My hands shoot out as a reflex—independent, still—and I feel leather beneath them, stupid leather, in this heat. I'm transfixed for a moment, as if I've stumbled upon something for which I've been desperately searching, and then the guy wearing it throws himself backward to get me off. The back of his jacket sports the white face of a playing card, ace of hearts. I shove back. He loses his footing, and slips into the ring. The instigator behind me has the same idea, and there I go, too. The guy in the jacket stumbles about three feet before he's rammed by the sweating naked tree-man, cock flapping, who knocks him aside like it's nothing. A girl about half as tall comes loping across the pit, head down, dancing in huge, hopping strides as if she's repeatedly trying to vault a parking meter, and it strikes me as hilarious, the absurdity of this flailing and dexterous figure, like the untouchable fiddler in a mob scene as the city burns in outline. I'm jostled forward again, or move forward in some way, and my hands graze the tree-man's hips like we're tender dancing partners and I'm thinking that I seem so relatively short and he is so awkwardly tall and unclothed and half-hard that it would be just so convenient to suck him off right here, that I'm close enough to detect the sweating fruit smell from the deep crevices of his body, even over everything else, and this, too, is hilarious, so I am probably cackling when he punches me in the face, probably cackling.

I don't go all the way down—doubled over, I raise my arms like a luxurious bird and taste copper while my feet do an unintended grape-vine to keep upright. When I finally drag myself back to eye-level, absurdly weighty, I see the moshing crowd again through some kind of tint, from the perspective of the stage, and every single one of them looks like Casey, dead Casey, or Candace (dead Candace, for all I know), or predatory August with his scribbled-on arms, or you, the version of you I mistakenly followed, like another self I'm drawn back to in counterpoint to current you, somewhere beyond. I grab the guy in the leather done up with band patches that stop strictly at 1988, who I notice is wearing giant safety pins as earrings, symbols that no longer mean anything, I seize his studded lapels and scream "WHAT YEAR IS IT?" into his face. I throw him away, I spit blood on the tree-man's flawless burnished chest, and I fall away. I have no idea what the band is doing.

*

When the show ends, the violence spills out of the building and into the street. On my way to the basement steps, behind it, I pick up an olive-colored backpack from where it rests against the wall, one that feels hefty but doesn't clank with bottleweight when I lift it, like it could still have something useful inside. In the anonymity and rush of the aftermath, I see no consequences in taking it.

A few minutes pass before we find each other outside, and when I spot you, you're a different height than I remember. We're still a little drunk with it as we walk toward home. Half of my face is raw and swollen, as if there's an island beneath it pushing up, new continents of unexplored terrain. Prodding my cheek, testing its density, I realize a new concept has formalized in my head without my noticing it, that a shift has occurred over the course of the night, or since the last time I found myself walking in this direction, toward a familiar place with this subtle feeling of regularity, of returning: our building has become "home."

You nod your chin at the bag. "Whatcha got there?"

I knead the bottom of it with my fingers; it's stuffed full of someone else's supplies. "Just some goodies," I say.

I hold the backpack in front of me until we're out of sight, to minimize the likelihood that it will look familiar to anyone. We walk north for a while, away from human activity, and then east, mostly not speaking. At one point a line of police cars barrels down the street in the direction we came from; the instinct is to turn and watch them disappear behind us, but we don't. Eventually the sirens fade into nothing, into the backdrop. As always, we scope out our street for on-lookers, and then, confirming that we're alone, we duck into the gated area in front to enter through the abandoned basement, pitch-dark, which we navigate like a haunted house, me first and you behind, your hand on my collar. We climb the four flights of stairs to the top floor, not really taking care to quiet our feet. On the landing, I drop the bag like a sack of groceries and unconsciously, mechanically reach into my pocket for a key—this idea of "coming home after a night out" having swept over me—but, of course, there isn't one. There isn't even a door. We walk through the open frame.

Two objects resolve themselves in the moonlight filtered through the blindless broken windows, this absence of barriers even further evidence of what this building is not, and has never been in our time: the vase overturned on its side, and a figure wrapped in my sleeping bag.

"Someone is sleeping in my bed." I don't know if I say it out loud or not; either way, all of my breath is gone.

We stand frozen in the doorway, totally silent, like we've accidentally walked in on an intimate exchange in which we play no part. I feel warmth in my left hand, and realize belatedly it's because yours is wrapped in it. The sound of our presence—our footsteps still on the stairwell, our bodies shifting—draws back like a curtain, and the sound that replaces it is louder than everything: a deep, slow breathing, as if a lead for us to follow, coming from the figure on the floor, peacefully asleep. A growing tower of dread looms above us. I feel deeply betrayed.

Neither of us speaks or moves. The image is too foreign to register properly, though it shouldn't be—this building wasn't ours any more than it was anyone else's, we've never had claim to it beyond the fact of our presence, our dwelling over consecutive nights. But my pulse is still racing from the show, I'm brimming with bloody energy, and as our eyes adjust to the dark I recognize more and more: our backpacks, torn inside-out with their contents scattered across the floor, the wind-up flashlight, our candles, water bottles, their shadows interrupting the room's barren order. I feel my body drain and refill with something uncontrollable, misguidedly righteous—for some reason, the overturned vase upsets me the most, seems the most intentionally arbitrary.

I grit my teeth, and take a step forward into the room, with you at my side.

Something adjusts behind us. I whirl around, panic flooding my chest.

Against the wall, a figure sits in the dark in a collapsible folding chair I've never seen before, something you bring to a kid's soccer game. They hold a knife in their lap, an unreal gleaming blot on the scene. You let out a gasp, an errant breath. I can't immediately identify the sound I make.

"What are you doing here?" a male voice says from the dark. The accent sounds transplanted here, like someone who's been training to talk tough. I can't tell the age.

"We live here," I say. I feel like I'm telling a lie: no one lives here.

There's a newspaper on his lap that falls to the ground as he stands. I imagine it's dated from the day Reagan was elected. The image of him sitting here pretending to read in the dark, waiting for us to arrive, in his ratty chair and its mesh cupholders, is flatly terrifying. "You've gotta have someone keep watch. That's the first fucking rule of this game."

In the light from the windows he looks ancient, but the voice clashes with the reading, probably less than forty. A mess of tangled long hair hides most of his face, the beard scruffy and incomplete, strived for. He's dressed in a bulky gray sweater, camo pants, and boots, ballooning his physical stature; I don't understand why no one here dresses for the season. He is pointing the knife—military grade, made for actual combat—directly at my chest, as if at any moment it could become a gun. The fact that he has a weapon at all seems absurd, an apparition conjured from the most exaggerated and predictable places, like he's drawn from the newspaper at his feet, with its messages of panic and urban rebellion. I feel you shaking beside me, a furious vibration through our joined limbs. "Also, you need to hide your shit," he says. "You can't just leave it lying around for anyone to take."

His tone is of begrudgingly teaching dumb children a lesson. I wonder how everything became such a cliché. I open and close my fists (letting go of your hand), snatching uselessly at air, as if I'm owed it, as if something will appear in my fingers. Without the physical attachment you seem separate, hovering at a distance.

"At least let us take what we brought with us."

Part of me thinks I'm being clever, because everything here—except the chair—everything is something we brought in ourselves. A part of me that believes we'll get away on this technicality, pictures us walking triumphantly burdened down the stairs while he shakes his head with a knowing smile, pure capitulation. To my right, I notice your body shifting, opening minutely up, arms rising, as if in support of what I've said, demonstrating reasonableness, that no one wants to die here, and I'm angry at you for it.

"I don't think so," the ageless man says. "Everything stays here." The knife still tipped at us, he kneels down to the newspaper at his feet. His eyes drop from us for a second. Your fingertips brush mine and startled fear pours adrenaline through my body. I throw myself forward and plow him into the wall. Dust and displaced plaster burst around our shoulders. I shove my forearm against his throat above the ragged collar, where the skin feels like it's barely intact, has ebbed away around the muscle, and I use my other arm to pin his knife hand. He seems to lean into the blow, to buckle around me as if for support. With my weight pressing into him, beneath the baggy clothes, his frame is wasted and crackable, bends to my will. His heart beats in its rickety cage. I imagine you behind me, floating like a planet.

The victory is short-lived. He wrenches his arm free and shoves the knife up through the gap between our bodies, into my face. The rubber handle jams against my mouth and smears it open, digging into my gums and teeth while the very edge of the blade slowly splits my top lip. A metallic chattering fills my ears; the taste spreads like a disease. "I will shove this piece of metal down your throat and I do not give a shit who hears the screaming. Stand down."

I stand down. My lips curl into my mouth. I'm amazed by how far I have to draw back until our bodies are no longer touching. I back into you, this time desperate for the contact.

He steps forward from the wall. An angry, body-sized patch of material has shaken free from behind him; the stirred dust lends the impression that he is stepping through a veil. His person clarifies: his eyes are vaguely familiar, dark and acquisitive. In his other hand, he un-crumples the newspaper, smooths it on one dusty thigh, and then raises it to his head—it's folded into a crown. "This city belongs to the kings now," he says.

My mouth fills with blood for the second time in hours. It stings wildly. I swallow in one gulp, the taste so strong that I feel dizzy. I take your hand again. For some reason, I'm not considering how many more arms we have than he does, that there are two of us against one of him; the darkness around us seems invisibly filled with others, pressing inward, damping our potential. The man, insane-looking, motions to the overturned Satsuma vase. "What's in the vase? Is that where you keep your stash?"

You answer, which makes it sound like a cover-up. "There's nothing in the vase."

He laughs—it's more of a wheeze—and my failure to restrain him suddenly seems merciful: I would have killed him. "We'll see about that," he says. "I am giving you babies thirty seconds to get out of my apartment."

What else can we do? We run, again, past the stolen bag just outside the doorway—unopened, forgotten entirely—with less than we've ever had before, and when we're midway down the stairs I realize that throughout everything, the figure bundled up behind us in my sleeping bag did not awaken, did not move or react even once. I wonder if their breathing was actually from the man in the chair, or something I imagined altogether. I tongue the seam of the cut inside my lips, relishing the pain, the minute warmth, evidence that I did not give up, wholly, without a fight.

When we hit the ground floor, we hear shattering porcelain from above. It's enough to resolve us. I will not swallow this city. I'm turning the corner toward the basement when you stop me. "Wait. Let's take the front door."

We exit through the front of the building. We slam the door behind us.

There's a collection of spraypaint cans just inside the gate, abandoned by someone caught in the middle of something. I wonder if they were dropped during the time that we've been here, if this conflict played out on the street outside the apparently empty building while we slept obliviously above. I'm about to pass them up, but you shove a few cans into my hands and tuck two more under your arms.

"Just so we have something," you say. We open the gate, and here, too, we slam it as hard as we can, so the sound saturates the street, sends its stupid echoes everywhere.

At the bus stop, we shove the cans under our clothes. We beg our way to a free ride, going north; it feels terrible, even when the driver doesn't seem to give it a second thought. Alongside the motion of the tireless bus in the night, I discern the indistinct, swarming movement of people in the opposite direction, the bus parting them like a sea.

Indoors again, back uptown, we move on to the next painting, scribble a giant cock across an immaculately rendered, classically proportioned, four-hundred-year-old face—as per the routine we've quickly established, you with the broad strokes, me with the line work—and you tell me there's a class war coming.

The prophecy is a familiar refrain. I sit down on one of the little viewing benches and idly rattle a can of spraypaint, my ears still ringing with the sounds of the vase breaking, the weird composite of his speech. "Everybody is someone else's pawn," I say—one of my answers that is less an answer than a gesture or an abstraction, that ducks responsibility. I imagine our roles in such a war: the man in the apartment, the people camped out in the street, the crowd at the show, would they be our enemies or our allies? A distant alarm sounds, not because of our entry, but because it's been doing that for weeks.

"We could have taken him together, you know," you say. "That man."

I don't respond, which seems to admit that you're right. How much less genuine was our poverty than his, because we rejected what we'd been given, because, if we'd wanted to, we could have taken it? We could have engaged that system. The next room over, on one of the famous French portraits of Greeks, I produce a token gallery-label factoid, this time about stoicism: "The Athenian government accused Socrates of denying the gods and ordered him to either renounce his teachings or die. He chose death."

You tell me that Socrates, like the subjects of most of these paintings, probably never even existed, and before I can tell you how fundamentally wrong I think that is, how truly absurd a denial, the Athenian scholar vanishes before my eyes in a thickening haze of black so dense that it drips off the canvas. When I'd first laid hands on one of the objects in the museum, it felt like crossing a million invisible barriers, committing some unholy act; now, the paintings just mark the walls, they're littered across the world. I worry that we're doing someone else a powerful favor, the inevitable collector surveying value in negatives.

Just before, on a whim, you marched from room to room spraypainting a crude X over "every exposed nipple and twat" in all of the European nudes, and you'd already circumcised and de-titted about six Venuses before I caught up to tell you that it came off maybe a bit fascist to do that, maybe a little like the hand of censorship.

"If it's indiscriminate, it can't be fascist," you said, castrating a cherub with a spurt from your spray can. I have no idea where you found that particular aphorism.

The first gallery we stopped in, I'd meticulously blacked out the eyes on a pair of Cot springtimes when you came up behind me and said, "No, no, no." You took my hand and sprayed a wide, sloppy arc across the two lovers, then a vertical line, then a swirl. "There shouldn't be any patterns—see? It's supposed to look random." As if the ultimate aim of this was to leave our mark as senselessly as possible, in the final tally our particular violence bleeding indistinctly in with the rest.

Currently, you spray a capital letter A on the flag in a Revolutionary War painting.

"You know, that could be misinterpreted," I say, watching it bleed over the faces of the Patriots like it's no texture at all.

"How?"

"A for America."

I say it as a joke, but by the time you turn away the painting resembles nothing so much as a black scour on the gallery wall. Compared to the others, it positively screams with intention.

You cap the spray can with a clack that rebounds through the galleries like every door closing. "Just meet me by the Egyptian thing when you're done," you say, and disappear, a tinge of resentment in your wake, for questioning your radicalism—the temple to Osiris, relocated from other shores via freighter to the museum's northern wing in the 1960s, has been a place of solace since we started coming here in daylight hours, when most of it was still encased in glass. The stone is now so thick with graffiti that it gives the entire monument a greenish cast, but there's something comforting in the fact that it's still standing, that despite best efforts no one has been able to take it down.

I walk through just the emergency lights like an ill-defined spirit of vengeance across beds of shattered glass. I pass a decapitated statue of Sakhmet, its head resting three feet away, one ear missing. Deeper within the museum crouches East Asia, Oceania, their pedestals empty, artifacts spewed across borders. I pause at each unmarked painting and object, unsure of how to proceed, as if totality had been something we intended when we arrived here, when I recognized the cross-streets and pulled the cord on the bus, saw the butt of a metal pipe against porcelain and knew finally where I was, as if this wasn't ultimately the perfect example of just using the items we suddenly had in our hands.

By the time we leave the magnificent cavern, our heads are filled with paint fumes, outbursts of black.

*

The second-to-last phone call I received—on the bus, as we crawled across Pennsylvania toward the city, numbed now to the changing landscape—was from a high school friend I hadn't talked to in three years, who told me that another mutual friend, close-knit into our group during school but, again, whom I hadn't spoken with in years, had died unexpectedly, at twenty-one. The circumstances were mysterious and difficult for my friend to corroborate: he'd seen him the previous night, they'd hung out for a few hours drinking, went to a restaurant, and then parted ways and gone home (they were both on summer break from school). That morning, the morning we left Indiana, the mother of the mutual friend had gone up to check on him, but his bedroom door was locked. Eventually, they'd broken in and found him dead inside. There was speculation that he'd accidentally or purposefully mixed some kind of pills with the alcohol, my friend said, but they weren't sure. People (he listed names) were gathering in Dayton for the funeral tomorrow, in case I wanted to be there.

I turned and told you what happened, about this friend who was dead (who I don't think I'd mentioned before), and about the friend who called to give me the news (likewise). I left it dangling at the end, the hint of proposition: "The funeral is tomorrow." You burrowed your head into my shoulder but didn't say anything, silently refusing to enter—I realize now—the trap that I'd created, that I would blame you for setting when Casey died a month later. How much grief, it seemed to imply, could I reasonably be expected to exhibit for someone I'd never mentioned caring about, who didn't exist between us until this moment? How deep and true could you expect this to go?

The last phone call came two hours after that, when you were asleep, the scenery in the window unspecified, probably still Pennsylvania, and was from another high school friend, with whom I'd communicated even less recently. He said my first name, then my first and last name, to confirm who he was talking to. He asked if I'd heard about Nik, who had died this morning. I told him that I'd just heard. He was less sure than my other friend, more audibly broken up. They still weren't sure. People were gathering in Dayton for the funeral. I filed the losses.

The peripheral world gets smaller.

Let's pretend we're walking home.

South again, you mount one of the stone lions outside the library. "What do you think it takes to bring one of these beasts to life?" You wiggle your hips.

"Probably a little more than you can give it," I say. "Probably nothing short of divine intervention or a lightning strike on an eclipse night."

You resolve to try anyways. You begin to grind back and forth on its back, grabbing the mane for leverage. I look side to side, embarrassed, as if someone will catch us in the act, but the street is deserted, almost seems to mock my concern. "What are you doing?"

Keeping the rhythm costs whatever breath you'd otherwise use to answer. You set your jaw and close your eyes, like this routine takes every ounce of your concentration. The scene is baroquely pornographic, as if we'd walked onto a tidily composed set on which we were supposed to play out the fantasy of some unknown director, where I'm the audience, and standing there beneath the streetlights and security cameras and around it capitalism and maybe somewhere above that the moonlight, tasting residual blood, watching your thighs tense—imagining, as anyone would, the lion as some beastly stand-in—I think, yet again, of the broken vase, glazed with an invisible layer of our dried sweat and oils, degrading it by degrees. I'd brought up your brother again once, obliquely. After we'd had the vase for a few days, when it had settled into the arrangement of the room, I drew my finger across the pattern of lotuses connected to cherry blossoms etc, etc and said, "It reminds me of something I've seen before—does it for you? Remind you?" The question was phrased in a way that made it incomprehensible. The only aspects of your brother I remembered were the tattoo and the fact of his death; I couldn't have picked him out of a lineup in long sleeves.

You answered, "I mean, it reminds me of Japan," which, fair enough, was what I'd replied to essentially the same question when we first brought it back, and that was all we said. Already a tacit understanding had formed, an unspoken agreement on what we would and would not acknowledge, a kind of commitment to choosing silence over dialogue.

By now you're straddling the lion's neck, totally spent, your hands splayed over the molded mane. You look up, panting, and brush the hair off your forehead. It takes you a minute to catch your breath, and then, saying nothing, you slide off the statue—I have the briefest image of your fingers untangling from long hairs—leaving a glistening streak down its side. You walk lightly, in a wider stance for a minute, then seem to forget. I wait for a breeze to clear the evidence, to crystallize this into an anecdote you'd once have shared among our circle of friends while I sat beside you, envied and silent, the chosen accomplice. The eyes stare out like statues do.

*

Three blocks later, we cross a high-end chain drugstore, recently shut down, its windows freshly blacked-out. We break in at my suggestion, a demonstration of our volition. The alarms go off immediately; in this neighborhood we still only have a few minutes before the cops arrive. You grab the back of my shirt and we stumble forward in the dark, as in the cellar—the only light comes from the jagged hole in the lower half of the sliding door. "Oh, John, let's live here," you say.

The shelves are still variously stocked; they haven't had a chance to come in and clear it all out yet, to distribute the remainders to other branches or ship it off to a landfill. "Okay…" your voice comes from behind me. "So, what exactly can we take?"

"Anything that fits in your mouth."

You dash off in the direction of the beauty aisle, while I lurch uncertainly toward the nonperishable foods in the back, for no particular reason except that they're the most recognizable in the dark. I paw the shelves blindly, not really trying to accumulate but enjoying the feeling of knocking items to the ground, as if

I'm some larger and more basic creature. After a minute I shout through the alarms, toward the general sound of your presence, "What're you finding?"

"Cosmetics!" you shout back. "I can finally do my eyes!"

I slam myself into the back wall, padded with bubbly packages of junk food. I let them rain down on me from the upper shelves. I clamber to my feet and circle the store toward your voice, upending sundries as I go. I hear you rustling behind a nearby shelf. You scream, "AERIAL ATTACK!" and something shatters at my feet.

"Jesus Christ!"

"Oh shit, it's a second barrage!" Another item hits the floor, and a third cracks against my head. I go down onto my hands and knees.

"Fuck! Joey!" My palms pick up little shards of glass and paint-smelling liquid. Something cool oozes down my forehead, hardening in the air. I hear sirens. "We have to go," I say, as the synthetic, faintly peroxidal liquid trickles into my eye. "We have to go."

Another shout—"BOMBS AWAY!"—but this time it sounds like it's from the street. Still, it must act as a trigger because you launch another bottle from the adjacent aisle. It ricochets off my back before breaking open on the floor.

My vicinity now smells very strongly of chemical flowers, something created in a laboratory without context.

Through the imperfect black paint on the windows, spears of bright light trickle through. The hole in the sliding door glows orange, then red, like an unearthly halo. The sirens are right out front. When you shout "CATAPULT!" I'm sensible enough to roll out of the way, and whatever you've thrown lands just to my left—it clatters like something cheap and plastic, easily broken apart, I guess probably a hair dryer.

A roar—from a car, I'm sure—tears through the wall, and I hear signs of an escalating conflict outside. My right eye is glued shut.

"Joey, we have to get out of here." By now, I'm speaking mostly to the ground.

One aisle over, however, you are having way too much fun. "Quick! They're mounting! I hear them at the gates!"

A handful of glass containers hits the tile by my head—the expensive nail polish, I think.

"What do you say, John? Are you hurting yet?"

Something explodes by my ear and I'm misted with glass particles and a scent so concentrated and powerful that I choke on it. My body reacts as if to vomit, but there's nothing to bring up; my chest goes rigid against the gray tile and my throat clenches repeatedly, mouth open, struggling to find something to expel. I get up ropy spit and drool until the convulsions subside, breathing shallowly, like the air can't find a deeper way into my lungs. I roll helplessly onto my back and look up at the ceiling. I chew a few times on nothing, slowly and carefully, like I'm working into a motion I haven't performed in a long time. Through an indeterminate haze drifting in through flaws in the black windows, I can just make out the shapes of the fluorescent lights above, empty and dead. The darkness is tinged with red, presumably from a safety light—no matter where you are, somewhere, something still has power. The memory of the gun rises up within me, a memory I've fought to keep buried: it was on a frantic night like this that it appeared in my hand, that the weapon revealed itself. I hear your footsteps first, and then watch you loom into view above me.

Earlier on in our days of exploration, when we were dividing the city into neighborhoods, you once got off the train at one station while I stayed aboard, bound for somewhere else. Immediately after the doors closed behind you, I turned to flirt unabashedly with the woman sitting next to me. In my head, it was a terrific joke of detachment—this complete stranger had been sitting next to us the entire time, had watched you rest your head on my shoulder and kiss me goodbye; it was unfailingly clear that you and I were a pronounced and public couple. Yet as I dug into this woman over the next several minutes—her book, her music, her destination, her home—my attempt at affecting her became, for all practical purposes, serious, the comedic timing apparent to no one but myself, and thus it slipped from my supposedly lighthearted, obvious joke into something else, something sinister that felt awfully like real damage, that felt like menace. When I noticed the shift—this dangerous, unaccountable shift—I removed myself from the train, I pulled back.

You did not. "I told you there was going to be a war," you say, standing over me, your feet at either shoulder, arms crossed, bearing of statue. "Just listen."

From the sound of it, your lions have come alive outside. You haul me up in the faulty non-light. I've got sea-legs, as in they don't work at all. The top half of my body slumps into yours.

"You've dribbled down your front, bless you. Let's get you home."

With that innocuous final word, I feel a shiver in your chest—transmitted through us both—indicating that every time we say it now, no matter how often, it will be an accident.

The good thing is: I smell like flowers, and they no longer seem that fake.

Together, we shoulder through the blacked-out doors and into the street, now lit by a false, electric daylight, the tone of a parking garage. My eyes are stinging, tearing up from the perfume and polish and sudden light, one of them stuck fast. Close at hand, I make out the shape of something burning beneath a glaze, hear a pattern of thunderous crashes, human yelling.

Beside me, you whisper, "I told you."

I want to tell you that I suspect it's not as big as you think it is, or that it's much bigger than you think it is, that violence creeps up in the oddest, most convenient places—but it sounds too much like a truism, especially from someone who can't effectively see anything. Still, I consider the heightened sense of smell particular to the big cats. And all at once, my legs are working just fine.

*

We move eastward, away from the fires, toward the northbound subway—not running, exactly, but walking quickly, as fast as you can walk away from a situation without looking suspicious. Beyond the immediate perimeter of the store, the burning and mounting whatever, the streets are empty—no traffic, no human bodies, no cops. The concrete-bordered avenue is bathed in a glow of red light that seems to come from beyond above, or to occlude the above, as if someone's put the entire bubble of existence here into lockdown. As if, all at one time, the city has finally decided to address itself. The air is close, busy with the sense of mass movement somewhere just out of view, but a distinct, concentrated chill pipes through the streets and directly into our faces, giving the impression that we're still indoors, that some controlled substance is being filtered in to appear natural, that the streets themselves are part of a greater structure. I look up—the persistent flow of air now pushing on my throat—and am not surprised: the sky, or whatever is beyond the glow, is matte black, no stars, so uniform as to seem artificial—again, this feeling of shuttering on an immense scale, a dome sliding over.

As we walk against this wind—which feels in its benign constancy like the static gust of an air conditioner—I notice that to either side of us several of the gated storefronts glow orange from within, as if someone had set fires inside them. The light reflects through the gates in pixelated patterns on the sidewalk. The color is inviting, like hearth.

Your commentary is constant, endlessly speculative about the nature of these changes, yet strangely offhand, as if the consequences lacked real effect, could only be interpreted symbolically: a class war, a changing of colors. I'm not listening specifically. I peel my eyelids apart into a clouded right field as a flaming figure hurtles around the corner, running toward us in rapidly increasing resolution. It takes a moment to put it fully together, build it up from an animal: it's a man on fire.

We tighten our grip on each other and jolt to the side, stepping toward the fires that aren't burning in the open. His path doesn't divert, continues to move in a line parallel to ours. The vent of cool air billows the smoke ahead of him and into our eyes. He makes no sound himself: the only noise we hear comes either from the background—the pulsing sirens from everywhere, the hum of the vent—or the physical act of his running and burning. His shoes hitting the street at a constant, unnerving rhythm, the melting rubber sticking and then breaking free; and, as he nears, the crackling of the fire, the flickering bursts of skin separating under so much heat. He pumps his arms, he doesn't scream—like something mechanical, wound up and then released, repeating the same motion until it winds all the way down, and comes finally to rest.

He passes dangerously close—just a few feet from my left side—and the heat feels like enough to break the skin inside my clothes, as if to draw it prickling outward from my body and consume it in the blaze. There's a sensation like light rain on my sleeve, sparks of him erupting onto me. Something runs down my leg. I can't remember if it's blood or piss that comes out cool. He leaves us in his wake.

"This is us," you say, turning abruptly to a subway entrance on the right, which, miraculously, hasn't been closed off.

We descend and enter another, deeper chamber. The station is still lit and not completely empty, which surprises me, as if I'd assumed we were the only ones to have sense to go elsewhere, to hide underground. There are people milling around the empty guard booth, down on the platform below; their movement doesn't indicate disaster or panic. We vault over the turnstiles, not because we have to, not because they don't work.

We wait on the uptown platform, where the mildly iron-like smell of tuna fills the air, like someone's broken open the rations early: undercutting this smell, perversely, that of fresh water. The idea of waiting for a train seems ludicrous—if there was any delicate piece of the city's infrastructure that would collapse first, it was the trains. At this point, though, I can't tell if what we're experiencing—the conditioned air, the planned and random fires, the winnowing of all our paths down into one, this feeling of controlled synesthesia—is the work of such an infrastructure crumbling or boning up; falling apart, or testing its limits. On the other side of the tracks, a woman sits hunched over on the platform, her top half hidden in a heavy fur coat, her leggings in a pattern of hundred-dollar bills, legs dangling over the tracks.

"That man," you say, rocking back on your heels against a tiled column.

There's still some resistance, some stick every time I open my right eye. I bat my eyelashes to ease away the sting. "What about him?"

"He was a cop."

I can't make out what this means—the implications of each action, already, are starting to lose their individual meaning in the collective well of paranoia. "How could you tell?"

You shift and put your hands behind your back, flattened against the column. "It smelled like bacon."

You mime turning a badge upside down and pinning it to your chest. The train drowns out my lack of response.

We step inside, along with several of the others standing on the platform. They move to empty seats as if prescribed, but we remain standing. It doesn't occur to me until we're aboard that the train, too, could be a hostile mechanism, an operative part of the defenses that I intuit around us. As it crawls out of the station, I see through the window, across the way, a drenched figure haul himself up from the tracks onto the platform, water splattering everywhere. The woman in the money-printed leggings struggles to her feet, screams silently, and falls.

The train fills further at each stop, but never reaches capacity. I watch the passengers, but whatever their disguises are, they keep them. A man drums his knee impatiently whenever the doors open; a woman consults the map once, then again two stops later, using the same series of gestures each time. No one exits the train. At the last northern station on the island, we disembark alone. We have to surface outside and go west for a block, to the aboveground trains that travel north more broadly, to other cities and states; it's been decided, somewhere, that we are leaving, that these are the steps we're taking. As we walk, the pedestrians surrounding us break off the sidewalk and move determinedly as one group toward the other side of the street, clutching baggage and children, curving in a line and cutting off traffic, as if they've collectively decided to change direction, alerted by a signal we don't have access to, that doesn't choose us. The implication is always that the crowd knows something we do not, has some deeper, more fundamental knowledge about how to practice life, how to guarantee safety, but here we don't listen—we go in the opposite direction while the rest funnel back, deeper into the city. Alone, we climb the stairs to the elevated outdoor tracks, and stand on the edge of the platform where the trains go north. The arrival and departure screens are all blank and dead. Again, we ignore the ticket machines, and again, we wait for the train we have no right to expect will ever come; this time, we're the only people on the platform. I look down the track in both directions, at empty rails.

A few minutes later the tracks illuminate and the train arrives from the south, shamelessly. We board. I pace the empty car up and down, looking for people lying down or slumped in the seats or crouched with a weapon where I wouldn't see them at first glance, an abandoned child, but there's no one. The speakers crackle in anticipation of an announcement, then fall silent. We finally slide into the plastic-lined seats. Regardless, the doors close, and the train begins to move. Regardless, we go north, approximately, exactly to where is neither profitable nor known.

*

Gradually, the city collapses and slides from view, and through the window the reddish glow fades, replaced in shades by real, heavy night. I'm unreasonably shocked when, what feels like half an hour later, the train pulls into a station and stops. The doors open, and I inhale sharply, pushing myself down in the seat—the feeling in my gut is that everything is over, they are about to storm the train, we'll be exposed and forced out, interlopers that we are, that this is where it all ends. You put your hand on my arm, feeling my body tense. No one boards, no infantry arrive. I breathe hard until the doors close again. The train begins its slow acceleration. Forest appears on both sides, occasional stretches of gray water. The towns we pass—visible through the trees, armatured by streetlights—don't look specifically unpopulated, but I don't notice any movement within them either. After the first stop I stand and make a show of consulting the map printed on the wall, a mess of primary-colored squiggles spilling in every direction. I trace my finger up the red one and into reaches unknown. "Do you know which line we're on?"

"I don't know, the main one."

Between each station, the panic builds, but as the stops continue, farther and farther apart, deeper and deeper into this endless night, and the train remains empty but for us, my physical reactions lessen. At intervals, we talk quietly about nothing, careful of disturbing the fragile complex of our existence here, of revealing our presence, as if we're a technical flaw in the system, slipping by and getting out unnoticed.

I lean my head against the window. At some unspecified point in the journey, a force pulses through the landscape outside, jostling everything to one side, a sudden ripple that I'll only think I saw in retrospect.

The train rolls into another station, without fanfare. The engine shudders to a stop, and the doors open automatically with an empty, metallic sound. There's no light from the platform outside. I wait for the doors to close again. The lights inside the train blink once, and then go off, too. A new layer of silence pervades the car, an absence of anything mechanical, while the sound of insects slowly wafts through the open car doors. We wait, past the point at which it seems obvious that the train isn't going to leave the station, that wherever the tracks go, this is the last stop. You clear your throat, uselessly—it's so obviously a space-filler that I almost comment on it—and we wait a few minutes more. Eventually, we peel ourselves from the seats and stand, shakily, as if we've been asleep for a long time.

We step out onto the unlit concrete platform and hear night sounds, air moving through trees. As we walk away from it, the train seems to become a husk—not something we ever rode in on or that ever traveled, but a static piece of the background, a painted-in part of the scenery. We feel our way to a staircase in the dark, your one hand at the back of my neck, the other in the air. I see a railing in the moonlight, and we follow it down.

The train doors do not close behind us. The train does not move again.

There was never any going home.

III.
NORTH

THAT FIRST NIGHT IN NOVEMBER A YEAR AND A half ago, in Richmond, the kid, dead Casey, still sputtering in the field behind us, we walked back to campus together, toward the dorms. That was it—we'd stood next to each other in the gathering outside after the show, we decided we'd had enough at the same time, and we'd walked to the show from the same place—all it took was space and convenience.

As we moved across the parking lot away from the crowd, you skipped into pace beside me, as if this was not your usual rhythm, you were used to moving faster—it was an obvious metaphor right out of the gate. "So...what did you think of the show?" you said.

"It was good! It's refreshing to hear punk rock with a Southern accent."

"Yeah, they're pretty great. I can't believe we got them to drive up all the way from South Carolina for this dinky little show." I'd gathered that you had something to do with the planning of the show, which wound up being one of the last either of us went to in Richmond proper—their performance had been in the works for a long time, but the turnout was bad, as it usually was those days, the few and the proud; it was clear by this point that the center of whatever flimsy scene once existed in Richmond had slumped away, everything had changed. Six months ago there had been shows every week, regular series, there were "up-and-comers" and "mainstays," no longer.

I was walking with my hands shoved into my pockets, empty except for my school ID and room key. I'd raked at the interior fabric until it was on the verge of disintegration. I was still in my ascetic phase, the aftermath of the gun—the weird impermanence, the sense that anyone or anything could disappear or materialize at any time—and it was comforting, the reassurance that I wasn't carrying anything but my clothes, a head I shaved every day, and the devices necessary to gain access, generally, to the facilities where I was housed and fed. It was part of what kept me at the local punk shows despite the way the community was fizzling out, despite what I had done to expedite this—there were bands, or figures in bands, or had been bands in the past, who subscribed to the same kind of lifestyle, which felt like deprivation or abnegation but carried a moral weight. Proudest moments, I told myself I was aspiring to some higher code, that my vision would be clearer and starker than anyone else's.

This was during your blue mohawk period, which I learned during our walk had been initiated a couple of weeks prior; it would stay this approximate color until summer break, when identifiers tended to change. Much later, on the bus to the city, maybe in the spirit of scrapping the past, you told me that during this year—and possibly the year or two preceding it, many eras ago—that you were trying to be "basically Tank Girl." The delivery of the remark was casual, but was followed by a silence that gave it a peculiar gravity, the air of a deep and long-held secret, a confession of precedent, that you aspired to this kind of fantasy, maybe some part of you saw yourself plowing through apocalyptic deserts in war machines you fabricated yourself, a copied haircut and patches with British slogans. (If you'd asked me at the time, I would have called my student ID a "tag"—as with anything, it went both ways.)

"You seem nervous," you said, as we walked.

I shrugged—the movement was probably imperceptible because we were in motion—and, to be sure, waited a few more steps before responding. "I like to make sure that everything is consistent," I said, slowly and very deliberately, stupidly implying something vague that I hoped you'd question (yet which was impossible to question in its vagueness), as if I was some dark reservoir of mystery and sadness.

You scoffed, laughed a little at me, which made sense, because it had been all of ten minutes and here I was in my melodrama making inscrutable and dire pronouncements at someone I was trying frantically to impress. "What does *that* mean?"

A laugh sputtered out of me—a laugh!—acknowledging the ridiculousness of what I'd said (or maybe acknowledging that it might sound ridiculous to someone who wasn't attuned to my deep inner torment), and I said, slightly shamed: "I don't know." I kicked the ground in a way I wanted to read "unconsciously frustrated" and almost tripped. I saw myself as if from a distance, acting this way: my self-involved tragedy seemed comic. The brick buildings of the college were coming into view—we'd changed from the gravel alongside the road to the sidewalk on the campus proper. I asked, "Does it ever burn you out, to be a part of the punk scene in a place like fucking Richmond, Indiana?" I was still implying a lot, but at least this time my sentence was answerable, had clear ramifications to respond to.

"Constantly," you said. "But I grew up here"—I'd insulted her town—"so I'm experienced with the burnout. You get used to the energy expense, you know what wears you down and what you can stand—it's a pattern. You know when you just need to give up and go someplace else for a while. Indy's not so far away. You?"

"I'm from Dayton." This meant nothing except a different state, but apparently the answer stood on its own.

I experienced a moment of panic after I answered, a couple of seconds delayed, a body-wide chill of realization that, though to my knowledge we'd never met before—and how had I never noticed you? how had I failed to map such a crucial person?— our set of friends and acquaintances, our familiars must overlap in some substantial way: what were the chances that you didn't know August, didn't know Candace, weren't aware of some rumor of what I'd done? In the thick of the blooming night I saw all of this unraveling before it even started, the destructive path of revelation twined with the perfect vision I suddenly had of our future together, the kind of fantasy a crush spins hopelessly into infinity. I would spend the rest of my life under this fear of discovery. I tried to bury the feeling by talking over it—to disguise my past steps with forward momentum—and gestured around us, the smallest canvas. "Where do you live?"

"Brinkman."

"I'll walk you there."

"How chivalrous."

In a few minutes we came to the most visibly decrepit of the dorms, a three-winged concrete block on the far eastern edge of the tiny campus, no more than five hundred feet from my dorm. Nine months later, we would move into an apartment less than two miles from here, and then we would stop paying. "Did you know," you said, at the door, "that this dorm was designed by a prison architect?"

"I didn't."

"Yep. Stand next to the staircase on any given floor and you can see straight to the end of every hallway in any direction. Every inmate accounted for."

You stepped away and swiped your ID in the reader to unlock the door—the lack of analog technology for this was briefly startling, like a moment out of time, a reminder we weren't living in the '80s—then turned back. "See you in the pit." You did a two-finger salute, and you were gone.

And that's it; born in fire.

We follow the railing a short ways to the ground, one after the other. We exit the stairway into a small commuter parking lot, maybe three-quarters full. Like the station, it's completely silent. The cars sit motionless, as if they've never moved, aren't capable of movement, their owners decided unanimously to remain in the city for the night. I hear you swallow next to me. It's truly ominous.

We walk past an unattended tollbooth, around the lowered gate to the heel of a two-lane road, new and black, paved two inches higher than the parking lot. The road is bordered by looming, impenetrable trees, and curves gently in both directions, like we're standing at the very crest, the access point to an artery that, way down, leads back to the city, and up, to somewhere else. There's no sound of traffic in either direction, none at all. The wind channels through the tops of the trees, shifting the spired skyline. The feeling of being trapped inside, of moving through the city during those final moments—it's obliterated as soon as we step into the road. The sky is a rich navy blue, and there are stars, actual stars. We're standing in the middle of the road, looking up at these stars. I wonder what time it is, if we should be expecting cars, other life, the sun.

"Do you have a preference?"

"North. My preference is north."

We turn to our right, in the direction we assume leads north, because it's approximately parallel with the tracks; I don't know the stars well enough to tell. The road is too wide for our footsteps to echo, but we can hear them on the asphalt, above all else.

We're wearing the same clothes we wore to the show in the city, innumerable hours ago, dressed in layers of paint mist and ash from the streets, the accumulation of travel. There's dried blood on the front of my t-shirt, splattered along with the cosmetics.

The skin of my face is hard in places, lightly crusted where the polish has dried and swollen around my cheekbone. I work my tongue under my upper lip when I need a reminder, pushing out the wound, repeatedly breaking it open. There's still some gunk in my right eye, and every so often I'm suddenly blinking back tears. You look less damaged—you wore your boots to the show; I wish I'd done that. That's the first thought of consequences I have as we walk, not of hunger or our lack of a destination: my shoes are shit, they're going to be the first to go.

I piece the preceding night together in my head—impossibly, we are still in the midst of it. It must be close to dawn.

The road is tracked by power lines, hoisted above the trees. When the road curves, we follow it, because the alternative is to have no path at all.

As the thickness of the night slowly rolls back, far to our left, an elevated highway fades into view out of the solid mass of trees, revealing mountains farther back. We stop for a minute. There's no distant glow of headlights, no sound carried through the wind. It wraps through the landscape like a concrete skeleton. I'm struck again by how everything a certain distance beyond us doesn't seem real, a painted sheet surrounding the set on which we walk, changeable only by distance and angle, variously lit.

Eventually, our road splits, offers an exit on the right down a single lane lined in thinning trees. We change courses here—we have options, and the highway is too eerie, too quiet. Around the curve, we find an abandoned gas station sunken into a gravelly offshoot of the road. The fluorescent lights inside burn into the declining night, and we hear it humming from a distance, its perimeter glowing like a ghostly shell. I step uncertainly toward it, off the road—there are two pickup trucks visible in the parking lot, and through the windows, I see the shelves are stocked—but you grab my arm and pull me back. "Don't."

"I'm sure there are supplies in there."

"I am not that desperate."

I don't press it. There's something unnerving about the building's illumination; the buzz of electronics that maintain it seems like a mechanical deception of life, of a structure grown self-sufficient. We walk resolutely past it, the hum following us for a while before it dissipates into the air, becoming ambient. I strain my ears to continue noticing it—the subtle, droning undercurrent—but very soon it assimilates into my surroundings, and I can't pick it out.

The road slopes down, and the woods start to separate, unveiling more landscape to either side of us. We keep up our pace for a while without acknowledging it, until the guardrail to our left disappears and a hundred yards later is replaced with a low white fence, bright and idyllic. Grass accompanies the road now, and looks to have been mowed in the last week. The sky goes pink with morning coming on. The tenor changes.

You don't speak until we're out of shouting distance of the gas station and the silence has returned, completely returned. "John, I—"

"What?"

"I—I don't think there's anyone left."

It's a ridiculous sentiment, and I answer, "That's impossible," without leaving any space for consideration, as if talking over you will prevent the thought from occurring to either of us. But there it is.

"I don't mean everywhere," you say, "but here—there's just, there's no sign of anyone. It's like everyone vanished."

This time, I don't answer right away. I take the processing of this thought and relegate it to elsewhere. We continue walking. I make a mental note of it, about my participation in this conversation, that I'm formulating my response and haven't said anything yet. The sky fills steadily with light, the sun rising from an angle I don't make the effort to discern, not even to determine what direction we're moving. It starts to rain, an inconsistent, patchy sprinkle that we can just barely hear, but which at least sounds natural. And I don't answer, and that conversation ends.

We've somehow transitioned without realizing it from wooded mountain highway to quaint country road. The white fence goes picturesquely along.

A very slight mist forms around our ankles.

"Let's get out of these wet clothes." One of us says this after a while, or both of us say it in unison, or neither of us says it at all, but it exists, somewhere, a concrete part of our ongoing human dialogue.

And then, as the clouds draw back, the light shines down, and we see the mansion before us.

*

You came from a family that seemed, comparatively, readily worth jettisoning. Your father was a fiery bishop at the Mormon church in Richmond four miles from the campus (and two miles from the house you grew up in, where your parents still lived), deeply conservative and yet the curator of an enormous personal collection of Prince memorabilia. You mostly stopped communicating with your parents when you started college, took out loans and moved out, though they lived five minutes away. To me, it seemed disturbingly, eerily close, and I was impressed by how thoroughly absent they were from your life despite the physical proximity, that there was willfulness to this absence. It felt like an accelerated path into adulthood, a daring and dramatic step.

Your brother had been closer. I'd never met him, but I'd gone to the funeral last year, which was quasi-military grade, and at which his commander—also a native Midwesterner—had told some really charming stories about your brother's casual heroism and infuriating-yet-noble dismissal of company groupthink in Iraq (chasing after kids' stray soccer balls, etc).

The circumstances of his death weren't specifically discussed; the undercurrent I felt was that of a suicide, in which—for the purposes and dignities of the funeral—the fault lay abstractly elsewhere, undiscussed. He was widely missed. After the commander, your father gave an impassioned speech about civic duty and service that, bizarrely, made no direct mention of his son, as if he'd already been subsumed into larger causes. Your presence at the funeral was that of a casual acquaintance. When we entered for the viewing, you shook your father's hand and he said, "Thank you for coming," without noticeable affect. I shook his hand next—his eyes darted quickly between us, as if mentally drawing the connection—and then he repeated, "Thank you for coming," in exactly the same tone. You hugged your mother; there were tears in her eyes. She paused for a second, and then hugged me too. You saw more of her than your father. She worked checkout at Walmart and so you encountered her incidentally; it wasn't clear how intentional or planned these interactions were.

The last time you were alone with your father, you told me, was a week after the funeral, when you'd been in the house to collect something and he'd grabbed you on your way out, crazy with grief, and tried to impart to you something like life advice but that sounded instead like a mangled sermon, free-wheeling and associatively insane, where he'd come close (not all the way) to claiming that homosexuality was to blame for his son's death, and that seeing your father crying in front of you, so absurd and lost and hopelessly bereft, had perversely created a ferocious ire in you. You hadn't spoken to him since—you were there in town, but not there—and, in time, you'd joined your brother in silence. My childhood, by contrast, had essentially lacked in nothing save siblings: both of my parents were doctors, had paid for my college education to leave me debt-free, had placed me here.

The sight is clearly one that you're supposed to approach and appreciate from afar—the way you'd come upon the remains of an ancient civilization in a valley—but we don't notice until we're nearly on top of it, when looking up we don't immediately see a house, but rather a series of barriers and overpowering, stark angles made from wide, blank surfaces, the whole thing too big to conceive, popped in front of us out of nowhere. We impulsively take a few steps backward; the first barrier becomes a spiked black iron fence. Moment by moment, we take in the structure in front of us, mapping it into our consciousness—where two white surfaces meet becomes a corner, a wall, columns draw up into other floors, strings of windows and ornamental borders unwind, balconies like the tiers of a cake. It's assembled before us, shining beneath a film of rain, steaming up from the ground. The instant that we behold it—and there is a definite moment where what it is becomes clear to both of us, the biggest house we've ever seen—you grab my hand like a child seeing a theme park for the first time, without taking your eyes off of it, as if out of fear that it will vanish. "You have got to be kidding me with this shit."

Thrilled by our discovery, blanketed in a kind of visceral relief, we spring toward the house (the arabesqued gate is already opened as wide as it can go), and follow a gravel path distinct from the driveway around the corner and up to the front door, which appears to be set on a throne, but is in fact two very deep stone steps. I trail behind, at arm's length, looking up at the windows—innumerable, towering, arched, occasionally stained glass—scanning for movement. They reflect blankly back, curtains drawn inside.

We pull ourselves up to the landing; we almost have to use our arms.

You're about to sail through the door but I pull you back at the periphery, my caution finally catching up with the rest of my body, our gestures suddenly too big for me. You give a dramatic kick in the air as you wheel around. "Wait. There could be someone in there," I say.

"There's no one in there."

I stare dubiously at the knocker, molded out of bronze in the shape of a bullish horned beast, probably a minotaur. There's no doorbell—either there was a speaker back at the gate or you're supposed to knock with the ring hanging from the snout. It's tacky as fuck. The door is slightly ajar.

You're wearing an eager, open-mouthed grin. I detect traces of cologne in the still air around us, and I think to point this out, vestigial remnants of another living organism, recently present, its aroma lingering behind, and then I realize that it's me. I flex the toes of my left foot; the rubber and fabric of my shoe separate, mouthing silently. The mansion and the gas station seem to occupy two completely separate worlds. I imagine some kind of invisible, filtered border between them—now, I can't hear anything beyond us, no matter how hard I try.

The door pushes open with barely the intimation of effort. You don't even have to touch the knocker. Of course, it's empty. We enter, our bearing wide, our bodies heedless and embracing.

*

An early part of our refusal: before we found the apartment in the city, we were camped for an afternoon on a busy street midway up the island—prime commuter zone—when a man, ostensibly walking by, stopped in front of us. We had our blanket beneath us, cardboard beneath that. Your feet were bare, you were "airing out," which gives the memory an unusual color.

The man held a white plastic bag out to me, stamped with a smiley face. "Do you want this? I can't finish it."

I looked up at him. He was dressed in a suit, the collar crisp and snug, his tie purple, and was built like a mannequin in a department store. His hair was groomed in carefully trimmed spikes, and he seemed to demonstratively maintain about five days' worth of facial hair; he couldn't have been more than thirty. He carried a gym bag over his shoulder, a model for the flawless balance of work and play.

We didn't have a sign. We didn't ask. We were just there. But I said, in the moment, out of an automatic politeness fostered over my entire Ohio life, "Are you sure?"

He ran his thumb and index finger down from the corners of his lips, connecting them at his chin. It looked like a gesture he performed often, like a trademark. His hand offered again. "Yeah, man. It's too much for me."

I extended mine to take the bag from the air where it dangled between us, as if by reflex, to prevent it from falling. I replied "Thanks," in kind.

"No problem," he said, seeming to de-stiffen, suddenly looking off into the distance, away from us. "Take care, man." He restarted and moved quickly forward into the passing pedestrian traffic. My eyes were drawn to the white sneakers he wore beneath the dark suit, bouncing along the sidewalk as if to prevent real contact.

I untied and picked open the plastic bundle at my feet, laying out its components on the ground before us like a surgeon. Inside the bag, alongside a packet of plastic utensils and a sheaf of napkins (one used), a falafel pita was wrapped in wax paper wrapped in foil, one obvious bite missing. Its juices were nearly soaked through. The sight, the smell of the food alone seemed to take the edge off my hunger. I looked from my lap to you.

"Did you ever expect to live off charity?" you said.

"Is that what you call it?"

"That's what it looks like."

"He was going to throw it out," I said. "People act like the moment something leaves your hand or goes into a public container it crosses some kind of magical barrier and becomes trash. It hasn't mingled with anything else."

"It looks like trash."

I ripped open the plastic knife and shaved off the bitten end of the wrap. The soggy bread peeled away in a toothmarked strip while the falafel crumbled into bits like dredged-up earwax. The sauce, the mush of diced tomato and onion pooled in the creases of the wrapper, torn. "You believe in guilt by association," I said.

"He's laughing at us."

I raised the package to my mouth with both hands.

You pointed to a halal stand on the corner a block north. "He bought it just so he could take one bite and then give it to us. Just to put his mouth on it and see if we would still take it."

A gap in the wrapper opened and the faintly orange sauce spilled onto my fingers, down my wrist, encircling it like a bracelet. He was long gone, but I turned to look at the man's retreating back, the brand of his sneakers carrying him across, above, beyond the street.

"It was a test," you said. "Do you understand?"

I watched the food wither in front of me. I noticed my teeth moving up and down inside my mouth, repeating an action that had once proved sustainable, now rendered meaningless. I swallowed spit. My hands smelled like onions for days, a pollutant.

*

Quickly, within a single flight of stairs, we find ourselves in the most gratuitous marble bathroom either of us has ever seen, a room bigger than the apartment we had in Indiana, with grossly oversized artwork and an ostentatious stone bathtub in the corner, complete with gold faucet—the whole thing is clearly the product of some '70s millionaire with more money than he knew what to do with.

Of course we fuck in the tub, with the bubbles on full blast. Afterward, we sit there in the tepid water, our dirt haloes merging, too many cosmetics mixed, and speculate on everything this bathroom has seen over the years, up until us. You suggest that the reason everything's so spotless is because somebody made a bloody mess and had to scrub away every last bit of evidence. You point to a miniature African nude posed on a pedestal and say it was probably used to bash someone's brains all across the marble floor. They probably had to hire someone to come in and clean it with a toothbrush.

Money-murders, you call them. "Like, you have so much wealth that the only thing you have left to achieve is killing someone. Where else would you do it?"

I dunk my head and bring it back up. I have to agree—the place is bright and ripe for nasty falls, and the bathtub is built like a sacrificial pool. It's not hard to imagine entering the room and finding someone reposed in red water, one knee breaking the surface. When we've finished, we wrap ourselves in the purest white towels—they must have replaced them daily—and head downstairs, leaving our own evidence: wet footprints on the tile, our hairs in the drain.

Naturally, the entryway has an enormous art deco chandelier ripped straight out of the roaring '20s, and an ornate wraparound staircase from another century. You sit on the towel and slide down the banister with perfect grace, and halfway down I notice you starting to topple outward at the same second that I see the wolf standing in the foyer.

Nothing in the world prepares me for your clipped shriek or the smack of your body hitting luxury tile—such brief and horrible sounds.

I've bolted down the stairs before the wolf has time to react to our breach of his habitat, or, ridiculous, we to his. You're lying on the floor with your legs crumpled the wrong way and the towel riding up between them.

I make for you first. The foyer is strewn with priceless objets d'art, and I send a few of them crashing to the floor to distract the wolf.

I scoop you up as gently as I can—the little splatter of blood on the tile is, as suspected, almost beautifully stark—and I hear the wolf snarling at my heels, while you don't make any sound at all. For a hot second I think you've been mauled, that the wolf somehow got to your shoulder, until I remember that it's permanent, that's a design you chose.

We stumble out of there on two legs, a pile of opulence and savagery behind us, as naked as beasts.

*

Before we knew each other, peripheral to the community my second and third years of college there was August, who sold cocaine and prescription drugs to the students there and at the local high school; as I saw it, this was his primary function. He'd attended the college as a freshman an indeterminate number of years prior, then dropped out but never left Richmond, didn't return to wherever he'd come from (which I only knew as some-where to the west, somewhere urban and moneyed). Instead, after officially cutting ties with the school, he'd nestled in, attached himself to the campus and, over the last two or five or eight or fifteen years, reinvented himself as a local. Most shows in Richmond, and he would be there, leaned against a wall in the back (as I would be leaned against a wall), his age—upper twen-ties? low thirties?—carefully masked in beard, arms crossed in broadcast detachment with the sleeves rolled up to reveal crude tattoos of big-eyed robots underneath, his style in artlessness. His insistent presence implied that he had always been here and always would be, his claim to this turf longer established and thus more genuine than anyone else's. He seemed to know everybody, to be welcome everywhere—it was impossible, on an incestuous campus like this one, in a subculture socially and musically fed by the neighboring high school, to be much more than two degrees separated, before you knew him and he knew you. He prided himself on his lack of physical boundaries; he pretended intimacy and touched wherever he could—it was hugs, hands on shoulders and skimming down arms, calculated leans, it was him breathing into your ear. The game seemed to be based on contact—if he touched you, he won you. His supply chain worked the same way: he bought from other, less friendly Richmond dealers and dealt to gentle high school punks and college kids afraid to cross the bridge; he made the community his currency, and via the threads of capital, tenuously held it together. The first two or three times I found myself around him my sophomore year—when I first started going to shows, my only steps out into Richmond, really—I'd sensed his stature, and I'd felt myself trying half-consciously to impress him, pitching my voice louder so that he could overhear, hypothetically admire my way of speaking or my patter, as if the reassurance of this longstanding person would somehow cement my own presence there, validate it in some way. It's a dynamic that hinges easily on hatred, which when it arrived, arrived indiscriminately. It was a time when all I could get was angrier, and when my anger, lacking a larger form, took root in specific people. He insinuated himself, he had a mushy swagger. He looked like he wanted to have followers; basically, he was too cool.

He had a type, and that was punk rock girls. This one was Candace, a pink-haired freshman from Gainesville, two years younger than me, who started attending the Richmond shows a month after she arrived, when I was in my third year. In this way, she entered both August's picture and mine. I was there when he spotted her for the first time, at a basement show in a house near the college. I don't remember who the bands were—generic Indiana hardcore, I couldn't keep up with the name changes.

I'd seen Candace on campus before she showed up there, enough to absorb some basic details and develop a crush. Our college was tiny, with most of its facilities distributed around a grassy, circular lawn, and the freshmen all lived in two dorms on its east side. The setup was constructive to people-watching, and this was how I'd spent much of my time in college thus far, purposely isolated, on a bench just apart from this central area. Over the first month of the fall semester my junior year, I'd watched Candace adjust to the campus, a pattern I'd seen many times: she spent the first weeks moving alone, shyly across the grounds—mostly shuttling between her dorm, the dining hall, and the two buildings where humanities classes were held—until one day she emerged with a pocket of other freshmen, five or six of them, and thereafter traveled with them almost everywhere (the two of us had never interacted). In the Richmond basement that night in September, I noticed that she had come alone. She stood uncertainly toward the back wall without leaning against it, as if to avoid bonding with the environment. She looked anxiously back at the steps. I was on the wall adjacent, arms crossed, trying to look tough and indifferent, my hair—in a mohawk then—as if I'd just been electrified. A small mob of people crowded the band at the front, throwing themselves over one another to the soundtrack of something choppy and indistinguishable.

I turned my attention from the band to August, where he stood in the far corner, as always, his sleeves rolled up, smoking and scanning the crowd. I considered his casual breach of house rules by smoking inside, though he wasn't the only one. A feeling like dread pushed into my gut. My reaction to him had become instinctive, a physical repulsion. I counted on his presence as a trigger the same way I counted on the effect of the music—his character seemed to contextualize what I was feeling, to hone my spite and rage and angst into an identifiable form. Hormonal levels spiked somewhere, and I felt on the verge of joining the crowd.

August's gaze detached from the mash of bodies at the front to wander the walls. His eyes passed me without registering and, some distance later, fell on Candace, standing apart, hands in her jacket pockets. Her bearing was nervous, one foot itching at the back of her opposite leg. His body stiffened. He visibly settled on her, and from there, he looked back and forth, from the crowd to her, as if trying to gauge whether or not she was attached to someone, if his was a move worth making. If I'd approached her at this moment, I thought, even just walked up and stood there saying nothing, just moved my presence ten feet in one direction, without even opening my stupid mouth—if I'd imprinted on August's initial read of her, I could have allayed everything that happened afterward: this is what I told myself. I didn't consider that if I'd done it, if I'd intervened earlier, at that first show (where the band, I'm almost certain now, was called Secondhand Destruction), rather than wantonly, disastrously later on, that August would have simply returned, that he wasn't so easily dissuaded; he knew what he wanted. This, in any event, is the moment I think of as I carry you down the crushed-jewel gravel path away from the mansion and into the forested property beyond, your angles digging into me, your arms around my neck like a new bride—this moment of scrutinizing yet opaque attention in a basement, this other fall.

Instead, I didn't move. Instead, I watched August stab out his cigarette on the brick, roll up his sleeves a bit more, and detach himself from the wall. He walked across the room toward her as the band recovered between songs, the feedback a lull as the singer returned to the front of the crowd. By the time August reached her, held his arm out and put his fingers on her shoulder, I was shaking at the blatant display of it, of his visual acquisition, the crudeness of this story.

Candace startled when he touched her, took an evasive step away. He smiled apologetically, laughed, said something I couldn't hear, and planted his entire hand on her back.

She seemed to rock on her heels for a moment, and looked down, maybe took another tiny step forward. The hand fol- lowed, like an entitlement, taking, and keeping.

Even then I knew that a part of my anger came from August's assertiveness, that this was part of the way he preyed. Hidden beneath the projected hapless cool I saw something sinister and calculating, a fundamental assumption that in any person there was something to take, a use to be exploited, and in watching this assumption play out before me—and in the end, seeing the person taken—I was fueled. I cast myself opposite him: I saw myself taken in, shrugging off the signals, as if, even while it was happening, I knew that I was setting myself up for some- thing I would one day try to forget, and every pair of hands that touched wanted the same thing, and there was no such thing as love.

*

You take your first steps anew on the fringes of the forest, while I stand before a full-length mirror in another borrowed master bedroom in a different mansion and try on bespoke suits tai- lored to the body of a man exactly my size. At first, I'd stood at the threshold of the walk-in closet with the same uncertainty that however long ago I'd once stood in a clothing store, felt the same pressure to decide amongst a series of variously colored and textured fabric objects that to me were all essentially the same, yet to which—by placing myself in this position—I began to assign arbitrary values.

There was no decisive moment when we determined it was safe to separate. When we entered this second property (through another opened gate), I stopped running, as if we'd arrived home, crossed a perimeter through which further pursuit was impossible. I didn't know how far we'd come to get there; the gate had appeared as the very last of my strength seeped out. I lowered you carefully to the asphalt, my arms and legs burning. I felt the accumulated grit under my bare feet. I found a gate-house with a blank computer and pressed a button inside of it. We turned and, naked, watched the automatic gate swing shut against the wild like the most fundamental demonstration of humankind ever conceived.

You could walk on your own again by the time we reached the door. A touchpad was mounted on the frame, and we took turns running our appendages in various combinations across its surface and listening to the interface reject us, but the door wasn't locked to begin with. The foyer felt even more familiar.

In some way, we were practicing a variation of the way we encountered the city: you traipsed alongside the treeline or through the labyrinthine gardens outside while I found security cameras installed in the fireplace and studied the texture of a room lined entirely with illustrated leather panels; I assumed that you would report back on whatever you found out there, and I would do the same.

Later, you sit on the edge of the king-size bed and tell me, as I adjust my collar, that only cutthroats and philanderers wear suits like these.

The second house is more modern than the first, younger, with rooms that light automatically when you enter them, a bathroom floor that's always warm, flatscreen TVs flush with the walls in every room that run blue screens instead of static, brittle flora in narrow boxes, island bars stacked below with whisky and vodka. This is the kind of mansion where there's a huge tropical aquarium in the living room, filled with rare and prehistoric creatures that cost thousands of dollars each but are fed the kind of shitty processed pellets you would give a goldfish.

You rip my suit off and we do what's expected of us on a bed of this caliber. I picture the noble octopus, propelling itself majestically across the tank, and the miniature bamboo shark, ramming repeatedly into the glass.

You deny that you ever saw the wolf, that your fall was anything other than a combination of poor balance and reckless speed.

*

I don't know why it was Candace, of anyone, who propelled me toward the path I chose to follow. Ultimately, when it came down to it, I knew nothing firsthand about her and August's relationship, less than nothing—by any estimation I had no connection with either of them beyond maybe a few people in common. After that first night, I only saw them together a handful of times, and there was nothing threatening in their interactions, nothing to suggest it was anything beyond what it appeared to be. They were two people onto whom I had foisted a history, an insidious narrative. Maybe it was because I watched their beginnings play out so plainly in front of me, that the obviousness of the relationship (whatever kind of relationship it was)— its implanting, its growth and acceleration—made me sick, or jealous. The assumptions were mine, too: I wanted to find the poison, and so I found it. Candace had been primed for my attention since she arrived here; how much did it take before I interfered, before I was going to interfere anyway? I was waiting for a trigger to pull.

Thus, I watched Candace flicker from college life and, in my way, I traced this to larger systems in the community. Her presence in the group of freshmen to which I'd watched her grow attached dwindled and then ended; they moved to meals, classes, lounged on the grounds without her as the weather cooled. I saw her less around campus, and when I did she was always alone, and seemed less present, isolated in an indistinct, shapeless way. I put probably too much stock in her pink hair, which began to grow out and lose its color, exposing the brunette roots, and wasn't dyed again. I told myself that once you know someone, it starts to matter—a drug habit, an abusive boyfriend—these things start to make a difference, to affect you, these changes signify evidence. I saw Candace at a few more shows—sometimes August was there with her, sometimes not. Sometimes they spoke, and sometimes they didn't. I remember thinking to myself that it felt like I was watching her turn into a ghost. I imagined telling this story of a girl I'd known who fell in with the wrong people and who I watched waste away before me. I don't trust my readings of these days.

Mid-October, I went to a show inaugurating a punkhouse in Richmond called Villa Scum. The show—whose bill included something like eight bands—was set up by one of the house's official tenants, Cole, who fronted Scum Artist, the house's namesake. He said he wanted to keep the proceedings "one step away from being evicted." He had clout in the community and had played in bands all over for the last ten years, so the place was packed with kids from Richmond, Dayton, and Indy. I kicked aside PBR empties as I entered through the sloping front porch. The place was recently inhabited and already filthy, its cheap two-story frame trembling with the music inside.

The living room—emptied of furniture, where the bands performed—was too packed for my usual kind of hanging back, and people leaned on the windowsills and bunched together in the corners. I didn't see August. I shouldered my way in, feeling the carpet sink beneath my feet from some unidentified wetness. The air smelled like sweat and stale alcohol. The bands were uniformly loud, and enough of them shared members that I quickly lost track of who was playing. I let myself zone out, the contact reassuring, a means of keeping upright, the noise like earmuffs, masking the detail. Somewhere in the din, three or four bands in, Candace appeared close to where I was standing. I saw her peripherally, her shoulder near mine, and a raw, sweating panic came over me, as if I'd been exposed. I smiled in her direction (we didn't make eye contact), and then, pulling myself from the trance, I drifted toward the far side of the living room, where during the course of the show four or five people had elbowed out a standing place just apart from the crowd. I put my back to the wall and found her faintly pink hair again—like, I will not be moved. She was as invested as anyone else, but I felt violently protective, as if I knew better; I wanted to wade in and rip away every person around her, as if her presence in this house, in this mass of people, was a performance she'd been coerced into giving.

I didn't notice specifically when Candace left the living room. Only at some later point did I try to reorient my bearings around her presence and find her gone from the crowd, and then dimly recalled (or fake-recalled) her head moving outward, toward the hallway. When I noticed her absence, I started counting the minutes by checking my phone, at first unconscious of what I was doing, that I was adding minutes every time I looked. At ten, I began to get that feeling, new sweat forming, because I figured this was ten plus however long before I'd noticed, *at least* ten minutes. The idea that she might have just left the house, left of her own free will, did not occur to me. I checked again at sixteen, then twenty. At twenty-eight, I decided to go after her. At thirty-three, I went. I told myself I wanted to get out of the room, wander the house and see what I saw. As I edged around the wall toward the hallway, my focus singular, the others ebbing away, I told myself to just leave, that this was as far from my place as possible, get the fuck out, let this stranger lead her life.

The walls in the hallway stamped with sound. They had been recently painted, probably by whoever owned the building, prior to Cole's move-in; I felt indefinably angry at the inevitability of its ruin. I glanced into the kitchen, where there were normal-volume voices and people at the counter, a sinkfull of beer. Both of the bedrooms on the first floor were dark, home to twin mattresses and cardboard boxes, variously unpacked. I found the bathroom door, locked. I'd passed it on my initial lap of the first floor and had sensed its potential, but had waited to exhaust my other options, to drive its latent tension as high as possible before I tested it. I knocked, and there was no response, but this didn't mean anything in itself, I couldn't even hear myself above the music from the living room. I tried the knob more assertively, turned it several times, trying to aggravate whoever was inside, to force a response. I put my hand on the door and leaned close to it. "Candace?" I said. I realized it was the first time I'd said her name aloud; it felt strangely proper, as if I'd expected more syllables. "Candace, are you in there?" I rapped with my knuckles.

There was still no answer. I knocked harder, and then pounded with my fist. I took a step back from the door. No one entered the hallway—the assumption at these things was that someone was always off somewhere destroying something.

I said her name once more, at speaking-level.

And then I rammed the door off its hinges.

The split came with a sharp, neat crack, and the door burst open and inward. Candace was lying on the scuzzy, egg-colored tile, her body wrapped around the toilet, completely gone. Blood ran from her nose, bright red on pale-pale. She was dressed in the jacket I recognized and a short black skirt. The heel of the door had gashed her leg as it swung open, ripped an arc from her leggings, but she hadn't stirred. I ducked quickly inside and pushed the door approximately into its frame behind me.

I knelt down by her side, my head full of noise. I checked for a pulse, as in I held my fingers at her neck, but the whole house felt like a pulse—the floor shook beneath us—and I couldn't feel anything from her. Her eyes were open and glassy, lips just parted, pupils bloated, her fists clenched. I took her by the shoulders and shook her, I shouted her name. It occurred to me that I hadn't yet called for help, that I was acting as a rescuer without any idea of what I was doing. I pulled her upper body roughly into my lap. The back of her head was bleeding from the fall, a darker pink.

I reached up and turned on the sink, sprinkled a handful of water on her face, diluting the line of blood from her nose. I thought sudden, unexpected stimulation might wake her up. I shook, and I shook.

It happened all at once: I was shaking her, staring into her face, the eyebrows like they'd been painted on, and it was as if her eyes emerged suddenly from behind a translucent film. She inhaled a huge lung-full of air and jolted upright. When she registered me, her eyes trembled with panic. She shoved me away and planted her hands on the toilet and sink for balance. The lid slipped and broke free in her grip.

"Candace—"

She gasped and scrambled to her feet, as if my knowledge of her name was what scared her, I shouldn't know this much. She pulled on the door for balance. It toppled open, and she ran, oblivious to the cut on her leg, the blood on her face. As I stood, I noticed further elements in the bathroom—a Family Video card on the edge of the sink, a rolled-up dollar bill on the floor, inadvertently bent in half: it all came across as too convenient, too typical. The door teetered once on its edge, and then fell forward, dangling treacherously from the latch.

I got to the porch as fast as I could, but she was gone into the night. The lawn was choked with cars. A few people were smoking beneath the porch, but they couldn't tell me anything. The bands played on inside; her blood was streaked across my thigh. I filled with rage beyond anything that I'd experienced before. I blamed August for all of it.

I stood on the porch until the world shifted around me, until I noticed the sound had ceased and people were moving past me, into cars and onto the street.

Given everything afterward, I'm not sure that this sequence happened as I remember it; I haven't earned the right to connect the pieces as I do.

*

North: overnight, the octopus escapes from his tank, and in the morning is nowhere to be found—they're crafty like that. The bamboo shark continues to bash its head fruitlessly against the glass. On your way out to the gardens again—a habit we're forming, me within the house and you without—I stand on the terrace at the edge of my kingdom and ask if this is the kind of wealth where people kill.

"Check the bathrooms and closets," you say, your back to me again. "That's the surest way to tell."

It's where I found the suit, the suit I put back on this morning. You disappear into the tiered grounds, as if on patrol, and I sit down on the stone steps and stare at the shoes taken from other feet.

I expect a howl, but instead all I hear is a crack from inside, the sound of something breaking and leaking out.

*

I took to August's house with wanton violence and crystalline purity of intent. I stood across North 19th Street just after one a.m., watching dim shadows through the pale curtains of his living room, the light a kind of sickly yellow, mixed wattages inside. Two miles from campus, his house—an untended copy of the white-painted ranch-style houses to either side of him, minus the pickups in their driveways—was a known entity, was accepted as "always open." Two cars were parked on the street in front of the house, one of them a tan whatever sedan with a long crack bisecting the windshield and Food Not Bombs stickers, a stringently punk-rock vehicle that I knew to be August's. As I rounded the corner onto his street, there had been a thrill in seeing the streetlight bounce in a jagged line off the glass, like the car was a distinct, recognizable piece falling into place in the schema of how the world was meant to function on this night, proof that my thoughts and actions were consecutive, well-structured, valid. I'd picked the night—a Tuesday—without real reason, when I could no longer physically stand to do nothing. I'd walked there with my headphones in but nothing playing, now a sweaty bundle of cables in my pocket. It was ten days after the Villa Scum show; I hadn't seen Candace since, and I had drawn my conclusions. It was freezing but my body was heated independently of it. I'd waited the week on my bench before I started counting the minutes, imagining the confrontation with August. Two hours earlier I had been in my room, watching another clock move forward, and in a single moment, on an even number, I had made my decision. I ought to have expected others.

I waited across the street for over an hour, shadowed by a tree in another lawn, until three people—two women and one man—came out of the house laughing, fumbling with their keys, their breath visible. They climbed into the other car and pulled away from the curb; the house appeared to have cleared out. When their headlights vanished, I stepped into the street, breathing in a way that allowed me to hear and see it, and was nearly sideswiped by a passing truck. The driver honked and shouted something out the window and I flushed with more heat, but I resolved not to acknowledge him. (Inside, I imagined August responding to the sound of the truck, glancing to the front window and then back again to whatever he was doing, while I moved unstoppably forward.) I crouched or collapsed behind August's car in the street, sweating through my jacket and clothes. I had dressed very carefully for the occasion, though at this moment I couldn't remember how. I saw through a sliver in the curtains that the TV was on.

I pulled myself up on the trunk of the car, feeling it sink a little beneath my weight. My legs felt numb. I noticed a couple of roof tiles scattered on the lawn. As I walked up the little slope to the front door, my left foot scraped on the ground sideways, half-asleep. I kicked it, took short, quick steps to try and bring the sensation back. When I knocked, I stomped on the stoop simultaneously.

August seemed shorter behind the door than I remembered him, but was dressed the same as always in flannel and jeans, except without shoes; he was a barefoot guy. He looked at me through the screen door without any particular recognition, which hurt me more than it should have. "Can I help you?"

It struck me that this was the first time he'd spoken directly to me, and reconciling this with the way "Candace" had sounded leaving my mouth, I felt a sharp contraction in my chest, a moment of doubt as to why I'd come here, in my purpose. I quelled it.

"August, right?"—there it was again, the proper names, and I may have accented the wrong syllable—"I heard you were selling." It was a terrible line in every iteration, like a vocabulary I'd borrowed from someone who had no idea what they were talking about.

He took it in stride, which made me question how serious a drug dealer he actually was. "I'm afraid you've got the wrong house," he said. His eyes flicked up and down, and he seemed to take me in, categorize my features and file them away, assess my commercial potential. "Why don't you take it easy for the night and maybe I'll see you around?"

His reply overflowed with transactionary codes. He made to close the door. I put my fist through the screen and grabbed the handle, aware that I'd just escalated the situation tenfold, yet feeling, strangely, as if I had others accompanying me, massed in my wake. "You take it easy," I said stupidly. "Come on. I've got the money." Rather than tearing, the screen had separated from the frame, and hung down like a bedsheet, imparting disrepair rather than destruction.

"You've got the wrong house," he said again. He tried to push the door closed, but I jammed it forward with my forearm. The inner edge hit him in the chin with the same sound as the door closing, and he vanished from the crack. I flung open the screen door and crashed into the living room. August was half doubled-over on the left, shielding his face, and to my right were the couch and the TV, showing something grainy and lit in red; past that, there was a counter with stools that divided the living room from the kitchen. The order and tastefulness of it all surprised me. There was a flurry of movement from that side, a body in the kitchen obscured by the hanging cabinets, and I realized that August wasn't alone. On the far side of the entryway—across from the door I'd just burst through—a hallway led straight back. I thought: *This house has been organized for exactly my purposes.*

I felt my surroundings accelerate, move suddenly into high resolution. Instinctively, I angled my body to the left, away from the kitchen, and as August rebounded I grabbed him by his shirt collar and pushed him down the hallway. He ricocheted off the wall like a rag doll, his hands held up in limp defense. The figure in the kitchen screamed, I heard bare feet on tile, a panicked collision with a chair and another fall. I followed August into the hall, my left foot still prickling, and he launched himself at me, clutching at my jacket with both hands (his chin cracked and bleeding, matting the beard, his hair unseated), a parody of his usual bearing in a crowd, negotiating by touch, clawing for the same responses in me, that I would kiss or hold him. I wrenched his hands free and pushed him through the door at the end. I followed, kicked it closed behind me. The wood was too light for the door to slam. It whipped the air and bounced open. I shoved it closed again. I was suddenly in a bedroom.

The room was fluorescent-lit, falsely bright. Opposite the door, shelves were built into the wall, stocked with books numbered on the spines, stuffed animals and action figures filling in around two plastic snake tanks; a *Dark Side of the Moon* poster hung on the wall to my left and Kurt Cobain across from that; the floor was littered with clothes, like the trappings of some twelve-year-old's bedroom had been lifted and transplanted here. For a second I relented, absorbing this dislocation, and in that moment, August punched me in the neck, his fist mostly open. I reeled into the shoddy white door, gasping from the weirdness of the blow and the sudden constriction of airflow. The door made a hollow sound against my weight. The shock of the retaliation spurred an equally violent response, and I shoved back harder than I should have, so that August went fully into the shelves, the tanks and animals and books all upended and crashed to the floor, scattering their woodshavings and plastic tops onto the white carpet. He fell to the bed, patterned in camo, a stain-concealing riot. I stood over him, and his eyes frantically panned the room, squirming, looking for snakes, finding me.

I planted my hand on his throat, and his eyes forgot everything else, wobbling in their sockets, unsure of what to focus on as I raised my other fist into the air. My future spiraled out in front of me. And drawing my hand back, August's face was not the combination of guilt and fear that I thought it should be—that I had counted on it being—but rather a muddle of absolute, uncomprehending terror, and there above him I realized the fundamental truth of the situation: he didn't recognize me at all, he didn't have the slightest idea who I was or why I was here, of the way I related myself to him. In its apparent arbitrariness—any semblance of a script abandoned at the door, no mention of Candace whatsoever—my violence lost every part of its potential meaning, its moral intent, turned into a random invasion. There was no reason for him to understand why I'd come, no dawning moment of comprehension or repentance; I was just this insane person, a psychopath, not even vaguely familiar (and ostensibly looking for drugs, I'd gone far enough to make that claim) who had burst into his house and attacked him, without cause. I realized that my role in this, now exaggerated beyond all proportion, had been nonexistent in the first place, I was no one, that the person in the kitchen when I entered, who had fallen, who I now sensed in the hallway just beyond the door, panicked, it was unmistakably Candace—the unspoken and available reason for all of this, the rampage—and she was just as terrified of me as August, and this, this was the sensation of bringing everything to a single, empty point.

Above my head, a cold, heavy weight materialized in my hand. When I brought it down to August's face, I was holding a gun.

He cried out, sucked air through his mouth and nose, threw his hands over his face. I stumbled backward, the gun, a pistol, falling to my side in my hand like dead weight, pulling on my balance while I scanned the wreckage around the bed for other bodies. A moment passed in which nothing moved, where I just recognized the orange tail of one of the snakes. I turned and barreled out of the bedroom, colliding with Candace in the hall, her face all confused fear, a mask, the gun dragging behind me like a sudden anchor, blindingly bright, and she fell to the floor. As I crossed the foyer I spared a glance backward in time to see her look from the bedroom door back toward me, her mouth frozen open in a silent sob, one hand planted on the wall, the other on her crotch, her legs buckled beneath her, like a moment after her body had reacted but before she was able to produce sound, a scream was wrenched there within her, tearing to get out.

I didn't stop running until I'd reached the campus, two miles away. The whole way, I did not let go of the gun, nor attempt to conceal it—the way it had appeared in my hand, my finger over the trigger, was the only way I knew how to ensure it didn't fire. I remember looking down at the tips of my shoes as I ran, which were spotless white and new-looking; it was a pair of Converse I didn't wear often, that I consciously left for occasions where I cared what my shoes looked like. In the night, they were like reflectors. Arriving in sight of the dorms, rationality took hold of me at last, and I shoved my hand inside my jacket. When I finally let the gun go, fifteen minutes after that, the grip dripped with my sweat, and my hands—both of them—smelled like metal. When I let it drop, the trigger guard hung off my index finger for a second, as if my body didn't want to let it go.

And then, shortly after, everyone started to disappear.

*

I'm sitting at the long table in the northernmost dining room of the main house, flooded with sunlight and dusty from disuse, when you finally return from pacing the perimeter, after the octopus has escaped from its tank and disappeared. I've been sitting here for hours, since I discovered this room by accident (by flinging open every door on the first floor); the way that the sun-faded carpet crackled when I stepped over the threshold and the burst of musty air when I opened the door told me that it was rarely visited. I don't know how long you're in the house before you find me, or how closely you trace the doors I've left open—it seems like a given that we would connect eventually. Compared to the rest of the mansion, the dining room is primitive and dated, a mismatched relic from an earlier era. Maroons, dark greens, and browns; wood paneling; black-blotted candelabras hanging from the walls with crusts of old wax; the petrified carpet. On the wall to my left, at roughly eye-level beyond the head of the table, the mantle is decorated with two austere urns, silver candlesticks, and a small portrait of Jesus with his arms raised. A faint halo of dust between the urns makes it clear that a third is missing. This is what I choose to bring up first, bursting with info, as soon as you enter the room, as if I've been holding it in: like, when they left this house, what drove them to choose one ancestor over the others.

You slide into the chair across from me. Your feet are bare from your travels outside the house; it's hard to tell from where I'm sitting how far out you need to go before it truly counts as wild. A giant shield hangs over the mantle and the urns like a vulgar, oversized medal, emblazoned with a grizzly. Below, the portrait of the savior reads like a last-gasp addition, the mark of someone looking for reasons after the fact.

"Maybe it was a kid," you say. "The third urn—better to cart along your dead kid than your nattering parents, right?"

"I'm not convinced," I say, as if my inside-house experience has offered me special knowledge of the routines here, as if to debate our two experiences of these new environs, loving the way the suit continues to perfectly fit my body into the third straight day, the way I can spread my arms like I own everything around me, like I'm sitting at my own dinner table. "Where are the family photos? Where are the young master's toys?"

"To succeed with a money-child"—you're talking like a guru again, picking up a thread from the previous mansion—"is to be able to hide all evidence of it."

I picture immaculate tile, scrubbed daily. "Then why would they keep an urn with his ashes?"

You shrug. "They didn't."

I realize that we're balancing on a delicate position, namely to admit whether or not we think the family still exists, here or elsewhere, kept or vanished, the manifestation of a larger conversation we aren't having. A kid-shaped silence floats between us. It's telling, despite all the open doors, how nothing I've yet found in this mansion looks remotely sized for child-like hands, or like it's ever considered the idea of children. The table we're sitting at, for example, is eight feet wide. Reaching over it, we could barely touch each other. To imagine a two-year-old clambering across the foyer or scaling the front steps, crying out from its princely crib in an empty echo-chamber of a bedroom—it seems worse than out of place, trivial.

The silence spreads across the room and takes on other dimensions. You shift in your chair, look to the walls. I think of the apartment in the city, how the living room could map to this dining room, how big it looked with nothing inside it the first time we saw it. How long had we been arriving and leaving just because we couldn't keep our bodies still, because we couldn't stand how the rooms were decorated? Our perceptions of the house settle again in the wake of our dialogue, its walls thicken and tighten, new chambers clarify, and at approximately the same time we notice the giant, gleaming kitchen knife sitting unaccountably in the center of the waxy wooden table between us, completely spotless, black handle, white knife, the blade caught in the sunlight from one of the bay windows, out of place in its perfection. In all the time I've been in this room, I haven't noticed it. There are cracks in the wallpaper, bubbled ruptures beneath the surface, an oily stain on the carpet, a gilded, tarnished mirror to my right, blue drapes—all things that I haven't taken note of, deeper makeup, thoughtlessly absorbed as part of the whole. Has it been here as long as I have?

My heartbeat quickens inordinately. Our eyes juggle from the foreign object to the bare expanse of table all around it, to each other. There's no way to adequately communicate that I don't know this knife, that I didn't position myself at its handle on purpose as some idle threat or joke, that I wasn't effectively waiting here with a weapon. It falls to me, as resident of this room, to make use of it, to qualify its presence here. I reach across the table (I have to stand), and grab it without a clear plan of action. It leaves a clean shadow in the dust. "I guess that answers it," I say, for lack of anything else. "It's a fucking sacrificial altar."

My fingers slip over the handle, already clammy. The metallics are far too reminiscent and I don't know what to do with the knife besides remove it from the room, so I resolve to make food-related gestures and disappear into the nearest kitchen (three doors). Passing from the stately oak into the nearly translucent tile feels like stepping through time, from one world into another; there's a change in air quality. I open the fridge and find nothing save a dejected bag of bruised oranges. I split one on the counter as an exercise, and it sprays faint brown juice onto the wall. I'm hustling to bury the knife behind the pipes in the back of the cabinet under the sink, chewing the inside of my lips, when you appear in the doorway.

"What are you doing?"

"Just putting this away," I say, returning to standing, kneeing the door closed, the knife out of sight and receding. The two orange halves rest on the counter, rapidly going black. I step to block them from your view, as if the food is incriminating, implies that I could turn anything in this house into sustenance, could prolong existence using its means. "These people survived on spite and valium," I say. "The essentials."

You turn back to the dining room, walking your fingers across the countertop. "There are flattened patches out in the western garden," you say, "where parallel strips of the land are just totally pulverized, like a segment of railroad ties. I wonder if this location sees a lot of saucer activity."

I wash the toxic metallic smell from my hands and return to the dining room. You've already left the table, but upon taking my seat again—like a reflex, it's my seat—I realize where the talk of dead children came from, its context beyond the missing urn and altar-like table: carved along the edge of the wooden table are dozens of cherubs, their minute details obscured by a fine layer of dust, swirling alongside each other like minions to the final judgment on the plains of tablespace above, where the gods feast. I scoot the chair back by its equally ornate floral

frame and crawl beneath the table to check the underside—
sure enough, there are branching plumes of the naked winged
infants roiling out from the table's legs, too, each leg footed in a
knobby gargoyle claw, the epitome of Gothic bad taste. I knock
my head on the edge of the table as I stand, and in the quick
flash of pain, the sensory kick, the dining room changes color,
and I see it through the lens of the past, as if the mansion had
been refurbished and modernized around it to leave this room
pointedly untouched, a shrine. My eyes land on the painting of
Christ floating heavenward on the mantle, arms beneficently,
generically outstretched, and I picture the two desperate parents
hurtling into the backyard to throw ashy fistfuls of their son or
daughter hopelessly toward the sky, praying for the wind to take.

You're sitting on the wraparound black leather couch in the
dug-out living room on the other side of the house, in front of
the ceiling-high aquarium, lit from below, which at this moment
is free of overt religious iconography, so that's where I join
you. You're staring intently at a branching series of tiny cracks
that have appeared on one side of the glass, about halfway up.
I examine the tank from all angles, and it's clear that in addition
to the octopus, the bamboo shark is now missing, too. I put one
hand against the glass, barely cooler than room temperature—an
unexpected betrayal—and I close my eyes, as if in communion
but really because there's nothing we can do to keep things from
coming or going within this house.

On cue, you stand, ascend from the room and walk toward
the front door, a little crescent of moisture from your instep just
visible each time your foot leaves the tile in the foyer; detectable
in your stride is the trace of a limp, a favoring of one side over
the other. Abruptly, I decide you've switched legs since the last
time you went outside.

"Where are you going?"

"To take a walk. Jesus."

The name unsettles me, because I'm convinced he's back in the dining room.

"I'll go with you."

"I'd prefer to go alone."

"Does it still hurt you?"

My question is vague enough to make you stop and turn around. I remember Casey; I wonder if the remains of loved ones in this region are kept in-house to avoid making lengthy commutes to the cemetery. The outside seems eons away. "Does what still hurt me?"

"Your leg."

You pause. "Does yours?"

Beneath the impeccable fit of the stolen pants, I feel the faces burn in psychosoma—it's a dig into our shared past exactly as cutting as it wants to be, as I'll allow it to be, for everything I've failed to address or let be, the times I haven't trusted you. It does.

I don't answer, which is answer enough. The front door opens excessively, obscenely wide, and then, barely here, you're gone again.

*

The gun (I learned) was a Glock, a 9mm semi-automatic, big and all-purpose and standard among cops. I couldn't hold it without shaking. I emptied the magazine onto my bed in a flurry of uncertain, clumsy movement, as if handling any part of it for too long would burn me or meld it to my hand, transform it into a permanent part of me. Even when I knew it was empty—the bullet impossibly in the chamber released as well—I didn't touch the trigger.

I plugged the serial number off the barrel into every stolen-gun database I could find online, smearing my metadata everywhere, but they all came up blank. Gun registration didn't exist in Indiana, so there was no chance of finding the owner without official intervention. I wouldn't go to the police, there was no way to explain. The night passed, and nothing changed. I resented a world that failed to restructure itself in some fundamental, demonstrative way when a gun was introduced into it out of nowhere. I hated that it was just one among the many, despicably at hand. I could walk into the Walmart where your mother worked and I could pay for a rifle at the checkout counter like I could buy a toothbrush. I could blow her away right there.

I decided that the best thing I could do was separate myself from it as fast as possible, release it back into the world. The next day I slipped the gun and loose bullets into the inner pockets of my winter coat and walked to the Whitewater River near Glen Miller Park, over the bridge. I counted the cars that passed me on the street, the number of witnesses, but I was already pushing myself away from what had happened, from my role in it. At the bank of the river on the bottom of the grassy slope, where I was invisible from the road above, I poetically threw the gun into the river. From where I stood, I could see it sitting on the bottom of the riverbed, maybe two feet down, its barrel reflecting in the sun. I fought the urge to trudge in and bury it in the muck. The further I was away from it, the safer I would be. On my way back, I threw the handful of bullets away, bunching them inside napkins and throwing them into different trashcans one or two at a time. The following day, I returned to the river, and could not find the gun. It moved, presumably, on to the next.

*

In its aftermath, when the gun had left my possession, I tormented myself with what its appearance meant. Had I carried it with me? Had I pulled it blindly off one of August's shelves, picked it up along my route somewhere? Was there someone who had given it to me, who had accepted money for its exchange? I construed that there were blank patches in my memory, fugues as if in sleep, spaces I couldn't remember or control in which I'd carried out this act so far beyond my realm of imagined experience and acquired a gun, then somehow secreted it away from myself, hidden from my conscious awareness but appallingly close—at times on my person—so that, at the proper moment, I could use it. The acquisition, the conditioning must have happened long ago, its circumstances repeated until I eventually became accustomed to the weird weight of carrying a gun with me at all times, or at certain times, or with certain outfits, and that, gradually and subconsciously, I'd molded it into my routine, to the point where I would pick it up, handle it, load it, and hide it on my person, all without acknowledging or realizing what I was doing, without experiencing it as a distinct activity rather than something I did mechanically, that didn't call attention to itself or create a specific memory. It had come as naturally to me as breathing or sweating, as addressing an itch or walking forward, shrugging on a jacket with something extra tucked into the interior pocket, as closing a door behind you when you leave a building. I hadn't even noticed the weight of it until I brought the gun down in my fist, could therefore draw it, had *practiced* drawing it from wherever I kept it enough times that this, too, had become a reflex, a motion I didn't think about making. It seemed almost miraculous that I hadn't pulled the trigger, that this blank spell ended where it did rather than one second later, the camo bedspread blurted with blood. And, it followed, if this was one period of memory I couldn't recall—not only the episode of the theft or purchase or discovery of the gun, but its acclimation—then doubtlessly there were others, other sequences I couldn't remember, other fugues, further deadly machinery being unwittingly incorporated into my system.

In contrast, at the same time I imagined with equal vividness that it wasn't a longtime process, but an instantaneous one, that at this given moment, the gun had simply appeared in my hand, relocated from elsewhere. It seemed even more improbable, but the implications expanded: I imagined living in a world where the things I needed—not even needed, or even wanted, but maybe distantly imagined in one specific, fantastical instant—suddenly materialized from somewhere else. That ownership, material and physical realities meant nothing; the objects of the world were constantly scattered and reconfigured at random patterns (or patterns that surpassed our understanding), disappearing in one place to reappear somewhere else. I imagined that I'd caught a rare, transitional moment—the instant where the object physically appears—the interlude between two states. When August looked up, what had he seen? Had he watched the gun appear? Had I been holding it when I entered the house? I wondered where it was ripped away from, that gun, if it had been in use or lain dormant, if someone had stared down the barrel visualizing their end and then watched the gun melt away, if it had disappeared from a glove compartment or a holster, a shoebox on the floor of a closet in a distant part of the country.

August stopped showing up on campus. There was talk that he'd skipped town—I heard his house was suddenly empty over the space of a weekend—but I never heard anyone mention why, no one had any explanation that neared me, or anything that sounded like me. His departure built into his legend. I didn't see Candace again, either; she dropped out, or changed schools, or was otherwise taken away. I realized that I had never heard her speak, not once. I braced myself for consequences that never arrived, for the connections to flicker up and the fuse to blow, but they didn't. No one asked me anything, not even peripherally—it was as if my entire history as it connected with these two people had been selectively deleted, as if August and Candace had taken all of me, my distinguishing features, my life of contact along with them into the afterworld, or it hadn't existed to begin with. I had never been a part of their story. A week after the gun appeared, Cole was evicted from Villa Scum when someone crashed through the porch during another showcase, and then he was arrested. Without his energy and organizational efforts, the local shows dwindled, and people stopped going, they went to further towns; everything from then on felt like a last-ditch effort to save something that wasn't worth saving. One night a carful of kids whose names I knew took a joyride in the high school parking lot firing a pistol into the air, which could be heard from some parts of campus. Someone asked me afterward, "Don't you know some of those dudes?" and I said no, and I let those strings go.

I dwelt on what had happened obsessively, long after I understood that I would never have an answer. I threw away most of my clothes and cleared out my room of everything I deemed non-essential, whose provenance I couldn't be completely sure of or whose origins lay in someone with whom I was no longer connected. I raided the room for other ammunition, other weapons, but found nothing. For weeks I barely slept, and ate only enough to keep from passing out, to prevent hallucination, afraid to introduce into my body any toxins or substances it didn't already know, as if this could all have been some chemical misunderstanding. Weight fell away quickly, the padded layers between the world and my person, leaving a dense core behind. I told myself I would never forget anything again. My life became about control. I collected most of my stuff into black plastic garbage bags late one night and brought them to a dumpster on the edge of campus, as far from my dorm as possible. As I let the plastic lid slam down, something crunched behind me, and a voice made a gruff sound. I spun crazily around and slammed my back into the dumpster, pawing pathetically at the waistband of my shorts, scrambling, for all intents and purposes, for something that wasn't there.

I fell messily, tearfully to the ground in front of the night security guard, a creature of impulses I didn't even realize I had, let alone was able to control.

I thought this specific paranoia—the impermanence paranoia—would last forever (the way you expect things at age twenty to last forever), but of course even this didn't, and eventually, over the next months I patterned most of my behavior away from it, stopped frisking myself each morning, my sweeps of the room upon arrival and before and after sleep, the strictest of my self-surveillance. But it never left me completely; it threaded into my muscles and stayed there.

Barely two weeks after the gun appeared, three students from our college were lingering on the tracks downtown in Richmond's depot district one night when they were hit by an eastbound train. One girl died at the scene; the other two students were airlifted to a hospital in Dayton where, two and a half weeks later, the second died. The third student survived, and after two more weeks he left the hospital, without clear memory of what happened.

The Norfolk Southern Railway system covers the eastern third of the US like a network of veins. On the news, when they covered the accident, they returned to the same helicopter shot of the railroad from above, filmed just after dawn, the train plowing across the screen from the upper-right corner, diagonally bisecting the view. The train occupied just a narrow strip of the shot, surrounded by flatness, wide roads, as if to visually reiterate that there is always warning, there is always somewhere else to go. I thought, of course, of the gun, conflated with the idea of the train. I assigned it the same design—the train appeared instantaneously, impossibly close, on an empty horizon. Why else wouldn't you run away?

The tragedy affected the campus and town like nothing before it, shuffled all the relationships around a few focal points and formed new connective tissue between them, and when it emerged in the wake of the accident, the lines had been redrawn like a bandage over what once had been. Anything I had done receded into the past; my actions—and the people attached to them—were lost in this new context, this new curriculum of grief, and at the height of my ascetic period, desperately unarmed, you and I met in our final capacity.

*

That night, I'm installed in the master bedroom and don't hear you re-enter the house. The first indication of your presence is the shower, a hum through three walls. It's an undeniably homey sound, the quiet reassurance that another body occupies the same space, forming hygienic habits and mutual routines, traceable and regular: an empty coffee cup in the sink at the same time each morning, a filter in the trash can. The bed remade, a light left on. The water shuts off, and when the bedroom door opens a few minutes later, I don't recognize the person standing there. For a second I feel paralyzed, inserted into someone else's narrative. It takes a few steps across the room toward me before I'm fully convinced that it's you. You're dressed in a sort of kimono printed with birds in flight, pulled up from an Eastern-fetish closet somewhere, but the most shocking part is the glasses—you wear them infrequently enough that I always forget you have them at all, the revision of your face behind the frames. Your bare feet slip out beneath the hem of the robe in a way that classically signals temptation, unmasking. A second of garbled reality re-clarifies itself before I speak.

"I didn't know you brought those with you," I say. I feel like I could be talking to someone else. Where had you kept them?

You sit on the edge of the bed a quarter-mile away, massaging your knee, risen like an island among the blue folds. "They're not mine. I found them in the study downstairs."

"Do they work?"

You shrug and settle into the pillow, borrowed and hotel-soft. You remove the glasses and place them on the bedside table. "Well enough." The setup—the glásses, the lamp, a photo in a frame of a toddler in a swing—it's all assembled to seem strangely domestic, though we're occupying someone else's former life and home, though everything is a prop. And there had been a child after all. "Do you want to try?"

"No thanks."

You rub your eyes. "It's the same as any ritual," you say, "it could be generic clear plastic and it would be the same. The strength of belief is all you need. The possessions—they work as well as you need them."

I choose not to parse this.

Outside, on the ground floor, there's a heated pool on the patio, lighted automatically at night. Steam rises from the churning surface and sends shimmering patterns of smoky light through the bedroom window. I wonder what comes to swim in the pool after dark, if this is where the other liberated creatures have gotten to. The house proceeds in its nocturnal patterns; I imagine a subsequent night where you fall asleep with the glasses pushed up on your forehead, a book open on your chest, an eighteenth-century novel pulled from the library downstairs, everything working as well as it needs to, and the image is repellent to me.

The next morning the glasses have shifted owners. The pool cuts out. The aquarium stands bereft, steadily warming and emptier than before, and we are on the move again.

*

We exit the property the same way we entered, in clothes taken from the bedroom closets. I salute the empty guardhouse. We step back as the gate swings open. We walk for hours—or what feels like hours, miles—along the shoulder of the road north, wooded on both sides. The asphalt turns steadily grayer, crumbling at its edges, as though gradually ceding to the wild, a battle no longer fought. You chose sneakers, but for some reason I kept the same pair of loafers, which have molded to my feet, relented to my ownership. When a path appears, branching off the main road, we follow it for a few miles (or about an hour, or the imagined space of an hour, etc), down a snaking dirt and gravel offshoot, a strip of grass at its center. We speak less than ever. Every step in this new, unfamiliar direction seems like a rejection of the previous mansion and everything it offered, to spurn every room that we learned; it dissolves behind us, and eventually a brick wall and iron gate twice as tall as we are rise before us in its place. There's a keypad and a speaker box on our side, but the gate operates via simple latch.

Inside, an enormous property has been carved out of the landscape, and the forest crisply gives way to an ocean of cascading lawn, the space wide in a colonizing way, oppressively rectangular. Set back into its green vastness is the mansion, as bound by its proportions as the lawn surrounding it, a white rectangular box, two broad floors crowned by a domed cap in front, everything so clear in its angles and constraints as to appear blocked in from elsewhere, lowered into place with all of its bearings. A long brick driveway leads directly into its mouth, marred midway down by a single stationary vehicle. We treat the car like a building; as we near it we divide, me on the driver's side and you on the passenger's. It's a dirt-spattered Jeep, the model at least ten years old, unlocked too, and we root through it more out of curiosity than anything else: no keys, a crumpled fast food bag in the front seat, an empty carseat in the back. Despite these signs, the mansion and its grounds don't read "people" to us any differently than the others, the Jeep doesn't register as "evidence," as a sign of anything really except for what once was but isn't anymore, the kind of certainty lent by undisturbed dust. The windows of the house are set eerily high and spaced widely apart, forecasting indeterminacy, offering no indication of what's inside, the nature of its interior architecture. The windows seem to rise as we approach and step up to the terrace, like the dots across your vision after staring at a light for too long. I push open the door this time.

The mansion opens itself to us; our eyes acclimate to the dark and filtered light in deepening shifts, like a series of curtains being pulled back. The front half is cavernous, and the door opens directly into a huge, hemispheric foyer two stories high and endlessly tiled, its sanctum-like ceiling pushed up into a dome, the rest of the house built to surround it. We stand just inside for a minute, absorbing it all, the way a visited house at first seems to inhabit a slightly different plane of reality, a moment in which everything still looks untouched, where normalcy can't immediately be established because there's no sense of the upkeep, the house's deeper interiors shapeless and unexplored. A magnificent crystal chandelier dips barely into our sightline. Across the foyer from the front door, a carpeted staircase of the stateliness and grandeur we've now grown to expect crooks up to the second floor, which is partially exposed, a hallway set off by a railing overlooking the foyer, marked by a line of doors awkwardly visible from where I'm standing—exiting from any one of them you could survey the foyer from above. There are depths behind the staircase, entryways and closed doors visible opposite us that presumably lead to the functional parts of the house, but the foyer itself remains bare, a naked expanse of tiled floor, as if the budget had run out before they made it this far forward. It lends the area a vaguely mythic aspect, like an empty template, a testament to the idea of scale.

You put your index finger in the air before either of us says anything, like "hold it," and then stalk carefully a few steps into the clearing, semi-crouched, like you're detecting infrared beams or picking up on air quality using receptors I wasn't born with. The routine is new, and its unfamiliarity renders me susceptible for a moment; I'm reminded of the time you told me that you knew "how to case a Target," as if this was an arcane and specific skill, shoplifting from this specific megastore as compared to another, and seemed to imply an innate level of intuition: walk into a big-box store and you'll immediately know where the cameras are, where you stand in their field of vision. That this, to you, had become automatic, a piece of the punkroutine I didn't have as a young adult.

The mansion is silent, as they have all been; the closing of the front door reverberates through the foyer like an indecent human interruption on a place that has been at rest for a very long time, a rock ricocheting through an empty canyon, the vibrations never quite settling back into nothing.

You say, at length, turning back to me: "I think we're good."

I breathe out, and the sound indicates relief, which I know is only encouragement. But then we spread, and the thrill of indiscriminate discovery, as always, begins to surmount the other feelings: the sense of being somewhere we're not used to, the familiar apartness, how unabashedly odd things feel here, how strange and funny in their difference.

A kitchen wraps around behind the staircase on the first floor, not huge by the standards we've acclimated to, but by the looks of it fully outfitted and perfectly functional. Peeking off the left side of the kitchen I find a dining room, six chairs around the table, a mantle and family photos, and it feels almost relievingly normal, until I hear you shout from somewhere far removed: "Oh my God—I found the kitchen!" I retrace my steps, somewhat confused, wondering how your voice could possibly seem so remote from one room away, how thick the doors must be. You're not in the kitchen, and I shout out, "Where are you?" My voice bounds across the tile, returns to me. You answer distantly, and I work my way toward you through the house using a game of Marco Polo (which we play by shouting out "Wilkes!" "Krier!"), feeling lost in the specific way in which I don't really take in anything around me, but rather move blindly in a single direction, following an invisible point. I find you, eventually, and when I do for a second I think I've somehow doubled back to where I started, until I realize that you're standing at the fringes of an entirely different first-floor kitchen, at least four times as big as the other, with an island-counter in the center that shines like a dark sea. On the far side of it, another dining room, which looks like the first one except stretched to dimensions that defy all reasonability. I show you the disparity—we trek back to the other side of the mansion, toward the stairs, fumbling a few times because the rooms are still unfamiliar. When you see it, you put your hand over your mouth and buckle, briefly, in laughter. "This must be where the dolls eat."

"Or perhaps the virtual family."

"Or Daddy, when he's on a business trip."

In time, we climb the stairs to the exposed second floor. There's an oil painting just to the left at the top of the staircase, likely visible from the foyer below but which I don't notice until I'm in the hallway-cum-landing above the ground floor. It depicts a hugely formal noble couple, two bearded young men, standing side-by-side in ruffled finery and clerical robes (one in shimmering red and velvet black, the other burgundy), posed among a carefully selected array of intricate and deeply meaningful objects and instruments both scientific and religious, an unabashed triumph of technical skill and humanist thought: a lute with a broken string, a hymnal, a pair of globes, a crucifix. It's late Renaissance, probably, when the symbolism was flat and apparent but itself a little arcane—an astrolabe represented the afterlife, a lily maybe purity or death. An angled disc of meticulous, amorphous gray and beige occupies the bottom quarter of the painting, placed directly over the oriental carpet at the subjects' feet without any bearing on the surroundings, like it was added to conceal a topical error, to trick the eye; it's the shape of a diagonal slitted eye, bleached and shadowed within like a craggy alien landscape. I open my hand over the shape. Beneath my palm, the texture of the gray disc on the canvas is indistinguishable from the rest. It must be part of the original painting. I feel my sweat merging with the centuries-old paint, chemically bonding. "Are you communing with it?" you say from beside me. We leave it be.

On the other side of the bathroom door in the hallway, set against the wall, a series of four white marble heads done in the neoclassical style sit atop white pedestals, each of them identical to the others. The effect is disarming; the duplication seems accidental, like they're collected here awaiting distribution to somewhere else, to other galleries or homes. To the left of the staircase, past the painting, we find two bedrooms, one decorated in a gruesome, exposed shade of red and the other surrounded completely in mirrors, floor to ceiling, the bedsheets and curtains in glossy black like a setpiece in a BDSM club.

When I open the door to this room, you have the same reaction as when I showed you the miniature dining room, covering your mouth, going to ground. "Careful, you'll smudge it," I say.

We take off our shoes and rank socks and stand at the very fringe of the carpeted hallway, our toes at the edge of the weird reflective floor.

"Is it glass?"

"I have no idea."

"How is it so fucking spotless?"

I push you forward into the room—you run a few steps and then stop in the center, your feet smacking and sticking as if on wet tile. We leave footprints, like a hand held to a fish tank, illuminating and then mostly disappearing; it feels delicious.

"This is definitely a sexcapade bedroom."

"For Daddy, when he's on a business trip."

The room is a perfect cube, and at first we just relish running around it in our bare feet, whipping each other into the walls, whose panels tremble and ripple in their frames, leaving random prints and smears, bits of DNA. In the corner of the bedroom, one of the mirrors makes a hollow sound when I smack into it. I stop, our reflections juddering momentarily. I run my hand along the groove beside it until I find a notch. I pull it outward, and the mirror opens on a hinge. Sure enough, it's a walk-in closet filled with leather outfits, sex gear and bondage equipment, almost as deep as the room itself. Above this stuff, a line of global-southern masks of various makes and materials leers out at us. The sexual character of the room becomes blatantly, hysterically obvious. I do a spit-take when I see the masks, we make a series of escalating puns about colonization. You strap over your jeans an enormous wooden phallus roughly the diameter of a canteen (it looks like an object of anthropological study jury-rigged into a sex-toy, namely by fastening it to a harness) and chase me up and down the second-floor hallway, screaming about English blood. I collapse at the top of the stairs in a fit of laughter, barely able to breathe, and you thwack my shoulders and face with it.

I tear off my suit jacket and once-starched shirt and throw them over the balcony (it's infinitely cinematic, they take on their full volume and twirl in the air) and unearth from the closet a tiny, furry vest. I slip it over my bare shoulders—it feels cheap and plasticky against my skin, the fur a bargain synthesis, like the tawdry rich who lived here had to drive some distance out of their way to buy it, far from what was familiar or where anyone would recognize them, someplace off the highway with a name like the Lion's Den. I dance down the second-floor hallway in a seizure-like, erratic shuffle, flaunting the vest and pumping my elbows, while you stand at the other end, your fingers meeting in a diamond above your head, thrusting into an invisible partner while the harness slowly slides down your legs. I feel giddy like I haven't in an unspecifiable amount of time, and I am aware of this—aware that for the longest time I haven't capitulated to a moment like this, let myself enjoy its absurdity so completely as to feel that it lacks consequence, and exists fully as a moment in and of itself, you and I dancing toward each other in this ridiculous configuration—while at the same time conscious that the physical qualities of this experience—of a mind wiped blank, free-associating, slightly dizzy, thoughts arriving sporadically and isolated and each one of them hilarious in its isolation, an overwhelming tiredness my body struggles to fully process and which is taken out on my brain, fighting with each unfettered and hysterical thought to remain awake, intoxicated by itself alone—these physical, sensate qualities are more recently familiar, that they are the same as delirious hunger. I remember us, days after the bus landed in the city, before we had a building to inhabit, after we'd ceased spending money, had decided that whatever we were carrying was all that was worth having, I remember us doubled over each other on the blanket beneath the awning of a building we'd never dare to enter, laughing uncontrollably at some snippet of dialogue we couldn't remember, which had taken form between us in the space of our hunger (isolate, hilarious, etc), and then instantaneously vanished, the laughter it caused the only residue of its existence, starved and horny with the thrill of having nothing, absolutely nothing.

We meet at the door of the other second-floor bedroom, the furry vest on my shoulders, the wooden cock jiggling around your knees, and then we burst into it—the wallpaper colored like something pulled up from deep inside us, raw stimulation—our hands at each others' shoulders. We collapse onto the bed on top of each other, the massive headboard carved—yet again—with cherubs. We fuck messily on the throat-colored bedspread, your pants at mid-thigh, buckled together by the harness. The wooden phallus knocks rhythmically against my kneecap. I look up at the canopy, lilting from an idyllic breeze through the window, and the ripples look like veins under skin. We roll up off the bed together and then break gooily apart, hands still together, my cock dangling out of my pants. I twirl you, we dip, and I spin away into the center of the room, furry vest flapping. I leap twice, and stick the second landing next to the mahogany wardrobe, my hip jutted out, one hand held daintily opposite, the other just tickling the brass knob with its fingertips (the promise of more rich secrets), and let out an exhalation I can't afford to waste that sounds like the final exclamatory motion of an elaborate and exceptionally well-executed dance. In one more overly choreographed movement, the coital rush, I pull the wardrobe open.

We are greeted by screaming.

It takes a wild, detached second for me to realize that the sound is generated from within the wardrobe rather than outside of it, and then I see the small, curly haired body crouched on the low shelf beneath the hanging clothes, eyes and mouth wide with terror. We cut a grisly pair, me in my furry vest and you with the fake penis dangling at your knees—something clearly opposed to the entire world this child knows, a costumed menace, and the kid screams, and we scream in response, and I whip the mahogany door closed again in impulsive disbelief, which muffles the shriek but not by a lot. Then I yank it open again, like I'm redoing a magic trick for a second time and hoping that the mechanism will trip and the false bottom will fall out, leaving me with an empty box. I refasten my pants, horribly late.

The screaming child does not disappear or abate, no matter how many times I slam the door on it.

Eventually, you grab my wrist—to keep the cycle from repeating into infinity—and I release the door. It slams once more, then bounces open. The screaming persists.

I shout, "SHUT UP! WE'RE NOT GONNA FUCKING HURT YOU!" while you shout, "BE QUIET!" and it doesn't even register a pulse in the noise, the scream just gets louder and throatier, more obviously the product of real effort, just like we're all taught.

I turn and look at you with new eyes, your fingers still wrapped around my wrist. I try to take you in as a stranger might: ridge of hair matted off to one side of your head, the rest unshorn for weeks and steadily growing out, tribal piercings, dirty, quickly wrecked clothes, and the giant phallus like a blunt weapon, your legs locked together. We've had no shortage of luxury bathrooms since we left the city, but the fact remains that we are bodies left to starve in someone else's finery. We arrived here with nothing—the afternoon sunlight trickles over your shoulder through the window that takes up half of the opposite wall, slightly open, covered with a peach-colored drape (it, too, lilts in the breeze)—and now we're standing in a room expensively designed to play off of natural light. I am wearing a furry vest over bare skin.

The screaming resounds so much in the wardrobe that we don't notice immediately when it stops, that the room has suddenly become relatively still, save our guilty breathing. Into this quiet comes a sniffling from the wardrobe, something less abrasive, weakened like a wounded animal, a sound that draws us both in, brings us closer. Our delicate parts are raw, we're still feeling sensitive and flushed; we are feeling the need to regroup, to protect something outside of ourselves and hold it tight.

I pull the wardrobe door open once again. It's been slammed so many times that it breaks fully off of its hinges, but I try not to act surprised. I lean it gently against the wardrobe on the floor. Inside, shrunken in the corner, once again, is the curly haired child, legs drawn up into a little ball, eyes poking over knees, shivering.

I push my head forward as slowly and gently as I can, forcing my every aspect to read deliberation, kindness. I use my opposite hand to swing open the other door, not too quickly, to let the sunlight in on this child. The head rears back.

For the first time, I realize that I have a beard now, unintentional and probably everywhere, neck and all—an unfair and hostile mutation.

The kid screams again, and you throw your hands over your ears and make a comical wailing face. I bring my finger to my mouth, move my lips behind the bristle, as if I'm saying something too quiet to hear above the crying, leaning deeper into the wardrobe. I do it again, holding my finger there, just keep moving my lips in the same pattern ("watermelon, watermelon"), until the screaming gradually starts to lessen, until the child is captivated enough by the movement of my mouth, the projected quiet, to try and discern what I'm saying. I start whispering when it's quiet enough to hear, just nonsense syllables at first. Slowly, the face starts to move out from between their legs—the face seems to shuffle every time I see it, changing slightly, as if settling on its final form—testing the air, trying to catch the words of this hairy stranger. I wonder idly what my voice sounds like at normal speaking volume in such a constrained space, but I resist the impulse.

I turn the nonsense syllables into a sentence, which I say again, in a whisper: "No one's gonna hurt you."

As I repeat this, one finger still pressed to my lips, sibilant air channeling around it, I reach my other arm out, inside the wardrobe, inch by inch, until, in one powerful lurch, the kid, a girl, springs out and grabs my forearm, desperately tight.

Her fingernails digging into my arms, I slowly withdraw from the wardrobe, dragging her with me. I repeat the mantra: "No one is going to hurt you." Her body unfolds as she emerges, the joints cracking—it's anybody's guess how long she's been hiding in there. She climbs out nervously, bringing herself to her full height—probably four feet—every vertebrae clicking into place. She looks nervously from me to you, and in the sharpness of her features, the tight cropped curls only recently begun to undo, I read an imposed history of strict control, of someone who has never been permitted to choose her own clothes.

She looks about seven or eight, and like her normal existence ended on the day of a family portrait: she wears a white summer blouse patterned with little blue birds, rumpled and yellowed in places. I lower my whisper; my hope is that eventually the sentence I'm repeating will become subconscious and repeat on its own.

I notice your two fingers are hooked inside the front of your pants, still unbuttoned. I snap my fingers once, to get us both out of it, to remind each other that we are not necessarily horrible creatures. You react as if startled from sleep, fasten the button.

I ask, in the same whisper: "What's your name?"

The question doesn't register, lost in my tone. I try again. The third time, she looks up at me: "Vivian."

Of course. She would have the name of a fifty-year-old. Her voice is scratchy, dangerously affecting. I swallow.

"How long have you been hiding in there?" you ask. We look at each other, and there's a quiet nod of assent, as if resolving to try and handle this situation as normally as possible—we'll take turns. A part of my mind is trying to count the days since we've seen another living human.

"I don't know," she says. Her speech seems unpracticed, like she hasn't had much occasion to use it; I'm already drawing shaky parallels between her and us. "Since Mommy told me to get in." She looks down at her feet—bare, chipped blue nail-polish. I imagine her toes grasping at dewy, freshly cut grass, suddenly snatched away and switched out for the dusty interior of the mahogany wardrobe. I begin to stitch together another abandonment. Vivian looks back up at us, towering over her, as if finally realizing our presence in this house where, presumably, she once lived with others. Her eyes quiver between us. "What are you doing in my room?"

"Your—"

I look frantically around the room again for a sign of childhood that I might have missed—a whirling floral wallprint, a mirror stretching up to the ceiling, the king-size bed slung low to the ground, so shiny that it appears to be moving. The color, overwhelming everything, that looks like viscera to me—I realize, abstractly, that it must be pink. I look back to the wardrobe, at the clothes hanging in it—sure enough, they look stunted, meant for the mother's miniature iteration. It occurs suddenly to me that if this child is to sleep in this house tonight, she cannot under any circumstances sleep in the bed where we just fucked.

You take the initiative to ask the next responsible question: "Do—do you know where your parents are?"

Vivian shakes her head as her eyes well with tears. She's still clutching my arm, and her thumbnail digs into the crook of my elbow. I reach my other hand out and pat her head. Her hair is gently springy. It feels like a startlingly ineffectual gesture for someone whose parents are probably dead, my hand placed as if prepared to scalp.

You reach out and take her shoulder. It works, because all of the bone fits into your hand, allowing you to wrap and hold, which is a form of real solace and comfort.

I don't move my hand, because I don't want to admit that your gesture is better, and Vivian doesn't seem to mind, so we just stand there like that, like three points in a poorly anchored triangle, until you give her shoulder an affectionate squeeze (again, this is nothing I can do without seeming murderous) and lean in close. With the hand not around her shoulder, you tilt Vivian's chin up to you, then kneel down to eye level. I notice Vivian's grip slacken a bit on my arm. You say: "It's going to be okay. No one's going to hurt you."

For a moment, I'm genuinely touched, until I realize it's a line you stole from me.

You take her other hand, which means prying it off my arm. It feels strange to be standing there with just the one hand on top of her head, so I pat it, once, and take it away.

"We're going to take care of you," you say, your thumb on her thumb. "My name is Josephine." The name is a step backward, something classed in the extra syllables.

I kneel down too, me and my terrible beard, caught up in it. "I'm Jonathan."

Vivian looks at us both, knelt on the ground, declaring our loyalty as if subjects, promising her everything. Her eyes sparkle like something we could never afford.

*

On a summer night in late May a year ago, three weeks after your brother's funeral, we sat on the steps outside Decker Hall on a campus that felt increasingly alien to us. We'd officially moved out of it almost a month before, but that night we'd been drawn from the apartment and walked back to the grounds, more or less abandoned for the summer but still lighted and available, as if to revisit the earlier spaces of our relationship, before we tied it to property. From here, I could see the bench where I'd watched Candace move across campus, where the ends of me were sharpened.

You were sharing a memory of you and your brother, of his dressing up in your father's white temple garment and prancing around the house while your parents were elsewhere. He was much too old for it, for this kind of game—probably twelve to your eight—and you recognized it, that the underwear fit him maybe too well, almost like it would an adult, but it had been a revelation, too, a marginal breach in the unimpeachable figure that was your father at that age, that in this one way some aspect of his religion, his character could become laughable, that when the absurdity of it was presented in this way—visually, which was the universal comic format—it was okay to laugh at it. And so, while he was away with your mother and thus powerless to stop it, while your brother farted into his holy underwear, your father lost a fraction of his power, his aura, and maybe God died a little.

You magicked a cigarette out of the air and lit it. I'd seen the same smashed pack of American Spirits in various places around the apartment over the last two weeks, but had never seen you smoke one, and hadn't noticed the cigarettes at all until we moved in together. I'd come to see the single, omnipresent pack as a totem, something you carried with you and felt in your pocket when you wanted to remind yourself of something else, of a habit you'd basically abandoned but didn't want to totally relinquish, the same way you no longer actively wore spikes but kept the jackets. Its deployment here signaled a reversion, a physical activation of the past, and the smoke, heretofore an alien substance between us, lent the scene a veneer of unreality. It seemed like a cliché. As often as I revisit this conversation, it's the cigarette that gives me pause, suggests that there is some crucial piece of information I haven't picked up.

Your loss expanded. "Jesus, what happened to this place?" you said, exhaling a cloud, which seemed to imply a lot, Richmond as a whole. "I saw Casey yesterday. Him and Ian. It was like they didn't even recognize me."

"What were they up to?"

"Just biking around by the cemetery, fucking around. I kicked one of his tires and was like, GO TO SCHOOL. It's exams this week. He almost crashed but he didn't even turn around. He just sped off. No acknowledgment whatsoever."

"Maybe he was just out of it. Maybe he was on something."

"He's going to be twenty by the time he graduates high school as it is. It's falling apart."

"What, like the scene?" I could hear myself putting it in quotes.

"Ha, the scene. What does that even mean. There are more faux-hawks than ever. It's always been something you could do at the mall," you said. "No, I mean my numbers are dwindling. Everyone's gone to me now. First August, then Ryan. Now Casey, basically."

The second name didn't register. The world adjusted in the course of an instant, took me in and spit me out somewhere new. I felt my phone in my pocket, which, since we'd started dating, I'd begun carrying again. Within a year, Casey, too, would be dead. I said, "Who was August?"

"He was another friend who went away." You arched your back and laced your fingers behind your head, like one would reminisce while looking up at the stars. The movement drew up the sleeve of your shirt over the bloody set of clawmarks you have tattooed on your shoulder, a design you described as "extremely teenager," its existence an indication that at some point in our lives we were allowed to have been really, really stupid. You couldn't hold the position long before you needed to address the cigarette again. "He had snakes. Did you know him at all? He used to come to everything."

I allowed a few seconds in which I didn't breathe, where the smoke—which I was obsessed with now—was siphoned in and out by purely your side. *He had snakes.* This piece of him like a myth. I answered tangentially, "When was this?"

"I mean, I knew him for years before you came along. October or November was the last time I saw him."

Before I came along. "What happened to him?"

If one were to dial back through this conversation, it would be here, in those last two extraneous words—"to him"—where they would find my agency in this. As these stories were all, ultimately, about agency.

You shrugged. "What happens to anyone in Richmond? I knew him for a long time, since high school, and then one day he just left, without a word. I have my suspicions."

The implications spidered out before me in the dark, memories rearranging themselves around the new facts now laying claim to my past, people and objects inscribed with new meanings, new possessions. I pictured the crowds, August at the back of some basement, and beside him—as if an illustrated transparency had been slid over the image—your face resolved into view, altered beneath a different haircut but suddenly unmistakable. The lapse in my perception felt enormous, treacherously basic—was I really so single-minded as that? Candace was thrown into your proximity, and her existence seemed to reconfigure, too, to shift one way, so that I saw you in places I hadn't before, places you'd always been—as if, once Candace had been removed as the active focus of my attention, I'd neatly found a replacement. You weren't there until she was gone. I remembered scanning the crowd. I remembered the night I met you, shooting firecrackers at Casey with the rest of that awful fake-Southern band, I wondered how I might have interpreted this scene in isolation, if I'd known nothing, if I'd been watching you, which pairs I would have drawn together. I wondered if you'd known her well. In the moment, I considered the consequences, what you'd say if I got his name wrong right now, if August became Arthur or Ollie. I replied associatively, sublimating his person, burying him, beckoning toward the future; I slid myself in as neatly as August had been X-ed out: "Well, you still have me. And besides, it's only one more year until you're out of here for good. We can leave just as easy."

You nodded without looking at me. It was amazing how much we believed in this endpoint, believed it would offer us something we could use. The cigarette smoldered away, casting its spells everywhere. Why hadn't we left then, at that moment? What were we waiting for? You said: "What about you?"

"What about me?"

"Have you lost anybody?"

The question seemed ridiculously huge. My past felt puddle-deep. I struggled for the names of the two kids killed by the train. There were stones with their names on campus now. I looked to my bench. "Did you ever know Candace? Candace Eriksson?"

I didn't know what I was doing; I had no idea why I'd suddenly claimed her as my own, brought her back to the surface to clash with your associations. Maybe it was because I'd racked my brain for concrete losses and come up empty and uncomplicated—as one could never answer a question like that with "nobody," "no one"—and had nothing else to offer, maybe because I desperately wanted to draw our circles even closer together, to create the kind of shared history that might cement us further, prove that we existed before we did, or justify to myself that Candace was important enough to have, for a time, overwritten you. Maybe I pictured your stock of ablated and fading humans and I envied it, I wanted the absence for myself, the same kind of impulse that would try to keep someone from a funeral, from that closure. I knew that the lie would lead to others, but for a second I didn't see it as a lie, rather a redirection of weight, of energies and emphasis, a casting of light; still, as soon as her name left my mouth I wanted to rescind it, invent someone else.

"Candace?" you said with spite. "Candace was a liar." You exhaled smoke through your teeth. I felt briefly weightless, waiting for the ground to come up and meet me, for my consequences. I pictured August's hand on her back, his mouth open in laughter; it became a betrayal. "Which version did she tell you?" you said. "The one where a maniac with a gun bursts in on her and August but she's had too much 'cop trauma' to let him go to the police, she doesn't even see this guy's face? Or the one where she has some Richmond dude buy a gun on her behalf because she feels 'threatened' by August? Or was it the cancerous father?"

Your voice changed on *cop trauma*, on *threatened*. I'd never heard any of it; the rumors had never found me. I felt my role shift again, from that of a person into some kind of force, something that lacked its own form but instigated environmental circumstances, like biting wind or heat. It was like I was coming to this story new—I was in no one's reading. The smoke blossomed in a cloud around your neck. It hovered around your eyes. A great density seemed to fill the air between us, a substance so thick that it was difficult for either of us to see the other, to gauge the impact our words were having. I said, "The first one."

You looked at me through this haze and smartly expelled more into it, a humorless, single-beat laugh. "Yeah. Did you believe her?"

"I don't know."

A wisp of smoke curled around your ear. "Well, I'm sorry she left you," you said. I flushed with the misunderstanding, or with my misunderstanding of the words, which I didn't correct. The implication was that I'd been played. "You know," you continued, "there's a version of that story where she and August disappear to the same place, in the same car."

"With a gun in the backseat."

"Exactly."

The night pushed on. It was easier to think of August and Candace as two waning symbols moving gradually into the sunset than as characters whose effect we'd ever let drip into our lives. I experienced, there on the steps, the distinct sensation of something fateful opening up inside of me, a vacuum in which my actions—storming August's house, the appearance of the gun, that night in November, Candace herself—lost all meaning except that which would, in the end, draw us together, your disappearance at my hands. I thrilled to you like never before.

It occurred to me then in a vague way (in the sense that, in the karmic ebb and flow of life, things will occasionally turn out better for one person than another, that sometimes we profit from someone else's misfortune in ways that we don't always explicitly recognize at the time), but now it comes to me ceaselessly, the steady development of circumstances that seem both impossible and yet difficult to deny: that the world in its present state has somehow been catered entirely to us, this other vanishing pair, a synthesis of everything I've ever made disappear, riddled with the consequences of a utopia that was everything we asked for, or ever imagined wanting.

*

The house, disturbingly clean, seems to exist one day fresher than its last inhabitants. I imagine, after it was vacated, the caretaker returning the next morning none the wiser, crunching up the driveway in their Jeep to clean the house one more time, to unknowingly scrub away the last traces of human occupation—you could tell just by looking at the soap, sitting neat and untouched in its tray by the tub. Only Vivian persisted beyond, moving without touching, her tragedy human and manageable, and when you pull her to your chest, wrap your arm around her back and say it again, "We are going to take such good care of you," it seems almost tenable, like something we could hold in our hands.

You ask Vivian—in the same quiet, sweet tone, a hint of magical intention—if she wants to get "cleaned up." She nods, and at once I feel a separation occurring, a collapse of suspicion about her origins, the opening of a new set of vulnerabilities. Within a few developmental seconds, I know that I will never be able to ask where she came from and how she got here and disbelieve her answer, that we are lost to this tenderness.

You march her by the shoulders out of the bedroom and down the hallway to the bathroom by the painting. With your every step away from me our journey down this path feels further determined, fated, the world outside the mansion gets miles wider while we remain stranded in its middle. I feel us fixing in place, the mud sucking at our shoes. The door closes. I sit in the same chair for a thousand nights, until it warps to my body. The water comes on hard. It runs, uninterrupted, on full-blast, for the rest of my life.

Abandoned in the hallway, I pace uselessly up and down the second-floor corridor examining the identical marble busts, as if I'll find some disparity between them that will reveal their true nature, their hidden significance. The chins tilt up in vague, uniform defiance, pupils blank. I press my ear against the bathroom door, but all I hear is rushing water pouring from faucet to drain. The stream is concentrated and undiluted, a domestic comfort turned hostile; deeply, I think I hear more than one source of water, as if you've turned on both the sink and the tub, a calculated maneuver to drown me out, to keep me from overhearing. I knot my slick hands and cross the balcony above the foyer back and forth until steam trickles out from under the bathroom door, seeping into the painting, weathering it.

On my twelfth lap of the balcony a possibility grabs hold of me. I bolt down the staircase, pound across the foyer, and throw open the front door to the terrace beyond. The air outside is denser than it is within. The forest stands before me in the distance like a dark entity against the late afternoon light, an impassable wall. I race around the front of the house, trying to find the easiest route to wind my way to the back, a means of egress I hadn't considered, each window an escape hatch. I plow through the flawless, dimming gardens around the corner in a wide arc, looking by turns ahead of me and up at the windows for movement. I emerge behind the house after what seems like an absurd length of time. Narrow pools and a brick avenue beneath an archway stretch to the vanishing point, tinged with gold. The property goes on forever. I stand very still on the lawn, poised for interference, a sudden start. The air swarms with heat like a grainy photograph, nearly audible. Sweat crawls down my face. Thirty feet away, a line of manicured hedges wraps around the back half of the mansion at waist-height, as if to disguise the seam at its base. I scan the windows of the second floor and spot it immediately—two windows are cracked open, and below the bathroom window hangs a deep red sheet, knotted into a rope. It reaches down about six feet from the window, ending fifteen feet off the ground, a lustrous color deployed on randy nights in the mirror bedroom.

I actually shout it out and point, I'm so pleased to have caught this deception: "Aha!" I look from the trailing edge of the sheet to the base of the house and, sure enough, the bushes directly beneath look disheveled, as if they've sustained a human-sized impact. I whirl around, thrilled—the grass at my feet rustles eerily, like stiff plastic—and scream "VIVIAN!" across the lawn, frantic with non-movement. I don't know why I call her name first.

My voice carries on without interruption down the land-scaped corridor. I advance on the bushes, hoping they'll offer some clue as to where.you've gone, how you made the decision so quickly without me. Beneath the window, the branches are sunken down and snapped, and as I approach, mounding above it, I see, unmistakably, the curved form of a human hip.

My stomach leaps into my throat—no one, really, comes to expect surprises like this—and I pause before taking a few more steps forward, as a rotting stench meets the suffocating air and filters into my nose, a radius around this bush, a pocket of sti-fling death.

It's the body of a woman, twisted among the leaves, wedged between the hedge and the house. She's bent at the waist, turned on her right side, angled toward the lawn but almost face-down, one arm twisted behind her back and the other thrown over her head. Her hair—fair red to gray—is pulled into a ponytail. She wears olive-colored pants and a faded hoodie, the color washing out of both. Her skin—the hands and face, the strip between the hoodie and the jeans—all has the same pallor, like bleached earth. Tiny ruptures dot the fabric of her clothes, minute threads curling out from the pricks of the thorny branches, barely blood, as if to add insult to injury, to mock what actually killed her.

I picture this woman scaling out of the window in a desperate escape attempt—having dragged the sheet into the bathroom or found it there, unable to use the front door for fear of being discovered, for fear of something—and then missing a knot, slipping to land awkwardly, embarrassingly, cripplingly alone in the gap between the bushes and the house. And then, unable to drag herself out, over a period of days, of weeks, left to die in the back long after the rest had fled out the front. Or: she'd made it to the ground intact, but someone had been waiting for her.

I imagine you and Vivian, your new pair escaping out the other side of the house, leaving me alone with this beastly place.

I forsake the body. I sprint as fast as my legs will take me back to the front of the house, trampling the same gardens. It seems to take even longer to cross the distance; I envision catching you on the great stone steps, imagine how I'd move my body to throw you off the railing and take Vivian by the hand, changing one partner for another, a choice I can't explain but that shouts THE FUTURE! THE FUTURE! with boundless ferocity. I reel around the corner in anticipation of combat, of having to act quickly, again lost in the emotion of my mistake, and as I climb the empty steps, something deep and generative yawns open within me.

But the front door hangs open exactly the way I know I left it, my breath still on the lawn below, my guts a mix of certainty and utter wrongness at the velocity of my movement, at the fact that when offered the opportunity, you hadn't run. I leave the door open behind me, because I'm convinced this means something. The foyer carries a wet heat from the boiling bathroom. I pick up the suit jacket and shirt I'd thrown from above; they feel like elements from a prior life, a former physical manifestation. I return to the second floor.

The hallway is enveloped with steam, trickling over the balcony. The marble heads all sweat on their pedestals. I run my finger through the carved curls atop a perfect specimen of youth, frozen in time. I listen again at the bathroom door. It's sweating, too. And again, all I hear is the sound of running water. I knock lightly, and then harder.

I feel a hum of vibration in response, someone speaking on the inside. I detect conspiracy in the tones. I turn the knob gently, silently until it stops. I draw mythic, angry shapes in the condensation on the door.

Eventually, I go back to roaming the second-floor hallway, ascending and descending the stairs, counting circuits and steadily dampening from sweat and steam. A ripeness exudes from me, and pressure builds in my bladder. Twenty laps later, the odor of anxiety around me now concentrated and powerful, I hear the soft click of the door being unlocked, then quickly opening and closing, the water continuing to run behind it. I turn in time to see you hustling off in the opposite direction. In a couple of strides I've leapt the last few stairs and overtaken you.

You're wet with perspiration and bathroom steam, hair dark and plastered to your forehead, furiously bunching and unbunching Vivian's blouse in your hands. I'm flushed from my journey outside. Our two-shot strikes me as strangely erotic, our respective bearings deep and earthly.

I test it. I reach out and put my hand on your shoulder. It echoes back to an equally basic gesture, some form of taking. You seize with the touch; an involuntary, disgusted look glances across your face like a flickering light, like I'm calling back the moments before we summoned Vivian out of the wardrobe, the sound of our bodies colliding. For a second, I forget who I am, of the way that we're related: I'm standing in your way.

"This is so fucked," you say, elbowing past me, my hand shrugged off, falling to my side like it's heavy with water.

I turn, the breach widening between us. "What happened? Is she okay?"

You open the door to Vivian's bedroom, shaking your head. "She'll never be okay."

Inside, you root around the wardrobe, one half of the door propped up beside it, flicking through pastel-colored blouses as if someone's going to judge the color.

"What happened to her?" I ask.

"What do you think happened to her? There's no one else here."

"Is that what she told you? That they left her?"

"You heard what she said. Someone told her to get in here, and no one ever came back for her. I haven't asked for more. I don't want to traumatize her by forcing her to live through it all again. I don't want to know."

"You went back to calling yourself Josephine."

You shoot me an angry look, like I shouldn't have noticed. "It was an impulse. I thought we—I don't know. I wasn't thinking." You turn back to the wardrobe. "I didn't know yours was short for Jonathan."

"It isn't." I step deeper into the bedroom. The bedspread is mussed from our contact, and a smell hangs in the air. The harness sits discarded near your feet. Death everywhere. "We need to be careful. We don't know what happened here before we arrived."

You whirl around and shake a lime-green dress you've selected in my face; it's an awful choice, begging for stains. "Stop it. I'm just trying to show a little fucking humanity. What else are we supposed to do? Do you want to throw her out? Is that what you're saying? Out of this house we just happened into? Is it ours now?"

Our list of options seems especially stark, and I don't have answers for any of these questions. "I'm just saying we use some basic caution. We don't know her story. We don't know who's looking for her."

You go to the bureau and pull open the top drawer, as if it's a place you've visited many times, and draw out a pair of kiddie underpants that glimmer in the light from the window in a way they really shouldn't. "I know enough of her story," you say. "She was abandoned. We don't have to do the same thing."

I stand at the bedroom door as you walk back down the hall, an entire outfit balled in one hand. One level below, the body bakes in the lowering sun. You knock twice, gently, on the bathroom door. "Vivian? I'm coming back in." When you ease the door open, into the steam, your face widens into a smile I've never seen before, beatific, I think, and then it closes.

*

There was something else, and that was your car, the indeterminate sedan with the cracked windshield. When I saw it for the first time in relation to you, I'd recalled it as if from déjà vu, assumed I must have tangentially processed it driving by on some other random occasion. But on our way home through the heat on the summer night you told me about August, I realized where I'd seen the car before, where the connection until now hadn't been present. The car had been parked in the street the night I descended on August's house the previous autumn, and I'd believed it to be his. The points connected as if on a map, expanded and took on the meanings I gave them: that you'd let him drive it the same as you let me drive it—which August had done enough for me to idly assign it to him—and that, in the fact of this regularity, the shared vehicle, even shared home, the two of you might have been closer than you let on. I wondered how you would have described him to someone else at the time, before he disappeared, using which word; if it was Candace who had eventually risen to supplant you in his life, if this was where the spite came from, if it was as basic as that. I wondered how long the overlap had been, the process of this replacement, if it had begun the night I saw August touch her for the first time, how much you, Joey—invisible to me until you weren't—how much you had known it was happening. If, when I'd broken into his house those weeks later, it was only a matter of statistical chance that you weren't the figure in the kitchen rather than Candace, that when I entered his bedroom you weren't curled up on the camo bedspread. I wondered if in the end I had become August's convenient excuse for leaving, a perfectly legitimate fear for his life, and if this might have been the reason he didn't tell anyone what I'd done, that he let Candace do the talking for him so he could slip away unseen, blameless, leaving you behind. If maybe, under different circumstances, had I been looking elsewhere, it would be the two of you who disappeared; the car that floated into the horizon would be yours, its broken windshield blaring the sun in two.

*

I collapse against the balcony railing opposite the bathroom door, level with the bases of the pedestals lining the royal blue carpet. On the floor, indentations notched at right angles show where the columns have been shifted recently, presumably for cleaning. The corner of one pedestal is worn and peeling, bits of white flaked off, tiny cracks radiating upward. I realize that they're just plaster, these columns, cheap stands holding up heavy sweating marble, where every minute renegotiation becomes a feat of balance—like the painting by the bathroom, an investment in the object itself but not its preservation. I fabricate an image of the woman I found dead in the bushes cradling one of the heads in her arms after it had toppled during some routine action, its impressive weight pushing her to her knees.

Behind the bathroom door, I imagine the intimacy being built under the auspices of your birth name. It occurs to me that somewhere in the act of choosing clothes for a little girl lies the path to a fundamental compromise, to my expulsion from the house. I run two fingers downward from the corners of my mouth to meet at the base of my chin, over the hair barely curling out of it, and my face feels unfamiliar to me, as if, without noticing, I've been shifted gradually into someone else. I look down at the leather shoes leftover from the last mansion that for some reason I cannot stop wearing, which have lost all of their shine and rubbed completely to matte, beaten and scratched from overuse, their upkeep a gesture once made in earnest but then forgotten. Everything around me bleeds with hard-won convenience—a moneyed stasis fought for so it could be ignored, expensively maintained by others and available for appreciation piecemeal, at random.

The presence of the body itself feels significant, in that it's the first body I've seen at all—until now, the signs of disappearance and death that surround us have been subtracted of their most obvious remainder. I consider a mass evacuation; I wonder if whatever happened could have occurred in waves, like a pandemic, by geographic locality, spreading into surrounding areas in a widening radius, and that even as I sit here, the radius moves farther south, toward where we came from, or has already cleared it. I think back to the train headed north, to the pulse across the landscape I recall for the first time, that I'm now convinced I witnessed. I try to remember which way the trees shifted, if the force was moving away from the city or toward it. Against the movement of the train, it's impossible to discern.

I feel my clothes dampening against the floor. My anxiety balls up in a noxious cloud, my eyes fixed on the door behind which the water continues to run unabated, concealing a detail, a mechanical fact that now stares me in the face, hanging there unaddressed since we found the car in the driveway: these disappearances do not leave bodies, not that we've seen, and the woman in the back, therefore, is not among them at all, and has either been there since before the people who lived in the mansion left it—that for some unspecified amount of time they occupied the house while she lay dying below their bathroom window, one bedsheet missing—or she'd died afterward, same as us, had entered the house and then tried to escape, from something inside.

Softly, without notice, the bathroom door opens. An eruption of steam, and within it there stands Vivian, hair wet and tousled, dressed in the lime-green outfit you chose for her, which is much too small, which doesn't even reach her knees and stretches to cover even her narrow torso, its straps digging into her skin, and behind her, you stand with your hands gracing her shoulders in an approximation of the tone I heard in your voice earlier, the smile, mother of mercy, the dusk light shining beautifully over your shoulder through the window, beyond which hangs, etc. You're illuminated with a new, rich kind of excitement, the sheen of knowledge. I understand, at once, that there is no breaking this bond, no matter where Vivian came from, no matter what has come to pass in this house before us.

*

Afterward, your bearing is as if Vivian has told you everything, as if the two of you are inseparable and always have been. She's one step away from being in your arms. "Let's have a nice dinner," you say. "A nice dinner."

We restrict ourselves to the miniature kitchen and dining room—the first rooms I discovered, behind the foyer—the smaller house within the house. While you explore the cabinets,

I enter the dining room. On the otherwise-bare table lies a broad kitchen knife, like an apparition. It wasn't there before. I grab it before my body reacts to the fact of its existence. I take it down the hallway; I stuff it into the back of a random closet, my heart battering away. My surroundings shift and refresh. I have to remind myself that I am not in the same house, that each has its own separate supply of weapons, cabinets full of guns.

The photos on the mantle in the dining room reveal themselves as family portraits, a parallel to the last mansion and its urns. A bride and groom; an older couple in front of an ivy-covered gate that I recognize from where we entered the property; a family with two kids outdoors. I scan for familiar faces, finding none, and turn the most incriminating portrait to face the wall, then return to the kitchen.

You're beaming over a box of spaghetti and an old jar of pasta sauce. Vivian shrugs into the corner when I enter, though I try to look as friendly as possible, mainly by smiling. I transmit with my expression that I won't betray her presence here, which is ultimately the same as ours, that maybe she has never seen this kitchen before.

You open a cabinet above the stove. "Do you remember where you keep the spices?" You look back at Vivian, who shakes her head. You smile like you understand exactly. "It's okay, we'll be spartan with our spaghetti."

You stuff the spaghetti into a pot of water and set it on the stove to boil. Your moves are panicked and rushed, out of order, frantically trying to project normalcy and missing crucial steps, but I don't say anything. I'm trying to remember the last time we ate, or what was consumed, or where it happened. You open four more cabinets before you find plates; with every miscalculation I see the stress roll across your back and neck beneath the white t-shirt you found in another bedroom closet. You don't ask Vivian for further help. It feels strange to be using someone else's dishes, to find the plates in the cupboard by chance—heavy and ceramic—a part of someone else's larger system. Vivian sits on the floor of the kitchen with her legs crossed, the lime-green dress ripping at the seams.

You apportion the spaghetti onto three plates and tuck the sauce jar under your arm. You coax Vivian off the floor and we go to the dining room.

The knife has reappeared on the table. Exactly where it sat before, gleaming almost white in the center, as if I'd never moved it. Adrenaline surges up to my ears and I freeze momentarily in the doorway. When thought returns I circle the table and pick up the knife without stopping, as if constant movement will disguise what I'm doing—I exit the room from the other side and stride purposefully into the foyer, to the still-open front door. I pitch the knife over the edge of the terrace, close the door, and return to the dining room, where you and Vivian are still arrayed standing and breathing, motionless. My re-entry seems to restore movement, you plate the table for our trio and in our collective sitting I steal a glance at the mantle, where the photo is still turned toward the wall. I did pass back through here on my way to the kitchen—could I have replaced the knife, opened the closet but never put it inside? I realize that one of my hands is shoved deep in my pocket, grabbing at the meat of my leg, an empty holster.

You take your place next to Vivian, opposite me, and hand the jar of sauce across the table. "Could you use your manly strength to open this?"

Under normal circumstances you would never say something like this to me, never. I accept the jar and notice the moisture from the sweat under your arm. I look across the table and watch your shoulders rise and fall, your body beneath all knotted with tension, trying desperately to fill this role.

"Of course," I say cheerfully, expansively, aware that my response is arriving several seconds too late to pass for normal.

The lid comes away like nothing. As I glop unheated, room-temperature sauce onto my plate, I discreetly sniff the lid—beneath the tomato sauce, sweat. I offer it across the table.

I jab my fork into the mass before me and mash the two ingredients together. When you and Vivian are situated, I raise a forkful into my mouth. It's unbearably sweet. My eyelids flutter. The pasta is totally undercooked—I feel it crunch beneath my teeth.

"I tried to cook it a bit al dente," you say. This, too, is something you would never say, and suddenly I see it, the scene we're trying to play out, the illustration we're attempting to become, here at our nice dinner. "Just a little bit crunchy."

I feel almost drunk, on the edge of dissociation, a tingling sensation on my skin. I say, "Delicious."

Vivian is wolfing down the spaghetti, her face about six inches from the plate. The sound of her eating fills the room; behind the wet mess of chewing, I hear it snap to pieces inside her mouth.

We are both staring. That smile again. "Well. Vivian certainly likes it."

I throw my head back and chuckle—there is no other word for it. It hits the air like a wave. I start to sweat afresh.

I try to divert your attention from Vivian—which somehow feels insidious—by slurping my spaghetti. I stick a loaded bite into my mouth and then begin to suck in, feeling flecks of sauce spatter my shirt and face. You slowly turn toward me with the same glazed smile. "Oh, August. You are disgusting."

It is Vivian who registers this first. She stops eating. "I thought you said your name was Jonathan."

Of all the names between us, it had to be this one that you get wrong. August, the disappearance, and the process that seems, obscurely, to be repeating. It takes until Vivian speaks for you to realize it, a visible shudder that Vivian is too intent on me now to notice.

I've still offered no objection. "It is," I say, as if my answer will prove some distraction to the question itself. My eyes flick to the mantle—just to prove consistency exists somewhere, I think—and then, so do everyone else's.

"What are these?" you say quickly, pushing back your chair and standing at the same time, zeroing in on the mantle. "Photos?"

I realize that, in turning the photo specifically not featuring Vivian to face the wall, I was not protecting her identity at all: instead, I was laying a trap.

You reach the mantle in one large step and begin to handle the photos in a way that suggests you already know who's missing from them. "Are these of your family?" in the same tone.

Vivian takes the opportunity to finally slop a spoonful of sauce onto her lime-green dress without taking her eyes off of you. A low cry of surprise breaks across the room—we are not making nearly enough noise to fill this house—and you spin around to the table in alarm. It takes me a second to understand that the sound came from Vivian. You rush to her, the photos forgotten. As expected, her front looks like a massacre.

*

We install Vivian in the mirror bedroom on the second floor, while we take up residence in the viscera bedroom next door, where we found her. There are plenty of other bedrooms to this side of the mansion, but these share a wall; these are part of the house we've carved out of the house.

The mirror bedroom retains our prints on its reflective walls. Prior to bringing her up, I'd made sure the closet was sealed. "Look," you say, kneeling at the wall across from the black and endless bed. "If you knock, we can hear you on the other side, and we'll knock back so you know you're safe." You knock twice. Your knuckles leave eight marks on the glass.

Vivian nods. She's wearing a set of horsey-printed pajamas that are, once again, obviously much too small. That the other bedroom is hers is the logical argument, but she doesn't make this claim again, and her introduction to the mirror bedroom betrays no familiarity with it; this piece of cunning does not occur to her. She reaches out and knocks twice in reply to you, and sort of smiles, banishing anything that's left of your doubt.

As you stand, she hugs your legs, spontaneously, and you press her head into your stomach. "Just let us know if you need anything," you say. "And knock before you go to sleep."

We return to our gore-colored room together, but before you have a chance to speak I depart for the bathroom down the hall. A crack of dark sky and a sliver of cool air greet me from across the room as I enter. I switch on the light. The floor is barely slick from earlier, and your last set of clothes lies in a pile by the drying tub, but otherwise, there's no evidence of human interaction. The end of the red sheet is tethered to an arm of the toilet paper holder and pulled taut. It seems impossible that you couldn't have noticed. In the drawers, I find nail scissors, old razors and shaving cream, a nest of expired acne treatments. I go about shaving off my nascent beard for the most obvious reason, which is to prove that I do not look at all like August. The cut on my upper lip has mostly healed over, leaving a thin, dark furrow bisecting the top half of my mouth. Its precision makes it look intentional.

I return to the bedroom, and you start when you look up from the bed, where you're sitting with your shoes on. "I didn't recognize you."

"Interesting."

"No, it's not 'interesting,' shut up. I'm sorry, I got flustered. It was just muscle memory," you say. "It doesn't mean anything."

"It's been two years." I want to bring up the car, August's replacements, the bodies, to lay out the connections I've made and be praised for making them, for having known all along. I try to remember you putting your shoes back on, at which phase of the evening you decided you needed them.

"I'm sorry!" Your heels dig into the mattress, and I hope there's a lot of dirt on them, that they're absolutely filthy. "You know how, with every person you know, you have a set of circumstances and settings that you associate with them, that are specific to that person?" you say. "Mine just got jumbled. I spent a lot of time eating spaghetti on the floor of August's house in college. He was a terrible cook. What do you want from me? What are you trying to prove?"

I feel an intimate sense of casual, thoughtless deception, like when I discovered that the really foul smell I'd noticed on occasion for six months was actually the smell of your bare feet. Still, I know what you mean, in the same way that I look at you sometimes and see Candace, for whom, I guess, I was probably once willing to kill.

"I made a mistake. Jesus. I have no idea what I'm doing." You hug your knees.

I look back at the closed door, behind which stretches the mansion, dozens of rooms we don't know, an inexhaustible amount of space. I feel suddenly, overwhelmingly tired. I turn back to the bed, another thing, your being: "What is our plan here?" I don't mean to repeat your sentiment, but that's how it comes out.

"Shit, I don't know." You rub your face on your knees, bite the fabric once. You scoot forward on the bed, look around the room as if someone's listening in, at the broken wardrobe, at me. "Did you feel it, when you opened the door and saw she was inside? Like something was being reset?"

I bite my lower lip in an unconscious echo. It feels like the closest we've come to addressing any of this in a broader way. I wonder if we put it all down now, everything, together, we might be able to make sense of it. Before I can reply though, you lower your voice: "Do you think this is some kind of a test? Do you think this is our chance to—to start over?"

It's the most uncertain you've ever sounded, uncertainty cut with hope—that somewhere out there is a larger meaning, a kind of final tally, a use for your full name, an aspect of God— and I don't want to speak and destroy it. And again, in my lack of response, my silence, we shift, you speak again: "I was think-ing—I thought we should stay here with her."

"Here? In this house?"

"Why not? This is her home. We can use the interior house." The swatch of the mansion that we've inhabited thus far—the two bedrooms, the bathroom, the staircase, the small kitchen and dining room, the foyer—we've never mentioned it specifi-cally, but I know exactly what you're referring to. "We have to stay somewhere. We can't just keep wandering forever. At least there's food here."

The mention of food surprises me; it seems to come out of nowhere and, thus, sounds like a lie. "Would you want to stay in the place where your parents disappeared?"

You absently start untying one of your shoes. "Another house, then."

"Do you trust her?"

You look up at me accusingly. "An eight-year-old girl? Of course I do. Why shouldn't I? Why shouldn't we try to help her?"

These are two separate questions, but before I can point this out, I hear two quiet knocks on the wall just beside the bed. Your face breaks into the kind of smile that tells me this is a decision I never had a say in.

"I'll go," I say.

"You don't have to go. You just have to knock." You turn on your knees and lean down, press your ear to the wall.

"I just want to check on her."

I don't know what I'm doing. As I open the door to the hall-way, you knock back. Almost immediately, Vivian knocks again.

You reply, two knocks. I think: *You are doing this all wrong. I should be stopped.*

When I open the door to the mirror bedroom, I'm greeted with an image of Vivian from almost every angle. She's crouched on the floor by the wall, her hand raised in this useless game with the wall, with the reflected version of herself. She turns to look at me across the darkened room where I stand rooted in the doorway, suddenly multiplied six times over, briefly uncomprehending my naked face, her eyes glowing in the dark, already gone.

"I wanted to see if you needed anything. Goodnight." I close the door without waiting for an answer, reach absently into my pocket. I stumble in the hallway, in the dark; I reach out and grab the banister. My throat constricts. I punch my chest, like there's some object caught in there, some hard evil I can cough up.

In our bedroom, you are still knocking. One of you will need to stop first. "How is she?" you ask, grinning.

I say, "Cozy." The word feels dishonest, as far from the truth as possible. I say, "Falling asleep."

*

Hours later, I lie in bed in the dark beside you with my eyes open, wracked with fear, our conversation unfinished, my hands so wide against the sheets that they ache, sweating out my palms. The canopy shifts above my frozen body, the air invisibly packed with motion, with vying forces pushing against each other. My existence hangs in a state of loaded potential, a behavioral holding pattern. The room feels poised to propel me forward at any moment, to bear me out of bed and into the rest of the house. If I fall asleep, I know the knife will appear in my hand, and that this time, I may not be able to control what I do with it. I can almost feel its weight in the bed with me, the weight of the gun; I can smell it. The reappearances—in this house, in others—are warnings: that this impulse has followed me, has been priming me for years, but has only revealed itself so gratuitously now that the potential for its use has narrowed to a single point, the randomness and bystander targets eliminated, the selection obvious and the reflex coaxed; that, when the time comes, there will be no real choice to make, and the act will be at its core, like the slip of a name, completely mechanical. I bid them to run. I should have run. I should have left this house lifetimes ago.

Darkness and exhaustion bear down on me, anticipating another knock through the wall, the door opening, inviting me inside. I can't do it.

I fall asleep.

And needless to say, in the morning, Vivian is gone.

*

I have a dream in which I am the train, plowing into the north. For the most part, it's peaceful, even comforting, a dream about being on tracks, in quiet, preordained control: there is a path, and I am following it. The dream begins at approximately dusk and proceeds through the night in an aisle between swathes of varying landscape, moving forward without effort, my field of vision fixed on the tracks ahead. The baring trees bordering the tracks at intervals, the cast of the sky indicate late autumn, northeastern climates. There's no sound, but my journey is enveloped in a constant vibration, the sound's physical manifestation. I sail along into the darkness, which deepens more quickly than in real life, as if the footage of the dream has been gently fast-forwarded, pushed insistently along. The progress toward the horizon is satisfying, game-like, the way I steadily overcome the sparse decorations of environment approaching to either side of me—the trees, the houses and mild traffic—as if I'll never need to stop, as if there is no end. I cross through small towns and the outskirts of larger cities, lofted slightly above, factories and old warehouses in the distance, occasionally long stretches of fields. The farmland, the flatness feels out of place, inconsistent with the region, but I interpret this as a regular malfunction of the dream, I don't know the geography of this area well anyways. At crossings, I watch the gates drop well ahead of time and the cars wait, stalled—I see them as I pass, like stationary objects. Everything rotates out at the same pace, time and distance condensing. The landscape blandly repeats its forms, and the night goes on. There's no telling how long the train stretches behind me. Innate of nothing, three figures resolve themselves on the track ahead where they shouldn't be, their backs to me. There is no time, but they seem to deliberate while I advance; it seems impossible that they're oblivious to my presence. They turn, sluggishly—I notice that all three are wearing flannel, that I am close enough to make these distinctions. It's here where I feel the engine—or the accelerated pace of the dream—start to slow, a subtle pitch in the scroll, the first sense that there is someone beyond me, controlling, but machines like these are nothing but momentum, variously disguised. They clear the tracks—no one stands there unless they want to die—but, again, not by enough. The friction drags them back toward it. I take them in and spit them out unseen behind me. All I hear, all I feel is the constant vibration, unaltered. My pace goes unbroken. I do not stop until long after, beyond the scope of the dream.

*

I'm on my feet before I realize that I've been asleep, that an unidentifiable amount of time has passed since I was last conscious and aware of what I was doing, and the vibration from the dream has turned into your scream from next door—long enough for the light to return outside. I stop in my tracks midway across the bedroom. I run my hands down my sides and legs before I exit; I'm carrying nothing, but my right side aches all the way down my arm and chest, as if someone beat up just the one half of me while I slept. My palms and fingers tingle; the room feels swampy and uncertain.

I emerge into the hallway with a mounting dread in my chest, the sensation of watching someone just out of reach go off the edge of a cliff, of entering an unfamiliar room where something sinister awaits. I follow the shouting automatically. One step before the door, it occurs to me that I should look in a mirror first, I should go somewhere private to compose myself, but then I'm standing in the doorway of the mirror bedroom, sextupled publicly, and so are you, and the room is otherwise empty, devastatingly empty: the bed lies undisturbed, the pajamas discarded on the floor in a huddle, and you, on your knees, at odds with it all. I notice that you're wearing sneakers, that you have already been outside.

"She's gone!" you say, your voice lowering now that I've arrived. "She's gone."

I stride immediately to the hidden closet and yank it open, as if the suddenness of my actions will reveal some additional, deeper secret passageway before it has a chance to close up. The door slides slowly, smoothly forward. It reads like I'm deliberating. I march in and throw the straps and masks and leather gear to the floor, leaving naked white walls beneath. I start shouting her name, which seems excessive.

"I've already looked there. I've looked everywhere."

I withdraw back into the room. My voice takes on a ridiculous tone, a pacifying authority. "She has to be somewhere. Have you been outside?"

You're speaking to the floor, to your mirrored version, for all intents and purposes still rehearsing. Your voice trembles. "She isn't here."

I gather that this isn't your first time in the room this morning, that you may have searched for hours before you woke me up, maybe I wasn't trusted to look. That once you had combed the house and its surroundings—made as sure as you could that Vivian had truly left—only then had you returned to the second floor, planted yourself in this room, and called for backup. Both of us know it.

"This house is a maze," I say, as if I don't notice this level of mistrust, as if our stories weren't already separated. "There are a million places she could be. She wouldn't leave the place where she grew up, not just because we arrived. We'll find her." More of this. I continue to pretend. My arguments—which it seems aren't actually meant to convince you, merely to temper what we both already know is absolute—are peppered with the most obvious inconsistencies, basic contradictions of what I've said before. They are color. I abruptly remember us boarding the bus in Indiana, stepping aside to let you climb on first, our destination as far east as possible, in thrall to an idea neither of us had ever fully articulated, but assumed the other took for granted, considered a necessity.

"She's not here," you say. "I can feel it. We shouldn't have left her alone. We scared her. We came in and we took over." I shift, I see bruises on my arm, and the room moves kaleidoscopically. "If she was afraid, she would leave. She's not here."

"What did you tell her? Did you tell her we were going to stay?"

From the way we're positioned, I can watch your face develop in the floor before you turn and reveal it to me. I speak before you can answer, before another story of eviction can begin: "I'll check the first floor again." And I depart.

I go downstairs, I open the doors and closets of the interior house, but without specifically taking note of their contents. I know there's nothing there, same as you; my instinctive destination beckons while I go through the motions and make these needless delays. I open a closet door off the dining room, I shove aside coats, layers of boots and shoes, but there's nothing inside that shouldn't be. I feel around for a panel in the floor, a crawlspace, a place of vanishing. I pass through the dining room, where the photo without Vivian still faces the wall. I stop and peer under the table, like looking for a pet cat you know will eventually show up on its own. I enter the kitchen.

The unwashed dishes sit in the sink—I can't for the life of me remember who put them there. I kneel down and open the cabinet beneath it, where I'd stashed the knife in the previous mansion, in a kitchen that was different but the same, in a house that was different but the same. I reach past the pipes and ancient cleaning products, through the grime that accumulates in these spaces no matter how rich you are. Wedged in the back, between pipes, I feel a blade.

I ease it slowly from its trap with the tips of my fingers. I hold the knife in my open hands, feeling the world viciously contract again.

It looks as though it's been used recently. The icy gleam is gone, replaced with faint brown streaks down its length, as if someone had tried ineffectively to wipe it off. I raise it to my nose—the smell is faintly copper.

"John—"

I hear a step, and turn. You are already backing away. "What the fuck?" Your voice breaks.

I freeze with the knife nearly at my lips, split and whole both.

"What the fuck are you doing?" You're shaking. You try to grip the counter, but it's weirdly low and so your arm fumbles there, like you're struggling to remain standing. Your reaction strikes me as bigger than the situation at hand, out of proportion to me, this simple misunderstanding.

"No, it's—" I climb to my feet, unintentionally matching your energy. You take another step away, edging back as if I'm advancing toward you, one hand on the wall. "It's not what you think," I stutter. "It's the same knife from the last house. She didn't live here at all. Vivian—" I have no idea why I've chosen this moment to link these things together, why I am not denying everything, why you are moving backward and I am not, why I am still holding the fucking knife.

"What does it matter?" you shout. "Neither did we!" Your feet trip over each other, and your cheek hits the corner of the countertop as you fall. You clamber back up, pulling yourself up on the counter, palms squeaking on the granite, your breath shallow and panicked. The side of your face is gummed up and already bleeding. The movements are so desperate and sloppy I want to tell you *Just slow down, Take it easy,* but in the seconds of your fall I've moved closer to you, unaccountably, I am ten feet from the sink and I don't know how, I'm reading violence everywhere and I don't know which part of it comes from me. I've never seen you so terrified.

It occurs to me in the space of a moment: you are trying to run away from me.

The knife clatters to the floor. I kick it behind me as hard as I can. I hear it skitter across the tiles. I hold my hands up. I take a demonstrative step back, like I'm hitting my marks. "I didn't touch her."

But somehow this denial is actually a confession, I've delivered the line totally wrong. Your face screws up and you shake it violently back and forth, backing out of the kitchen the opposite way, toward the foyer.

"She hasn't gone," I say. My mind goes blank and then spits out a name. "What about Collin?"

"Who the fuck is Collin?"

But I've forgotten the name of your brother too, as well as the reason I drew this pointless connection. I look briefly to the floor, as if to study its meaning, and you bolt.

I come after you—in the foyer, I reach out and just barely touch your fingers, at which you scream, legitimately scream— but even after all of it, you're faster, and you throw open the front door into blinding sunlight.

The connection, but not the name, resurfaces as you're eaten by the glare across the lawn: two people who no one actually saw disappear, who for a time existed somewhere unknown to us, alive and whole (when they pulled your brother out from under the tank, at first he was completely unrecognizable, and I imagined the frantic momentary hope that it wasn't actually him, that he'd changed uniforms with someone else at the last minute). When I reach the top of the stone steps I've lost it again, and by the time I can see properly, you're long gone.

All at once we're separate. All at once, there's nothing to navigate but the wilderness we've chosen for ourselves, to walk endlessly up and down these steps, entering and exiting.

*

I turn against the mansion. To follow you now seems impossible, a gambit that could only confirm everything you think I am; it would be a chase, and I would be the monster that never stops. My back to the woods, in the relentless sunlight, the cancelling shadows, I stalk back into the house.

Every time you've left I've thought it was for good: every time you left our apartment in Indiana, the building in the city, even on some mundane errand, I felt there was an equal chance that you would never come back, you would return to the plot that had been laid out for you originally, before I had intervened, and that would be it. There was a guarded part of you I'd never known, a history I'd only seen in fragments, like another life we were always at the edge of. I felt like the tangent where you hid from the rest of it, and when we weren't together, I imagined you out there interacting, fighting or embracing it; your stories to me were codes I couldn't read, a mask I couldn't push back. And after each absence—whether it was an hour or a week—every time the door opened, a shadow flickered in the stairwell, the data would scramble for a moment, the lines would reconnect, and then it would be you again, suddenly and unexpectedly as a death.

I don't bother to close the front door behind me; there's nothing moving in the world now besides us, and eliminating these barriers leaves me open to the larger labyrinth (the outside), rather than isolating me inside a separate labyrinth (the mansion itself)—in some abstract way, I tell myself, it bolsters the chances of consistency between the two, the inside and the outside, decreases the likelihood that whatever is behind me will reset again. I retrieve the knife from beneath the dining room table, and with one hand each on the blade and handle, I pull it apart. The raw metal at the base grates against my palm. I throw the handle into the unused fireplace beneath the family photos and stuff the blade into the sinkmouth, clench my fist until I'm sure it won't bleed. I don't follow immediately, and here, another path forms.

After Casey, when you learned of his death, you sputtered back to life for a moment to the people we'd left in Indiana, crossed severed channels with your messages of sympathy and return, exchanges that I read through that same night as you slept, in the moonlight through the curtainless windows and the glow of the four-inch screen—perverse among all of that self-inflicted poverty but admit it, before we threw our phones away we were both still on our parents' plan, they could have tracked us—just to get a sense of how you recalled yourself. They read like you'd wanted me to find them, like little burrs in people we'd known:

"Holy shit! You're alive! I thought you were lost to us."

"Lazarus, bitch. How have you been?"

"You coming back for the funeral? This place is nothing without you."

"I am def coming back. I miss all you guys."

"Where have you been?????"

"Ha, living. How have you been?"

"Did you get a new phone or something??"

"No, just been busy. Why?"

Most of the conversations didn't last more than two or three texts, always ended with questions you didn't respond to, mild and disappointed followups—a flicker, and you were gone again. I imagined all of the crushes and former acquaintances, flushed with the reconnection, thinking to themselves, "She's asleep, she'll reply in the morning," and then waking up to nothing, waiting for a response that never arrived.

I remember the last phone call I made to my parents, from our apartment in Richmond, the night before we boarded the bus and left for good, the same night I'd introduced you as my wife at the party. I hadn't gone home since graduating—Dayton was just over an hour away, across the border in Ohio, and I wouldn't go. I didn't intend to make the call. I was sitting on the couch—the couch where we'd screamed at each other in the ecstasy of possession, which we would leave behind the next day without a second thought (we'd decided not to take anything we couldn't carry ourselves)—looking through the contacts on my phone, trying to find someone to tell that I was leaving, to switch out this sense of permanency with something else. My finger hovered over "Home." I scrolled back and forth around it, I told myself I wouldn't call; if I could make it through this one night (I was alone, you were absent at the time), the rest would be easy, and freedom would come, or the future would come. These lapses would happen from time to time, I knew, it was largely a matter of persevering through them. I told myself I wouldn't call. I watched the clock moving forward. I called.

The phone rang less than once before my mother picked up. I interpreted this as reflex rather than eagerness or desperation; the phone was sitting right next to her, and she grabbed it. She must have been at the computer. "Hello?"

I lost my composure the instant she answered. Any plan I'd had for this conversation, for what I was intending to tell them, evaporated. I wet my lips from corner to corner. "It's me."

"Oh! John!" I heard her move the phone away from her head and call for my dad. "Beau—John's on the phone." And back to me: "Daddy's going to get on the other line."

Another click. "Hello, son." My hand was pressed over my mouth as I began to cry. I knew that whenever I moved it, everything would be obvious.

"How have you been?" my mom said. "We haven't heard from you!"

I took my hand away, couldn't help the wet sound of congestion when I sniffed. "I'm leaving." My voice broke at the end, and I clamped my hand back over my mouth. My whole face quivered, my throat clenched and hurt.

"Leaving? Where are you going? When?" My mom again—I could tell my dad was still there, though he wasn't speaking: I pictured him exactly, downstairs, in front of the TV (muted), on the one phone that still had a cord, which, when I was five or six, I'd drawn all over with my interpretation of Egyptian hieroglyphics.

"Tomorrow." It would have been plain to anyone that I was crying. I looked out at our apartment in the dark, the lights off, like I hadn't moved since the sunlight went away. My vision blurred and resolved into wet coronas of light from the streetlights outside the window. I felt tears running down my cheeks.

"Are you all right? John, where are you—"

I hung up; I left them in silence. I pictured my dad, once he'd realized that I'd cut them off, hanging up the phone, pulling himself out of his chair, and going upstairs, where he'd found my mom trying to figure out what buttons she needed to press to call me back. He'd put his hand on my mom's wrist—not trying to take the phone, that would have made her hysterical—and said, "He's just upset. Let him sleep." He'd said, "I'm sure he'll call back tomorrow."

They'd gone to bed after a while. The next morning, they woke up to nothing. I hadn't called back. When you returned a few hours later, you told me to start calling you Joey, that Josephine was a past version of you that had been too long ("sprawling," you said), and now ceased to exist.

*

On my way back up the stairs to the second floor, the house uncloaks another of its secrets, this time in the Renaissance painting of the two nobles in the hallway. Ascending from the final landing, as I step across the balcony toward the painting, the incongruous gray disc in the bottom quarter of the canvas suddenly takes definite shape, and in the space of one step, like a mental pivot, reveals itself to be an impeccably rendered human skull, painted in forced perspective, only readily identifiable when the painting is viewed from above at this angle, from its far right edge—a visual gimmick and shameless piece of technical bravado, classical painting's favorite memento mori. From where I'm standing the skull looks physically separate from the painting, floating in non-space beyond the frame. I almost laugh at the brazen symbolism, as if someone's trying to teach me a lesson so broad and obvious that it's completely over my head, but this quickly turns to anger at the cheap deception, the plastic of the house even with the front door open.

I walk down the second-floor hallway to one of the marble heads on the far side of the bathroom and use both hands to topple it. The head busts through the plaster of the neighboring pillars and takes down the other three all at once, like dominos—the heads clunk to the carpet with a loud, muffled stamp, undertones of cracking beneath, and roll thickly on their stumped necks. The destruction is enormously, physically satisfying. A cloud of burst plaster fills the air, the scent of paint, like a house simultaneously under construction and mid-demolition. It feels as if I could dig my fingers into the walls and tear them down like a roll of paper, revealing the shoddy joists underneath, the ultimate truth that this was just a set all along, an imitation. I feel intoxicated.

I kneel and pick up one of the severed heads, an exemplar of classical male beauty—it's absurdly heavy, I have to lean back and carry it with my legs bent—and stagger to the balcony overlooking the foyer. I heave it over the edge. The head hits the ground floor and breaks before I even have time to appreciate the beauty of it falling. The crash echoes throughout the house (the chandelier rattles above) and several tiles leap up with the impact, cracks branching from the new indentation in the floor, the wide-open front door spilling light inside. I'm laughing and clutching the railing, which vibrates beneath my fingers, until I recognize the fall, the accident I'm replicating.

I feel wolf eyes. I leap backward, as if the banister had suddenly become electrified. The chandelier twinkles like the most garish and obvious object ever installed in a home. I pick up the single remaining undestroyed plaster column—it weighs about eight pounds—and hold it over my head like a weapon, inching back toward the balcony, expecting to see something alive in the foyer below, drawn out by my noise.

There is light everywhere. The head is split in three pieces, clustered together as if by magnetic force, but otherwise the lobby remains empty. The foyer. I turn back to the second floor wall, cross the hall, and decimate the pillar against the painting. I step into the explosion of plaster like a shower, and inhale. It cuts into my nasal passages, tastes of chalk and blood, craft projects of old. The petrified white men get whiter.

In the haze, I spend the next hours combing the house for Vivian, though I know I won't find her, that my search is like fulfilling an empty promise I made in a distant life. As the day collapses, it doesn't seem consequential that the longer I wait to pursue you, the farther away you become, the wider our paths are drawn apart. I feel time advancing independently, for me alone, the house like a cell apart from its passage. I move methodically from room to room, past the interior house and into areas we've barely touched, the interior house's larger counterparts, looking in every closet, under and behind each piece of furniture, in each wardrobe, each drawer. I crawl down on my hands and knees, plaster in my hair and caked to the inside of my mouth and nose. I find nothing but inconsistencies, proof that this house all along was just like the rest: an enormous empty frame in a prominent spot on the wall; windows mounted in the hallways that look directly in on bedrooms; an unused fireplace in the back of a closet; empty, oddly shaped rooms with acutely angled ceilings, too many corners, and no furniture; a chute on the second floor with no obvious egress (I shove one of the marble heads into it, where it lodges with a clang that rings through the walls for a solid three minutes). All things you would find interesting, hilariously out of place, but nothing of any use. All the while, through the afternoon, the front door lies open behind me the way you left it, allowing anyone and everything easy entrance or escape without my noticing. The sun sets, the fragments of the marble head draw long shadows across the foyer like a sundial reading my fate. If Vivian were here, she could have left a hundred times. You could have returned in the midst of my dismantling, my fight with the house, and then left again. You could have left over and over.

Outside, the sky pitches to dark and it begins to rain, horribly. It smacks against the windows in sheets, and lightning illuminates the mansion like an armature. I stand at the open doorway on the first floor, buffeted by the wind, my eyes trained on the treeline in the distance, waiting for you to come running out. There's always been this suspicion that when you left to explore the exteriors of these mansions, all the time you remained somewhere close at hand, the actual risk minimized. I watch the top of the trees jig violently in the storm, the Jeep centered in the path swaying back and forth. I imagine the blood-red sheet flailing against the back of the house, the body filling with water. I leave the front door open and the light on in the foyer, like a beacon.

I sleep in the mirror bedroom, where we kept Vivian. It's not the best idea—if the house goes in the storm I'll be cut to pieces by a thousand little shards of mirror-glass—but there's no way I'm spending a night in the viscera room by myself, and at least this way I can keep close watch of everything around me. It's a small comfort. I close myself in, amongst my reflections. I accept the labyrinth of myself.

I lie on the bed and look up at my body in the ceiling as if adrift on a black sea, listening to the storm, which grows in ferocity, sending its surging forces through the ceiling and walls as if it's a fundamental part of the house's structure. To my left and right I can see myself in supine profile in the mirrors, to observe in full-body view exactly what the last six weeks or month or seven or four days or lifetime has done to me: my stomach somehow seems both hollowed out and bloated, an incongruous pocket of air; above it my chest sits awkwardly mounded like a frame I haven't grown fully into. Red patches on my right side, sore to the touch, whose source I can't recall. My left side scratched at random, the same, wounds of the road. Breathing in makes me go concave, drags volume from parts of me that don't feel related to the act—my thighs, the base of my neck. I look like I've been ravaged from a holocaust, the tattoos on my arms and legs like massive lesions; I check their proportions, the faces on my leg, to see if this kind of loss would compromise the space they take, would wrinkle them into each other. I'm reminded of an animatronic replication of a human, encountered on a carnival ride, its components both weirdly disconnected and eerily in sync, eyelids blinking mechanically while an arm moves up and down in gesture, posture rigid. Looking forward, down the bed and toward my feet, I see my body reflected in the mirror as if stacked, in this case a pair of feet, some balls and knobs for toes, fingers and arms, a crotch, the hump of a ribcage and a projecting, naked chin. The soles of my feet are completely black, bulbous and blistered.

I hear mighty cracks outside, great rumbles of thunder. It rains impossibly hard. At one point, I detect the sound of a continuous trickle of water somewhere nearby, outside the bedroom, crackling across the tiles in the foyer like a faucet behind a locked door, or a distant fire. I don't investigate. A few minutes later, a tremendous rattling is followed by the loudest crash I've ever heard; the force rattles the door and I'm worried the mirrors will jump from the walls. It must have been the chandelier. I repeat over and over that if I just sleep, finally sleep (the opposite of what I told myself the night before), that when I awaken in the morning everything will be different, will somehow revert to another version of this story. I'll awaken in another bedroom, and the cliché will not be that I'm waking up with an erection I can only satisfy to about forty angled images of myself, but that I'm waking up next to you, vibrant and unchanged.

*

I return to consciousness after a thick, strangely dreamless sleep with my face in the crook of my elbow, and there's a moment of obliviousness about my situation, genuine obliviousness, in which I could be anywhere. I feel it—the cool on my back, the emptiness of the bed—but a few seconds pass in which I don't recognize it, and then a few more where I don't acknowledge it. And then I turn, I move my arm, and it's everywhere, and the hollowness in my stomach is back again, and I'm staring down at myself in the morning dark.

You have not reappeared. Water is still leaking from some-where nearby.

When I'm fully awake to this bleary reality I sit on the edge of the bed for a while, digging my palms into the mattress, molding around the pressure. I crane my body forward over my knees; I wonder vaguely if my newly emaciated figure would allow me to suck my own cock. The top of my feet look slightly greenish, as if the black from the soles has seeped up through skin and bone—more likely, the color from the shoes and socks I rarely remove has started to dye them.

Out of the corner of my eye, I see a slip of paper curling out from between the mattress and the box spring beneath it, which I register as a mattress tag. I wiggle my index finger into the loop, still seated. The paper is crisp and thicker than I expect, and this itself is a satisfying tactile sensation that, for a moment, completely focuses my attention: I interpret the texture as "rich people paper, a bed fit for a king," and I think of mattress labels printed on authentic Egyptian parchment (to accompany the lyrical cotton), wondering, without clear resolution, if the sheets are actually satin, which seems like a word for the wealthy, for this level of glossiness, and then I look down and see that the slip of paper I'm fingering is not a mattress label at all but a hun-dred-dollar bill, unfurling from where it's been tucked beneath the mattress. I pull it from its hiding place and hold it between my thumb and index finger, stiff in the still air. The sensory memory is barely familiar, feels false.

I rise from the bed, holding the bill slightly away from me, almost embarrassed at what I've uncovered. It should not be this easy: like the idea of waking up next to someone who's magically returned, I didn't think this was a cliché that existed anymore, the stash under the bed.

I wedge my hands beneath the mattress at the foot of the bed, coffined in satin black (which sounds more correct the more I say it), and overturn it onto the floor. The hidden nest of money explodes into the air in ridiculous, gratuitous array, countless, shockingly green, more than I've ever seen in real life. It's unbound, all hundred-dollar bills, like you'd see in a movie depicting complete and utter decadence, reflected in every possible combination by the mirror walls. The room turns suddenly into a perverse disco ball as the bills come fluttering down around me, my arms outstretched. I cannot stop laughing. Still, as I stand there in this absurd vortex of money, I can't help thinking, aren't you supposed to put the money *inside* the mattress? Shouldn't it be organized, contained in some way? How else are you supposed to take it with you?

The bills stick to my bare feet as I walk across the room, and at the door I stop to peel them off. The option should occur to me to take the money, like one would take food from the cupboards, to take it all and run toward civilization, but this doesn't seem like a real possibility—my curiosity stems mostly from its strangeness, its randomness and obscure origins, the same as every gaudy object here. The idea of its activation, its use in a meaningful, consequential exchange seems absurd. Where the money has settled, this is where I leave it, dirty under my dirty feet, a testament to its own uselessness.

I open the door to the landing. When I step out, it's into a completely different environment. While I was sleeping, the house has shifted again—I knew this was coming, I shouldn't have closed the door. Above the foyer, a bolt-shaped gash has appeared in the domed ceiling, through which pours a thin, steady stream of water. Above it, I see sky. Beside the gash, a jagged hole bores to the foundation, the anchor for the chandelier, whose carcass lies directly below, bulbs and crystals sprayed across the foyer. Its skeleton sits in a crater created by the impact, which in turn has filled with water, forming a shallow, glass-ridden pond on the first floor, glimmering slightly, a sinister preserve among the wreckage. Somewhere at the bottom of it sits the split marble head, like an artifact from an earlier time. The front door is flung entirely open, the hinges pulling up from the wooden frame. Bits of debris, branches, leaves stray in a gusted path across the tile and surface of the water. The only sound is the stream from the ceiling, like that of a fountain, cascading over the empty tubes and sockets, swelling the pond, faintly pulsing out its perimeter. The electricity is gone; some of the bulbs are blackened from when they met water.

Toward the edge of the rippling pond, slowly creeping into view from the far side of the chandelier, a single flamingo walks through the foyer, bright and rudely pink, an animate stain on my reality. The sight of this life drives the same piercing cold through my chest as abject fear.

The bird raises one long, spindly leg and sets it down carefully, silently, avoiding the scattered glass. Long neck doubled over, it dips its beak around the broken field of the chandelier, beached as big and strange as a whale. Stark and glamorous, the flamingo doesn't dignify me, another escapee from someone's impossible private menagerie, each step cautious, traversing new terrain. To my left, the Renaissance painting sags in its frame, hopelessly waterlogged; I realize now that it's just a reproduction, a copy on flimsy wood. The carpets are totally soaked through, shades darker.

I take a handful of money from the floor of the mirror room and throw it over the balcony. The bills become leaves and drift down toward the gray water. The flamingo looks up at me with two distinct bobs of its neck, unimpressed.

I root around in the closets upstairs for new clothes. I find the pieces of another outfit, a pair of shoes to replace those I've been wearing since the last mansion. When I'm newly dressed, I return to the mirror bedroom. I pick fifteen bills off the ground—I'm dimly aware of counting—and roll them tightly together. I slide the bundle into my back pocket. It's not enough to matter: the weight, the tumorous bulge it makes in my pants isn't enough for me to notice or acknowledge that I'm carrying it, always.

I walk down the stairs, into the foyer. The flamingo stalks the pond with utter deliberation, indifferent or oblivious to my presence. Glass crunches beneath my feet with each step; the new and unfamiliar shoes make me feel like an observer, a non-participant. I try to remember footage I've seen on TV of these birds in flight, if they can fly at all, but I can't convince myself either way, and this indeterminate fact floats in my brain as something I'll probably never confirm. I wonder about the route it intuited between houses.

I walk to the interior kitchen in the name of observing what's changed after the storm. The jar of pasta sauce has exploded on the tile, pooling in the groove between wall and floor like a murder scene. The first cabinet I open is brimming with spices— the shelves you failed to locate two nights ago. I look at the basil leaves in their little glass jar. I consider rolling them up and smoking them, not for any specific reason, but for the novelty, to see how it would burn, the taste of the smoke, because no one would ever know I'd done it.

I tap out a little mound of garlic powder onto the counter, shape it into an approximate line with the tip of my finger. I lean down, close enough to smell it, and pinch one of my nostrils closed. I stand up quickly and banish the whole mess with the side of my hand. I'm dialing back to the moment in the city when we stopped talking about food. I was rolling a bruised apple in my hands like an old piece of clay as it browned in patches.

You gave me a sidelong look and smiled a little, like a challenge. I felt myself teetering on a moment of commitment. "Are you going to eat that?"

I passed it from hand to hand, and then I let it go. It rolled across the sidewalk, skipping on the grit, until it went over the curb and, as we'd discussed, turned instantly to garbage. It was all garbage.

I don't take anything. The sun shines wetly outside.

*

The first time you disappeared—really, truly disappeared, no contact at all—came after I laughed about your brother being dead at the party our final semester in college. You were gone from the apartment by the time I returned an hour later (and I couldn't explain how it took me an hour to get there, where the intervening time had gone), but had left your car, the keys inside on the table, as if daring me to guess where, to come after you.

My first, insane impulse that night was to drive to 19th Street, to take your car right up to the house August had vacated over a year ago, as if the whole thing was some perverse re-staging of our personal histories, as if I expected you at any moment to spring into reversion and return to symbolic empty spaces of your past, my past, etc. When I turned onto his old street I'd already decided I wasn't doing it. New cars were parked out front; the house was a different color, and nicer than I remembered. I hardly slowed down as I drove past.

I didn't stop. I'd met your parents at the funeral the year before, and knew you'd pledged not to see them again, not intentionally at least, but for some reason—no less symbolically but maybe more plausibly—I thought you might have gone to their house, somewhere private I couldn't breach, your brother's bedroom with all his old shit, the comfort of pain and nostalgia. The next morning, when you didn't return, I followed your specter there. I parked your car across the street and waited, convinced despite everything that you were inside. The house was a brick one-story ranch alongside other brick one-story ranches, inhabited by the same people forever, with a chainlinked yard behind it and a trimmed lawn in the front with ornaments, a flag in the window, exceedingly normal. The layout was the same as August's house but with a paved driveway, different building materials. You hadn't spoken with your father since just after the funeral, and I knew this.

My tendency for determined waiting from the past three years, the passivity and angst of sitting and watching for hours without clear intent (the phase that had led me to notice Candace, to follow that path) I'd thought was behind me by the time we met—or another version of it was playing out in the aftermath of the gun—but it's easy to settle back into old habits. For the first few hours, I sat outside your parents' house with the air conditioning on and my hand resting on the key in the ignition, running down the gas in your car—the idea was to be primed, as few moves as possible away from active pursuit, as if at any moment you'd come hurtling out of the house and I would have to follow. Over time, the air conditioning came to feel too convenient, and further, like it might be concealing something, a telltale noise from the closed house I might hear from inside a sealed car across the street. I turned the engine off and let the cold air bleed out. I preferred to sweat; it was the route that gave my actions physical consequence, pretended exertion. Nothing was behind me.

The car quickly became suffocating, even after I cracked the window, and my back stuck fast to the faux leather. I traced the long, cartoonish line created by the crack in the windshield, never repaired. I had to fight to stay awake, kept shoving myself up in the seat, my eyes fixed on the house. Late that afternoon, your mother pulled the car out of the garage and drove off, the first sign that the house hadn't been empty to begin with. I saw her in the window as she drove past, and I remember thinking that she was so indistinct-looking that I probably wouldn't recognize her if I saw her again—this, after having met her in person once before—that I could check out at Walmart with the same woman and not realize I'd attended her son's funeral. I kept fastidious watch on the house after she left; I thought this seemed like a time when you might do something, might make your presence known, as if by sliding up one of the windows and shooting off flares.

Your mother came back an hour later and pulled into the garage. I had the impression that she'd seen the car I was in, had slowed down as she passed it, made note of the addition to their street. I wondered how long the crack in the windshield had been there, if beyond the model and plates this was a distinctive or recognizable characteristic to your parents. The garage door slid closed, and thereafter the house didn't move. I texted you again, then held the phone in my fist, hoping for a response and silence in equal measure, something to drive me to either extreme.

Around six, your father came home. He parked his SUV in the driveway, and when he got out—tall and thin, a white button-down and tan pants, brown shoes, bald head (when I'd shaken his hand at the funeral the idea of a bald Mormon had, for some reason, shocked me)—he turned and looked at me directly, at his daughter's car. He looked to the house, and then back at the car. He took a few steps down the driveway toward me, craning his head to look at the license plate while I tried to stare directly ahead without moving my body. There was little I could do to explain why I was here, at his family's home in his daughter's car, where his daughter was obviously not.

He stopped at the edge of the street at the mailbox, and then retreated, as if the car held an answer he was better off seeking elsewhere. I remembered then, without a specific memory to attach it to, you mentioning having inherited the car from someone else. That was the word you used, "inherited," which sounded like blood, and which—it didn't occur to me until I was sitting there watching your father going into the house—must have meant from your brother, after he'd shipped off, before his departure became permanent. On the bumper of your father's SUV, I picked out the silhouette of a POW/MIA sticker.

I waited for the blinds to move. I wondered if he was telling his wife what he'd seen across the street, their dead son's, now their daughter's car, obviously populated, parked like an omen. In some part of my mind I knew the fear I was inspiring, how simply improbable it was that you were actually in the house—you'd told me repeatedly that you no longer spoke to your parents, that their role in your life you preferred to keep at "less than zero"—I knew this the same as I knew what the reappearance of this car could trigger, the ghosts I brought with it. Inside the house, I imagined your father picking up the phone, standing just in a spot where he could see outside to the street without having to adjust the blinds and reveal his position. Your phone ringing somewhere distant, your father watching a motionless figure in his daughter's car not answering, nothing where it was supposed to be, there but not there. At an arbitrary point, I raised my own phone to my ear, silent, held it there for a minute and pretended to speak.

The lights went out late. I knew it would be unbearable for them to wake up in the morning and find me there still, that if I continued to wait, I would risk almost certain discovery. I checked my phone one last time; you'd said nothing. I drove back to the empty apartment, dragging a sea of implications I wasn't able to face, but knowing that I had just stood upon a threshold and had not turned away.

The next day, a Saturday, I emptied my bank account, crossed into Ohio—within half an hour of my parents' house in Dayton—and got the Yama tattoo on my left leg. It took four hours. Afterward, I stood at the counter in the front of the shop and methodically, one by one, emptied the bills from my wallet. I counted them at first, and then I stopped counting.

I drove the hour back to Richmond in your car with my calf bandaged in plastic wrap. Rather than going back to the apartment, I went directly to your parents' house, again. I parked in the same spot across the street, facing the same direction. If I was going to come back, I was going to come back different.

This time, my observations were sloppy, and I didn't know why I was there; it was almost an hour before I even noticed that the SUV was parked in the driveway. Shortly after I did, however, as if waiting for my acknowledgment, the front door of the house flew open, and out came your father, holding something in his hand, not stopping at his car but walking directly toward me with furious determination, almost running. I heard his footsteps on the asphalt. I turned the key—it took a second longer than it should have, because I'd turned the car entirely off—and hauled out of there, leaving him behind, standing halfway across the street, watching me go.

(Obviously, I'd never filled this gap.)

In the rearview, he raised the thing in his hand to his head.

A phone. A phone.

Somewhere else, a phone rings.

A line flickers, and then becomes permanent.

It's in my hand.

That's why I'm coming after you.

*

My first step off the terrace, my foot sinks three inches into the grass. The lawn all around me has turned to mud. When I look back, I expect to see the mansion at a tilt, sliding into the ground; instead, I see a white fortress stained by weather, busted off its hinges, its troops gone from their posts.

Enormous branches lie strewn about the lawn, blown in from distant reaches, tearing up furrows in the ground and leaving behind clumpy eruptions of wet earth. Puddles of brown rainwater line the driveway and grounds, pooling in every available imperfection, spotting the landscape. The Jeep has been shunted off to the side, a blocky piece of litter. The chessboard-like swatches of flowers just beyond the terrace are unanimously pummeled and flattened like a bed of cooked spinach. Around the house itself, the water has filled in to create a moat, as if the estate had planned for this, to detach finally from land. Opposite me, the forest into which you fled the day before looks bedraggled, its wetness sapping the lush volume of the trees, dragging their branches down toward the earth like outstretched arms; where once it was thick and unforgiving, now it seems as if I could stand at one edge and see all the way out the other side. The trees look like soaked mannequins. The sky is a flat white, and the air is finally enough to breathe.

On my last look back the mansion greets me with a final image: the body from below the bathroom window has been improbably washed forward, navigated by the makeshift rainwater current around the perimeter of the house and overturned on the grass before me, face-up and ripe with water. I'd walked by without even noticing. It's obvious now from the way her body is positioned that she was stabbed—many, many times—that this was how she'd actually been killed; her sweatshirt is torn to shreds in the front, where it had been angled away two days before. The fall, the hunger hadn't killed her after all—she must have tried to run, and then been viciously caught. The bathroom, true to form, had been scrubbed clean. Her face is caved in, partially eaten away. I imagine Vivian, from wherever, in the moment she decided she would live in this mansion for the time being, for as long as necessary, no matter what stood in her way, a story that runs in parallel to ours, the survival instinct taking over. We're capable of anything if threatened enough. My hands unconsciously search my pants like a tic, finding only the useless wad of money in the back pocket. I'm tempted to throw it away each time I touch it, but I don't. I tell myself that I'm being more pragmatic than that, that someday there might come a time when I'll need it. I nudge the body with my foot and immediately feel nauseous, there was no reason at all for me to do that.

I turn back to the forest. To my left: north, again. Or, it may as well be, as much as anything is north. The morbid treeline stretches on endlessly, disappearing into morning fog.

This was the direction I'd seen you run, and if there was any path you'd take, it would be deeper, toward wherever the sun would be highest. The longer I remain stationary in this mansion, the further I revert to the jumble of speculation I became in the weeks before the gun appeared a year and a half ago, the more my options decrease.

In the end, it didn't matter that much: a day had passed, a storm had shifted things. We were two points in an empty area that might as well have been infinite. We would find each other—I would find you, I was fated to—or we would not.

Ignoring the road we came in on, I move in this direction, into this approximation of north.

I always keep a wall to one side of me, and so this is where I place the treeline, at my right, to orient my progress and ensure that I'm moving forward, perpendicular to the distant gate where we entered the grounds. I cross the drenched flowerbeds and expansive lawns, and finally, at one crisp, well-maintained edge, I exit the mansion's box-like vicinity, escape into the thick tangle of wild land that separates this household from the rest of the world. The sunshine is dimmed by an overhanging network of branches, tightly webbed together. My pace is slowed. I move parallel to the treeline. The soles of my shoes are quickly heavy with mud, and a thick crust forms beneath each, lending the impression that I'm walking slightly above the ground, over something that is not the ground.

It occurs to me at one point that the treeline might not proceed in an absolutely straight line, that it might subtly curve and thereby point me in a different direction, which could eventually turn me around. The thought is so disconcerting that I decide to immediately ignore that I've had it—if I don't choose at least one orientating factor and stick to it, I will be completely lost.

Wet branches and stickers tear at my legs as I traipse through the brush, pushing weeds and stray limbs of honeysuckle out of the way. I turn frequently to look back, to confirm that I'm still making progress, and I gain some satisfaction in this, in marking time and ground covered. The thicket slowly takes on the character of a smaller forest itself, and my heart rate quickens when I look back and in one decisive moment realize that I can no longer pick out where I came from, that I'm definitely further from the treeline than when I entered. I block it out, and try to orient myself straight, plotting an invisible line—whenever I have to move left or right of this line to negotiate some obstacle, I try to find it again. The ground remains wet and soft, but I feel the sun on my back. My throat goes dry. On an impulse, I pull a handful of leaves off a branch and stuff them into my mouth. I chew four times and spit them out, and for the next twenty minutes—or another indefinite period of time, it doesn't matter—I'm spitting leaf bits out of my mouth. Ultimately, it's counterproductive. I lose more than I gain.

The entire time, despite the stops and starts, the circumnavigations and innate bad sense of direction, the treeline stays to my right, a distant and taller darkness. The thicket feels endless, especially once I've lost sense of how long ago I entered it, and I had no idea to begin with how wide this space might actually be, if there was a neighbor to be looking out for; it begins to reconstitute itself in my mind as some sort of antechamber to the forest rather than anything in which I could truly cover any ground. I wait longer and longer between looking back, or at least I imagine I'm waiting longer. I think of "acres," how many of them you could own if you were rich. Thousands, or millions, I guess, though truth be told I've never known how this works.

An indeterminate distance later, when I'm hopelessly sweaty and tired, my legs streaked in mud, my salmon-colored shirt hanging with sweat and woodland distress (it was a stupid color to choose), I hit a brick wall, taller than I am and covered in ivy, the real perimeter of the mansion's property. It's infuriating, because I'd assumed I crossed this line a long time ago, when I left the lawn and entered the thicket, and I feel like my progress has been deleted, nullified in some critical way. Hooking my foot repeatedly into the noose-like tangles of stem, I pull myself stubbornly up onto the wall, and eventually gain enough purchase to topple onto the ledge. The light is instant and bright. I lose my balance and fall over the other side, landing on hard, empty grass with a startled, expulsive sound I'm thankful no one else can hear.

I lie on my back, catching my breath, staring up at the sky. It's a different kind of helplessness. It's blue now.

I climb to my feet to find that I'm in a wide, grassy expanse—to my left, mossy rocks that have been strewn there for millennia, scaling gradually up into hills, and further back, more forest, mountainous, too far away to seem real. To my distant right an opposing treeline, the one I tried to follow to get here, rises up full-bodied and ominous; I have no idea how its border could have swerved so goddamn far away.

I break for the right side of the expanse, my ever-persistent version of north. The clouds have dispersed overhead, and it's hot enough for me to sweat just moving at a normal pace. I roll up my sleeves, which seems like a decision I could have made years, decades ago, but which never occurred to me. Again, I reach the edge of the treeline, and I walk within the fringe of shade alongside it, the wall to one side of me. The ground hardens, and after an hour (or what I take to be an hour), most signs of the previous night's rain are gone.

This time, I stare at my feet as I walk. I think about nothing, really. The shoes are wearing out fast; they're meant for stationary outings. The leather is not hearty.

It hits me, some period of time later, that I'm not looking for you very hard, that despite my progress forward, I don't really know what direction I'm going. There's no reason to believe that when you disappeared you ran in an absolute straight line (as I'm trying to do), and even if you did, there is no realistic way that I'm following that path. The earliest you could have been here is a full day before me, and between then and now the rain would have obliterated any evidence I could reasonably track. I'm not even looking as I walk, really, but watching the ground, eking out a narrow strip of surveyed land along the treeline, the practical version of walking forward in the present to mask the past. I would've had to step on you to see you there. I stop walking, a hollow sensation expanding in my gut, and this time I recognize it as loss, crushing loss, an absence I'm only now beginning to acknowledge. You could have been three feet away, on either side, standing silently, and I never would have seen you. We passed, like two anonymous people on the street, bit our lips, didn't speak, while in reality we were the only two people left, and the street didn't exist. Finally, I look up.

The sight before me is familiar, uncannily so. To my right, the treeline, dense and unrelenting. On the left, the usual expanse of grass, lush but yellowed in places, noted, maybe thirty feet away, by a little triangular crumple of bushes, out of which projects a thick, crooked black branch like a giant waylaid spider leg, stabbing into the ground. I've been here before.

The same feeling crawls up inside me, that I've been missing something for an unspecifiably long time. I turn around, but of course the area behind me is as indistinct and unrecognizable as the area in front of me is familiar. I turn back, in the direction that, until a minute ago, felt like forward. I look in both directions for footprints, but the grass is dry enough here that there's no sign of my presence that couldn't be misinterpreted or fabricated by an anxious mind. In fact, it doesn't look as if it's rained here at all, not recently, despite the wayward branch. Had

I somehow become turned around? I start walking in the direction I came from, waiting for the sensation to occur again, for the terrain to suddenly appear familiar, as ground already covered. It doesn't—which makes sense, I wasn't looking anyway when I approached, but had been staring at my feet, and anyway am coming from the opposite direction. I turn around again, and a few hundred feet up, there's the bush and the spider branch, oriented just as they were two minutes ago. It's more familiar now—for what might be the third time—and already the déjà vu that made it familiar when I approached it minutes ago (the elements in those approximate positions) is being replaced with this new memory.

I resolve to keep moving forward, in the direction I've heretofore assumed is forward—walk enough, I figure, and things are bound to recycle. I walk past the spider branch, now hyper-alert of my surroundings. A few steps later I'm suddenly expectant—in the way that one recognizes familiar sights in a neighborhood—of a rightward shift in the treeline, of a dead stump and the gap it leaves on the edge of the forest, like a missing piece on the border of a puzzle. A minute later, the trees wrap right, and, sure enough, there's a dead stump, a chunk absent from the forest. I stop in my tracks, again. This, too—I am more certain than the scene with the spider leg, which could be any windblown branch—its formation, the way I wrapped around the corner and saw it: I have definitely seen this before. I have taken this exact bend before.

But if I had—if I had previously taken this curve, been somehow turned around—wouldn't it have been from the other direction? Wouldn't the treeline—on my left, from that perspective—have curved outward to the right? Wouldn't my remembrance of this scene have been reversed? The only possibility I can imagine is that, by continuously following the treeline, I've somehow walked the forest in a circle, looped what must actually be a relatively small cluster of trees. That the forest is

nowhere near the size I thought it to be—someone else's property, even, meticulously surveyed and analyzed—and that this
tragedy is acting out on an even smaller scale than I thought
possible. I turn around, start walking back to the spider branch,
and to my right now, ten feet away, basically right in my path, lies
a small pyramid of stones, a cairn, stacked largest to smallest,
flatly intentional. The sight is completely alien to me.

I turn, and run straight into the woods.

*

Entering the forest is like changing rooms. Everything darkens
and lengthens its proportions, and the sky virtually disappears.
When I break the treeline, a flock of starlings bursts outward
in the opposite direction—I label them starlings completely
without evidence, though I couldn't distinguish this type of
bird from most others. Again, I move in as straight a line as
possible. The forest is easier to negotiate than the thicket, the
trees are further apart, allowing full-body motion rather than
half-paced plodding forward. Thick roots and fallen branches
criss-cross the forest floor, and hopping over them lends a feeling of control, of bounding, of surmountable obstacles as part
of a grander sense of progress—each pace is a little longer and
higher, therefore that much more successful. I tap the bark of a
tree with my palm every so often, like each of them is a pre-set
waypoint in a journey someone else planned, but on which I
am a fully knowledgeable and briefed participant. The canopy
of branches above me shelters the light from the ground, but
it's less disorienting than following the treeline from outside,
because there's too little light: the trees, tapped and untapped,
now move too quickly for anything to look too familiar—if it's
only the fear of recognizable objects that throws me, then this
can be neutralized by rendering everything generically recognizable, still repeating, but broadly, in natural-occurring patterns (as

forests are composed of such patterns). I have so little idea of where I am in actual, spatial reality relative to anything else that if I'm able to accept this leap in my own logic, I will be able to continue.

I often thought (or I often think now) that when I found the gun in my hand I'd started something over, had both gained and lost some fundamental knowledge about the world and its physical properties, its parameters: here, my entire sense of direction.

I accept it, and I run until I'm exhausted, until my side starts aching again—probably short of a mile, but enough for the forest to close completely behind me—and then I walk. The sense of progress dims a little, but lingers, takes definitive form when I set my eyes on a distant tree and then pass it. I still have no sense of what lies behind me—each small goal deletes record of the previous one—but I'm transfixed by the path I carve. Whenever I'm able, I walk atop the roots or moss-covered logs, avoiding the forest floor, the leaving of silly footprints. I notice the birds in the trees. Unaccountably, the word "pleather" appears and settles into my mind. I know, not from one clear source, that this is some kind of artificial leather, but the more I turn the word over in my head, "pleather," the less certain I am about its origins, whether it's a combination of "plush" and "leather" (the idea being that it's very soft; if "plush" is a material of its own or some other synthetic I don't know either), or, possibly, of "plastic" and "leather." I wonder, horizontally, about "patent leather," the material I understand to be, above all, very shiny, and how it relates to this family, if "pleather" could actually be a contraction of "patent" and "leather," if in reality they mean the same thing. I try to locate the contexts in which I've heard both terms used—I'm in a dorm room and someone is zipping up enormous glossy boots on Halloween; someone else is sorting through black pants in a drawer—but I can't evidentially separate the two. This is something I'd ordinarily look up, uncomfortable with the uncertainty, but here, as I move through the wilderness, none of this technology is available to me, there are no signifiers of its truth. If I could, I would ask you—you're familiar with these materials, are unquestionably handier—but you aren't here, aren't anywhere that I am, and the knowledge seems to exist in some distinct body just out of my reach, a trove only you or someone else has access to, the loss comes at me from a different angle: like the flight of flamingos, it's something I might never ascertain, that I could die without knowing.

Darkness falls in time and the forest takes on a new character, shaped by what moonlight penetrates the canopy. The bird songs quit for a while and then become darker, too. I look back and see that most of the forest has vanished into black except for the trees maybe thirty feet behind me, a neat approximation of my attitude toward their existence until now, and it's clear that I won't make anymore real progress until morning, that to proceed with my current approach would be beyond idiotic. I feel my way forward to a fallen trunk, climb over it, and slide into place on the opposite side, facing the direction I've been headed in.

I stare at the blackened and massing forest until it's too dark to see anything, listening for predators; with every sound my drained body shocks itself back to consciousness, frantically tries to echo-locate the source, holding for the pattern that signals an approach, an imminent attack. My eyelids flutter open and closed. Beneath me, I feel the wad of money I took from the mirror bedroom pressing like a knob against the ground, forming a little bruise, a bedsore. It seems impossible that this item could ever be of use to anyone.

Gradually, the darkness filters out the information in layers, first the last vestiges of sight and then the sounds, turning them all into one ambient landscape, beckoning sleep. In the end my body takes over, working in coordination, gradually turning off its receptors, and I forget that my ultimate goal is protecting myself. In the last glimmer of consciousness, when

I'm powerless to act on it and just dropping fully to sleep, finally, I hear a howl.

*

Improbably, I have a sex dream: I am in college again—the way many of my memories seem to lie "back in college," as if it's some temporally remote place—and there's a starved-looking version of you that I notice (though the word that occurs to me in my dream-consciousness is "tap," as if I've singled you out and brought you to my attention like a cult initiate). We're back in a darkened copy of your dorm room, only with towering, church-like windows. There's very little pretense there on your bed—in the dream, the implication is that we don't know each other well, but met at some unspecified point just before, rote stranger fantasy—and I flip up your skirt and press my face between your legs, your face too dark to read. The pleasure in the dream is basically nonexistent; there's no sense of tenderness or physical response, no joy between us, and I've hardly begun when the walls vanish and we're suddenly lying in an empty field somewhere, on a hill, a distant train on the horizon, laid in the same position, trying to fuck and failing in practice, as if your body has gone away and left a plastic shell in its place. The landscape is desolate tawny grain.

The black skirt is a tell. I've never seen you wear one.

I awaken on the ground wracked with intensely physical guilt and dread to the call of a bird that sounds like a malfunctioning synthesizer. Warm sunlight pushes in through the trees in front of me, and suddenly it is stupidly, comically obvious: east. I am moving east.

I continue walking. Late morning, I come to a stream winding through the forest, the waters brown and still. Its appearance is unexpected, but causes me to question the lack of others, because this is supposed to be a coastal region, there ought to be famous rivers everywhere. I climb down to the rocky bank, kneel there peering at the glinting surface as if trawling for familiar objects beneath, and then plunge my face into all of its three inches—it feels like a massive interruption—rubbing my skin raw with cold water, my hands disturbing the mud at the bottom. When I draw back, eyes shut, my hair dripping down into my face, it's like stepping out of a shower, a liminal sense of normal, balancing on a sensory experience I remember. I feel heavier as I move away from the stream, charged with a new life, a reclaimed power. That afternoon, when the sun beams directly overhead (I'm watching it now, tracking its movements, and therefore time, in a somewhat more accountable way), I see the trees thinning ahead, and the outline of a structure that reads differently than the mansions. I'm overcome with a feeling of purpose, as if I'd been moving toward this location with singular intent since I entered the forest, since we first stepped off the train.

A minute later, a man-made construction looms up among an avenue of cleared forest, a concrete overpass at least twice as tall as me and supported by arches, flanked by treetops, stretching in both directions farther than I can see (north and south, I tell myself). As I near it, I realize that it's an elevated train track, conceivably the same track on which we arrived, or one of its neighbors, stretching lifelessly through the forest, cutting from end to end. The landscape filters deferentially around it, has sculpted itself to this imposition over time.

I stand beside it, my hand touching cool, reassuring brick, looking up. If one made it up to the track—railed off on either side—it would be possible to traverse the land from above, to search on a broad scale. I wonder how long it's been since these tracks were laid, where the nearest station is. It occurs to me that I'm standing at the conduit, or a point on the path that leads to the conduit, the beginning and possibly the end.

And then, just inside the shadow of the brick archway below the trees, on the forest floor, my eyes adjust and I see it, another foreign item.

A shoe, lying on its side.

Your shoe.

Or, more accurately: the last shoe I remember you wearing. A sneaker—white with blue trim and a swoop, impressively generic—from a first-floor closet in Vivian's mansion, one of the pair you'd said fit "better than a greased fist." The shoe lies at the center of a nearly circular sweep of dirt, a spin and a fall, maybe. My chest swells with a feeling of victory and, in equal measure, perverse hopelessness, knowing ultimately that the shoe is nothing if I can't attach it to anything, if I don't find its partner.

I pick it up and hold the opening over my nose, inhaling deeply, prickling with the sensation that I'm being observed from just out of sight, that I am trespassing on a private moment. It's slightly damp, and the sweat scent is there, still harsh, faintly like yogurt. It feels as though I'm picking up the final traces before these molecules join the air around me and are subsumed into the environment, like I'm interfering with some natural process by putting them into me. The sole is dirty but not caked with mud, as if the bulk of the rainstorm had been waited out elsewhere. It can't have been long since you were here, or since whatever or whoever had your shoe was here.

I call your name into the forest, the shoe. It would never be that easy.

I search the area for other signs, for more unsettled earth or broken branches, a rune carved into a tree, but there's nothing glaring or obvious enough for me to notice. I backtrack to look for evidence that someone else has been here, of a struggle or a chase, a body being dragged, just movement beyond myself, but the forest floor is random, devoid of even my footprints, and I understand with a kind of resigned reassurance that this is all I'm going to get—short of finding a sleeping bag or a makeshift hovel my tracking skills are nonexistent—and I feel certain that I've been left some kind of gift, a sign. I consider the place-ment of the shoe—beneath the arch, heel angled toward me, toe pointed east. I proceed in that direction, the direction I've been headed, because it's easiest to draw that conclusion. I take the shoe with me, assuming it's charged with magical power and because, wherever you are now, you're missing one. In my head, I turn over and over something you said about possession.

A short distance later, a single-lane paved road appears in the forest. I skitter across as if afraid someone will see me, ignoring both directions, thinking only, *Forward, forward.*

*

The afternoon passes, with this as my mantra.

At first, I register the smell and then forget it. It's filtered through my senses and disappears, like the last of your sweat, assumes the identity of the forest around it: the bark, the leaves, the dirt. Above it all, the sun is lustrous. It's a day for optimism.

I only notice when the insides of my nostrils start to burn, one sense reminding me of the betrayal of another. I press my nose to the tongue of the sneaker, holding it like a gas mask. Suddenly I'm squinting back tears, the trees above whispering all the same thing—the remnants of smoke. Something has burned here.

I blink away the clouds from my eyes and feel my contacts shift. As I walk on, the smell remains the only indication that something is different. Looking up through the branches at the sun has the same effect on my eyes, and again, I'm able to deny what I sense. Again, I register it, and then forget. I walk blindly on.

I emerge into a clearing.

The first thing I take in, beyond the unexpected openness, is the roundness of the space, a platform there in the forest. I look skyward—at an utterly empty patch of blue—before I look anywhere else, before I look directly ahead and see the blackened, scorched hulk in front of me, smoking quietly into the sky.

The clearing isn't natural. Around me, across a diameter of maybe a hundred feet, the smaller trees have been imperfectly downed, and the tops of those surrounding are missing at erratic, choppy angles, as if wildly scissored away by a giant, spinning blade. As the thing resting at the center of the clearing has one long remaining strut projecting from its top like a single finger pointing at its own wake. It's a downed helicopter.

Apart from the blade, the rest of the machine has burned and warped torturously together into a single, twisted mass of charred matter. The shape of it still reads "helicopter," its general structure intact, but the body has burst, and the entrances on its sides, the windows at either end are stuffed with its half-ejected human contents, as though the helicopter had been packed as full as possible and then, interrupted mid-flight, just barely touched down when it exploded from the inside, propelling its passengers out through any available space. Through the rear window, facing me, someone's back half has been forced mostly out, while someone else's arm reaches pitifully into the air, pinned by the bulge of the other body into the corner of the window, like a strand of clay extruded through a press. From the cockpit window, half of a masked body outfitted in uniform black lies on the nose among the glass of the shattered windshield. Between the front and tail ends, the insides of the helicopter's cabin spill en masse onto the forest floor like garbage, at least a dozen bodies, a wreck of tangled limbs in a pile as if awaiting mass burial, a mix of uniforms and silk suits and dresses, summer clothes burned away. Shreds of fabric waft in the breeze in clouded colors. Scattered further into the clearing, around the mangled helicopter and its dead passengers, overturned suitcases lie among the wreck of the forest, burst open, like a luxury cruise washed deep inland. The fallen branches, splintered trees are arrayed around them in vibrant destruction, revealing their orange and yellow insides, the charred bark like reptile skin. The ground goes alternately gray, black, brown, and green. The smell—of smoke, for one, and of bodies rotting in the sun for days—blankets everything without warning.

I vomit just shy of my shoes—I make a point to avoid them, I careen away at an awkward angle. My body seems to make a concerted effort to bring up the last thing I consumed, and so it's the acidic sweetness of the pasta sauce that fills my mouth, somehow undigested pasta that I spit onto the forest floor, held onto for days out of spite, refusing breakdown into anything useful. I stay on my knees for a long while, because the smell is actually better down there, closer to the ground, and because, I realize, I can hear birds again. Crouched here, there's nothing forcing me in any direction; I can stay in one spot as long as I like, just breathing. I wonder if you'd come across this wreck, if the shoe had been some kind of indication as to what lay ahead, the swooping pattern in the dirt a cipher I'd failed to decode.

Eventually I push myself up, joints cracking, brushing ash from my knees. I pinch my nose with your sneaker, inhaling your scent, your fear maybe, and make my way cautiously forward, stepping over branches, discarded clothing, and debris. At the base of the slopped pile of bodies, one of the black-uniformed figures lies face-down, as if he'd been standing on the edge of the aircraft when it exploded. Even the hands, spread to either side in permanent don't-shoot, are gloved in black. A zipper runs down the back of the head. I use one shoe to lift the body at the shoulder, but it hardly moves, the legs pinned down by others. I try again, harder. I kick and drag my foot—a motion I repeat with increasing viciousness and pressure—until the body turns over; when it does, those behind it shift and topple. The sound, like potatoes falling to the ground, cuts through the clearing and then quits, infinitely still. I vomit again, my body empties another refuse chamber, followed by a hacking round of coughing.

I turn back to the uniformed body, now face-up, pointed toward the sky. The mask only leaves space for the eyes, intact and glassy, ringed with dirt. There's a bulletproof vest and zippered pockets across the front and sides. The chest is strapped with sleek black canisters, tear gas or grenades; I'm surprised they didn't explode on impact. A combat knife, too, is sheathed on the leg. I'm looking for insignia, for a distinctive label of some kind, corporate or government branding, but there isn't any. The belt is hung with ammunition, an empty holster at the waist. My heart skips a beat at the sight of the missing weapon, and I step back and pan the forest floor before me. My stomach drops out again: materializing all around me, pistols and machine guns, weapons of all kind shimmer into view out of nowhere, gleaming in the grass, hidden in the suitcases, transmuting out of branches and black shadows, everywhere, outnumbering everything.

I stagger backward and trip over a fallen branch. My elbow lands on the barrel of a rifle. My breath feels trapped inside of me. I scrabble at the ground, pine needles and ash, I push myself to my feet, furious that I have to work so hard just to keep standing, to move past anything. I snatch your shoe from the ground. I trip again at the edge of the clearing, the trees ludicrously tall.

I don't stop running until my legs give out. Behind me, the killing machines bloom like flowers at my feet.

Before I know it, the forest ends, as cleanly as it started, and the next thing I smell is the ocean.

The sea breeze breaks against me and doubles me over, drives a chill through my body and the outfit now completely saturated with sweat and dirt, stiffening it like a shell. The ocean is maybe a quarter mile away, sprawling before me in both directions, as limitless as the overpass was before it. The sky is a deep, majestic blue, like a painting, something you pay for. I stand there rigid, wind channeling around me. From the edge of the forest, thinning grass slopes into a bulky rock fringe, and beyond it and below, a narrow strip of beach glows in the moonlight. The sleeves of the ocean pull forward and back; I imagine the land beneath, coding and re-coding as it's alternately revealed and hidden. To the south, my right, stoops the foreboding outline of a rambling coastal estate, dark enough to nearly pass itself off as part of the landscape, to disguise the threat. As I stand above it, deep in the black, in some miniscule fixture many levels below me, I recognize a pinprick of light. The moment I step forward, it's gone. I step backward again, retracing my steps; I tilt my line of sight left, then right, but the light doesn't return from any angle. The mansion crouches in its creeping darkness like a family who's snuffed out the final candle as the troops arrive.

I pick my way forward down the hill, away from the forest and toward the rocks, parallel to the mansion. I clutch your shoe in my right fist like a talisman (my fingers wrap almost all the way around it, the size is just too perfect). The dirt changes to sand. My feet sink into it and I trudge forward, a physical experience many years dormant. The sound of the waves is borne up to me like television static. I fill my vision with the ocean and try to move into it, toward the water and nothing else. I divide the world into two halves: the sky clouded and phantasmal with stars, and the water below it, offering a smoky hint of reflection. I feel myself going deeper. My right shoulder knocks against wrought iron in the dark, and I'm awakened as if by a bad dream. The collision cascades outward along the fence; the sound is swallowed by the ocean but the vibration continues, an insidious undercurrent. I step back and feel out the bar with my hand, ceasing the resonation. Faintly, against the night, I can pick out the spires of the fence, ending about six feet above me. Just inside, the property is bordered with hedges of the same height, obscuring the grounds. I angle away from it, now that I know the approximate perimeter, and continue on at a diagonal toward the sea, the wind, the roar now coming from all sides (when I'm near the bars, it's filtered through them, ringing slightly). I paddle out into the air.

I remember a beach trip my parents and I took up to Connecticut to visit my grandparents, at least a decade ago. Over the course of the morning we dug an enormous hole in the sand, my dad and I, deep enough that I could stand inside of it, up to my eleven- or twelve-year-old shoulders. Afterward, my dad went out into the water and dragged a neon-orange bucket back and forth until he scooped up a wayward jellyfish. He wandered back to the beach, the bucket overflowing, I clambered out, and we dumped the jellyfish into the hole. I shoveled sand on top of it while he went back to the shore to find another. The process repeated: we kept layering them like this until the hole was entirely filled in. The thrill of it lay in the pacification of the jellyfish at my hands, that isolated in this mass grave the jellies were no longer dangerous to me, the natural aquatic environment where they acted as predators to carefree swimmers switched out for another that they weren't suited for (where they couldn't even move!), and I was enamored of my role in this, in their relocation and burial, in making these fearsome, nebulous creatures harmless. (The thought didn't occur to me at the time—or to my dad, apparently—that someone else might later dig in this same spot and be stung by the buried jellyfish, that their poison lingered, their tentacles wound through the sand.) Around the hole, under the span of two umbrellas, our beach chairs are arranged in a lazy half-circle: one with my mom, reading (her chair partially in the sunlight out of self-sacrifice); my dad's empty chair; my grandfather, looking at a magazine; my grandmother, likewise, while unwrapping a sandwich covered in foil; and two more empty chairs, one of them mine. It must have been longer than ten years ago, I think, because my dad's father was still alive; it must have been twelve or thirteen years, when I was nine or ten. There came a period a few summers later—a dark period, sometime around sixth and seventh grade—that I can't remember with any specificity, that afterward my parents avoided referring to explicitly. Following this, after thirteen or so, everything comes into sharper detail, and from then on I can approximately trace my development, my sentience as a human. But this day on the beach, it must be a moment before then, before the silent period in my memory—even years before, because there were visits when my grandfather wasn't mobile at all, when he wouldn't go to the beach and we were further inland—a rare, clarified scene. Across the hole from me, also digging and filling, reacting to everything in the same ways I do, there's a face I don't otherwise specifically remember: blonder, longer hair, brown eyes, but built the same way I am, a little thinner. He climbs out of the hole as my dad walks up the beach, the bucket sloshing over the sides, and then he takes one of the empty chairs, kicking his feet, to watch my dad empty it. The memory smacks of conspiracy. I find myself looking at this boy more than I should, slightly uncomprehending, as if my present self has gone back to inhabit the memory, overlaying its current perception on the child I was, pausing a moment to examine the reality around him, to reflect on this distant, strangely familial face. I had a brother like you.

The next moment I'm standing at the arched front gates of the coastal mansion, completely perpendicular to where I last remember walking, without clear recollection of how I changed direction. The ocean is at my back. The sound of the waves hiccups behind me, cutting out and returning, doubling over itself to fill the missing space. The gates here are closed, but they're unlocked, and so I push the right half inward as if on command, moving forward as the external world catches up, readjusts to my new position. I enter the grounds. I leave the gate open behind me, a habit now more than anything.

The courtyard between me and the house is decorated with fountains and pools in elaborately planned formations, all shut off, the water stagnant and evaporating. There's no direct path to the front door—the meandering pathways are meant to be contemplative. Weeds have started to sprout among the zen-garden flowerbeds and through the cracks in the flagstones underfoot. I walk over a once-charming varnished teak bridge above an artificial pond—below it, in the dark, I discern the shiny, whitish shapes of enormous dead koi that once populated the pond, now floating on the surface. In the moonlight, their scaled bellies, barely drifting, look like giant maggots. At other displays, thematically and historically at odds, mythological nudes and Hindu gods stand with stark resolve in emptying stone basins stained and striated green with algae. The lack of arcing water, of at least a common movement to unite them, if nothing else, makes each tableau look especially empty of meaning, especially forgotten. Bordering the courtyard, the towering hedges create a pocket of isolation around the property, locking out the breeze, the tangential ocean. When the estate was at its highest level of operativity, I imagine the people entering these grounds through the front gates would be greeted by the sound of trickling water through treated silence, the coast a separate aesthetic to be viewed from afar.

The handle on the front door—in this case, a metal ring on a little knob, a bit of stronghold about it, the door perhaps an antique shipped in from another country, another century—is pitched low, below my waist. I pull. These doors open out, but this is the only difference.

In opposition to the imperial-dilettante exterior, the inside is old-money stately, sized in different proportions. Rather than tile, everything is carpet over wood, every surface is patterned or paneled where it's not covered in somber oil portraits of the family ancestors locked in thick oval frames, the forebears of this region. A monstrous coatrack greets me just inside the door, beside a chair and a wooden endtable, used for sitting and anticipating visitors, correspondence sorting. When I take a step forward, the entire entryway creaks, and I freeze, a bolt of fear paralyzing me. The sound crackles through the carpet and up the walls, past the sconces and browning bulbs shaped like candle flames until it disappears into the far reaches of the house. There's a different character in the house's pre-modernity, in knowing this mansion could have been built on the upwards of a hundred years ago, that it keeps its own mysterious ways of carrying messages from end to end. I listen raptly for sound from elsewhere, as though, if I'd been hiding in this mansion, I would have come running at the slightest noise rather than burying myself even deeper, as if I've forgotten my entire purpose for being here, the warped sneaker in my hand: to find other life.

I move out, in the usual way. Further endtables, thick lamps with yellowed shades, Tiffanys, rolltop desks, looming clocks, and tasseled, stiff furniture occupy every free space, accumulated like dust. The kitchen cabinets are filled with chipped ceramic plates and heavy cast iron hanging from hooks. Any improvements to the house seem to have ceased in 1976. A pioneer motif dominates the artwork beyond the portraiture, the settling of new lands, merchant ships and formative exchanges with the natives. In a sitting room I find an enormous tapestry covering one wall, a pack of noblemen with spears and dogs arrayed around the bloodletting of some beast at the center. A library occupies one wing of the first floor, with great bay windows that look out on the treeline in an expectant way, the lawns a staging area, as if those who lived here were accustomed to sitting in their easy chairs and watching things break through. The middle pane of one window is shattered, the window unlatched, glass sparkled over the bench sill in a plume. The library hasn't acquired books since the Kinsey Report.

There are three floors above the first, the staircases set wide under bulbous oak railings and thick, well-traveled carpet fraying at the edges. From a second-floor bedroom wardrobe—I brace myself before easing it open—I take another set of clothes from beneath plastic: a 1940s button-down with some sort of checked pattern and sleeves that I roll up, dark pants, an old set of Oxfords; in every item I default to black. And still—it's inevitable in a way that seems defeated—the longer I'm in the house, the more I explore of the mansion dressed in the manner of its previous inhabitants, the less it feels like a novelty, and slowly, the rooms, the furnishings begin to repeat. On each landing, in a niche on the wall stands a marble head on a pedestal, Grecian and familiar.

My second time through the foyer, I follow the curve of the balustrade backward into a wide, peaked hall leading south, lit by electric torches. A deep coatroom wraps alongside it, the wooden hangers bare and inexplicably sad. At the end of the hallway, a closed set of double doors begs to be thrown dramatically open. I oblige the instinct, and burst through them into a huge and empty ballroom. I twist a knob on a panel beside the door and light springs from a million invisible recesses; I dial it way back. From outside, this section of the house pulses once. A bar reaches to the left, its surfaces reflecting, and past it, floor-to-ceiling windows with the curtains pulled back look out onto the ocean. An illustrated series of panels compose the wall to my right, molded with arches and complex layered borders in velvet red and gold. Maroon patterned carpet spreads in all directions, nicked in places. A few sparse tables and chairs fill about a quarter of the room in no particular order, left over from the last event. A rectangular dance floor begins about halfway across the ballroom, scuffed everywhere, and beyond it, on the stage, a sleek black grand piano sits alone, top open. I imagine a body crammed inside. Above it all hangs a set of four colossal tiered chandeliers in a style now familiar to me, which I'm confident in pinning to the 1920s. Keeping the wall to my side, I make my way around the right edge of the room, wary of the space below the chandeliers.

About a third of the way across the ballroom, opposite the ocean, my hands unconsciously locate a slot in one of the wall panels, a narrow groove leading about eight feet up. I hook my fingers into the molding and pull. A section of the wall swings silently open on artfully disguised hinges, like the closet in the mirror bedroom—I think that this must be a feature of rich houses, this mystery-novel way of hiding secrets. Through the door, another carpeted staircase leads down, alongside a more basic wooden ramp. I follow it to the bottom, expecting something truly sinister, but it's just a storage basement, albeit one finished with tasteful floral wallpaper and green carpet. The room is large and at its capacity likely held all of the furniture needed for the events in the ballroom above; as is, it's about half-filled. High-backed chairs are stacked to one side of the stairs, circular tables rolled together and nestled beside them. Near the base of the staircase, where I'm standing, sits a long dining table draped in a white dust-sheet. Other unidentifiable furniture is similarly covered in the far corner, where I imagine it's remained for years. Directly across from me, a closed door marks another passage, a closet or the entry to some deeper basement, a sub-basement. Light from the ballroom filtering around me just illuminates the room—if I stood still for long enough, I could probably see particles moving through the air. Because I'm interested to see how deep this house goes—because I've already counted the levels up—I walk across the room to the closed door: for once, plain wood in the wall, brass knob and all.

When I open the door into the darkness, I hear the sound of ragged breathing cut short into dead silence. My entire body braces, and my senses instantly retract, leaving me to move forward by pure momentum, all that's left over from before I heard that sound. I feel my way slowly onto the staircase, wooden, no railing, an abrupt shift, as if this was the one part of the house they didn't care to improve since its construction, because from the basement below was all service. I put my hand out to the wall on my left, cold concrete. It's like being somewhere close to home again.

I am three steps down when a deafening sputter of gunfire erupts from my right, exploding into the wall next to me, illuminating it briefly, pocked with bullet holes. Ears ringing, hearing shells clatter to a hard floor, I scramble blindly back the way I came. I slam the door behind me, my senses returning to full alert. Panting, I back blindly across the room until I hit the edge of the sheeted dining table, and, feeling it there, I drop to the floor and scurry pathetically beneath it, ensuring that I'm hidden from sight before I let myself fall apart, before I collapse into that most basic position. I take huge, gulping gasps of air, more rawly panicked than I've ever been—than when I was holding the gun myself—because it feels abruptly like warfare. Lying on my belly, I peer out from under the edge of the sheet, eyes locked on the sub-basement door, my chin digging the carpet. That's what I'm thinking to myself, a frantic chant as I scrutinize the stationary door, the forces mounting behind it: *This is war. This is war. This is war.*

I stare and stare, forcing my eyes open as wide as possible, to preclude blinking, as if otherwise I might miss it, the split second in which I'll be forced to react, to flee or engage or conceal myself, to start the car. I shudder, but attempting to regulate my breathing only makes the rest of me harder to control—the sensation is the same as fighting back tears, and when they follow, it's almost a relief. I let it happen, I'm so petrified that I will let my body do what it wants, will take anything it offers as evidence of being alive, of still breathing. I squeeze your stupid shoe so hard I'm afraid that it will pop in my fist.

When I'm beyond myself, I listen to the house, trying to detect the vibrations below me. I wonder if my shaking can be felt from the sub-basement, if the path of my footsteps running across the room was easily traceable, where I've been positioned by whomever waits below. I imagine him training his sights on the ceiling. I feel the bullets erupting up from the carpet, clear through my body, to lodge in the table above. I hear the spilling of shells again, the transition from live to dead weight, the slump of my body perceptible from below, final.

Whatever waits for me in the sub-basement, there must be more of them in the house: they must occupy every floor. They must have watched as I explored, as I moved up and down. I remember, completely unheralded, when I was about four years old and we were visiting my mom's parents in Mount Vernon, I'd wandered into the living room and sat in front of the extinguished fireplace for twenty minutes before I realized my grandfather was sitting in the chair beside me, completely silent. It was a moment of utter, basic terror. I think of the figure wrapped in my sleeping bag, clutching it to them like it was the only thing they'd ever possessed in the world, motionless throughout the entire scene, during our combat around them. There have always been others.

I blink, and among the covered furniture there are men standing with their backs pressed to all of the walls, perfectly still, blending with the wallpaper. I blink again, and they're gone.

The carpet under my chin is salty-wet. Demolished, I rest my cheek in the grit, the brief cool. The rendered foot of the table next to me catches my eye: it's in the shape of a monstrous claw, a form that I recognize from somewhere. I follow the carved pattern up the table leg, raising my head, letting the edge of the sheet fall back to the ground, vanishing me beneath it. I trace the wooden shapes in the almost-black to the underside of the table, and discern at its edge a bubbling mass of cherubs sculpted into it, one breaking from the rest, his chubby arms reaching toward the long side of the table as if to escape his brethren, sucked down toward the monster below.

I have seen this table before, in the mansion where we found the urns, where the knife appeared for the first time. It is exactly the same table. I launch to my knees, my breath a mess again, rearing back. My shoulder hits the underside of the table; it rumbles through the house. For a baffled second, I think that I've somehow circled back to the same mansion, to the same point in time but now populated, always populated, that I'm so disoriented I can't even recognize a house I've slept in before, to which I've been brought back to be killed. I hear footsteps thundering from the floor above, raining down the carpeted stairs.

But I know that it cannot be the same mansion, and that the truth is even worse: the table, the marble heads have followed me here, as has everything else. Every building I enter is the same but with its ingredients shifted around, arranged in different patterns, the floors stacked in a different order, the artifacts and artwork shuffled randomly—a changing set of labyrinths built from recycled parts and fixed variables. The walls here are the floors somewhere else, the carpet a magnified copy of a throw rug, a vase transposed from a gallery to a vacant building, a camo-print bedspread knit into someone's pants. The judgment table. An overturned throne. A bedroom surrounded in bathroom mirrors. Marble heads repeating exactly on every landing, miles apart. A wolf in the foyer, an octopus inching slowly through the sunroom, a gun in my hand—the elements, like a dropped deck of cards, repeating numbers in different suits. Some are populated, some are not. I'm sure that if I opened the wardrobe on an upper level, I would find Vivian. Or I wouldn't.

I wonder where—as that mansion came into view around the final bend of the path off the highway, as it was generated into our consciousness, or as we fucked on the bed, or entered the bedroom—where Vivian was yanked from and put there, which subway car, from whose scattered aspects she had been composed. If August's bedroom was actually someone else's, reconstituted, that of a brother I'd once had.

I wrap my fingers around one talon of the claw-like foot, anchoring myself in this reality, and once more, I sink back to the carpet, my ears straining to hear sounds that aren't there. For a moment, I don't recognize the tattooed shapes on my arm; if they were rearranged, I would never be able to convince myself they'd ever been any different.

At length, I slowly raise the white sheet a few inches and scrutinize the basement again. Everything looks the same. I walk the fingers of one hand out on the carpet a foot or so, and then leave them there, ghosted in the dim light, fighting every urge to pull them away. After a minute, I gather the courage to drag myself forward out from under the table. And then my foot is on the floor again, and I'm getting up, mostly because I'm certain that when I yank the white sheet off the judgment table I'll find the knife sitting calmly atop it, faintly smeared or gleaming as if it's never been used, and in a populated house like this, it's comforting to know at least one thing, to know where one weapon is, to possess this limited certainty.

Instead, I leave it concealed, and walk across the room, my eyes everywhere, toward another dust-sheeted table. I don't uncloak this one either; I grab two corners and walk it in minute shifts backward, as quietly as possible toward the sub-basement door. Its feet leave indentations in the carpet, notching time on the floor. I move the table length-wise to block the door, as close as I can without touching it, for fear of sending sound downstairs. I stack three heavy chairs and a square-topped endtable on top of it, all hefted with ancestral value, decades of human cells, blocking the shooter inside. A wave of nausea overcomes me—the physical manifestation of a reality that I've been putting off, space that the rest of my actions have been masking to fill until this arbitrary moment of disruption, like light breaking through—and I realize that I have no idea where you are, and probably haven't since I left Vivian's mansion, that I've made it to the coast for another reason altogether, or for no reason at all.

I return to the judgment table, and whip the white sheet off with a flourish. Another plane rotates out.

A cloud of dust explodes visibly into the air. The table is completely bare underneath. My stomach lurches and, instinctively, I spin to face the sub-basement door. I know what I've seen. I drop your shoe. Hands gripping the naked wooden edge behind me, I lower myself again to the ground. Like everything, I wait for it to burst open.

*

The first time we had sex—which had occurred in the prison cell-like environs of your dorm room in Brinkman, six weeks after I'd first walked you there—in the slightly giddy aftermath of the act itself (because I always believed in a slightly giddy aftermath), during the minutes I assumed were meant to be filled with tender and earnest flattery (though we'd both known this was coming for some time, had planned it specifically), coated in a pleasantly sleepy sensation, my breathing still residually ragged, my head pressed into your neck and my face angled down, I traced my finger around the curve of your clawmarked shoulder and said, "My favorite part of your body is the collarbone."

I knew, by this stage of our relationship, that you weren't really receptive to compliments, especially those about your body, but, again, I was feeling sensitive and earnest, so I said it anyway.

"I'm afraid I've got bad news for you," you said. "That's everyone's favorite body part."

I think the double meaning occurred to us both at the same time: one, that this was a clichéd body part to choose, in general, that I was not unique in this regard, which, fine, and if there was a time I was allowed to be clichéd, after losing my virginity was probably it; and two, the meaning specific to you, that everyone you'd been with before me (or, even more broadly, everyone who had ever admired your physical character) had picked out this same feature and identified it as their favorite—worse than a cliché in and of itself (even having a "favorite body part" was a cliché, maybe), it was a reflexive kind of cliché, one that had developed in response to your person alone, and then was repeated so many times that it had become a predictable, boring quality in your admirers, along the lines of "I like girls with tattoos," or "I like the Misfits." The implication here being that I was just like everyone else.

You didn't follow up to clarify—there wasn't a graceful, immediately apparent way to do it without referencing in some way the past guys or girls who'd complimented your naked upper form—and I didn't reply, either. It had become more or less a habit, after the appearance of the gun, that occasionally, in conversation, I would spend so much time dwelling on my possible replies, and the replies to those replies and so on, that eventually I'd awaken to the fact that I hadn't said anything at all, that I had let our conversation slide into silence, carried on, only hypothetically, into a conversation in my head. We fell into one of those silences then; when I realized it, I didn't speak (not knowing, ultimately, what to say) but instead tried to make the silence resolute rather than defeated, natural rather than disruptive. I continued to stroke your shoulder, and I kissed you again in the dark, and I squeezed your body at intervals, like I hadn't noticed the history that had crept into the room, and I repeated this series of motions, again and again, until my physical gestures (the stroking, the squeezing) became background action, reflexive reassurances, the way you reach out to catch something when it's falling. I fell asleep.

Which is to say: seated on the floor of the basement, with my back to the claw-leg table, eyes tracking the stillness of the sub-basement door blocked by furniture, assuring myself over and over that it's not moving, exhausted beyond anything, I fall asleep.

A moment later, I'm back in the bathroom of Villa Scum in Richmond, with the noise all around me, the walls vibrating and Candace's head in my lap. I'm trying to shake her awake. My hands are on her shoulders and I'm staring into her eyes, as if the harder I concentrate, the better this will work.

The moment still takes me by surprise: she awakes, the film dissolves across her eyes, clearing them, but this time her face changes—or I'm aware, somehow, that it's different from what I remember—transforms to someone else's entirely, to someone I don't know, like a veil drawn back from my memories, revealing details once obscured. I am on the floor in the bathroom and I am holding this perfect stranger in my lap, participant in an escalating history of intervention in which my role grows more and more irrelevant and uncertain, more and more sinister. She jolts to life, struggles to her feet, and runs. The rest of the scene is exactly the same.

*

I start awake an indeterminate amount of time later. It could have been minutes or hours, I have no idea. The same light filters down the stairs.

The square endtable I'd stacked on top of the three chairs— the top of the furniture pyramid blocking the door—is now upright on the floor in front of the blockade, the drawer closed and fully intact. My skin chills and then prickles with the onset of sweat, like each pore awakening to action. The movement is thick with intention. The house has rotated again, shifted its furniture around, or else someone has been here to alter it. I can't tell what else has moved; I look at the floor—suddenly sick of breathing, of my constant awareness of it—and see only the marks from the table I dragged to block the door, a code inscribed into the carpet, a written record. The three chairs are stacked on the table the same way I left them—a gap in the rest of the sheeted furniture across the room, the space they used to fill—and the sub-basement door is still shut. The sheet from the clawfooted table behind me is crumpled on the floor, its dust settled, time passing.

I rise to my feet, trembling with anger, my head swimming with phantom noise and the wrong memories, the fear that while I slept dumb I've somehow changed houses, that the mansion I'd fallen asleep inside was switched out and reconstructed around me, but imperfectly, and I'm resentful at having spotted the error. I feel like I'm being taunted. Beyond what I perceive in the room, beyond the objects shifting and repeating, I sense mean human calculation.

I grab one of the heavy chairs from atop the barricade and hurl it as hard as I can across the room. It doesn't go far, but one leg cracks against a corner of the table and snaps off, and the body thunders to the ground—however thick the floor is, anyone below would be able to hear it. The sound roars through the basement and up the stairs, as if calling *Come here, come here.*

The second chair doesn't break when I throw it, so I lift it by the shoulders and bash it into the carpet, into the other chair, over and over. When the legs crack against each other, my body shivers involuntarily as if it's a bone being snapped, clinical and ruthless, and then, as I repeat the action, I acclimate to the sound. There's sweat running down my face by the time the legs break, the energy pouring out of me raw and unfiltered. I pick up the displaced endtable by two of its legs and slam it to the ground in the same place, then three times more, until the legs separate like those of a smashed insect and the drawer bursts open and spills forgotten placecards to the floor, bearing handwritten names like Weatherby and Morris. I pound the third chair into the wreckage of the others until it splinters, making as much noise as possible, screaming, the wood dividing into shafts, into its basic shapes, as if there's a target beneath me, a spraypainted X marking demolition, and if I keep hitting, eventually the floor will give way, eventually I'll come through the ceiling, the process will be complete. My voice creaks when it first leaves me—my last word was your name, shouted into the forest—then catches, holds steady. When the rest of the blockade is destroyed, I walk to the long table, the single piece of furniture remaining in front of the door. I hoist one end of it above my head—legs digging into my shoulders, my strength feels infinite—move my hands to the feet, shove and jump back with a final, anguished yell.

The table crashes to the ground with unearthly force and a painfully loud crack, like a tree falling—the vibrations surge through the floorboards at my feet, rattling everything smaller than I am. Elsewhere in the house, something has been set off and continues ringing, but there's nothing beyond it, no responsive movement, nothing racing downward or upward, and in the force of the moment, its physical tremble, the lack of retaliation only makes me angrier.

I take a severed chair leg from the rubble and negotiate around the fractured table to the sub-basement door. I raise the leg in my hand like a murder weapon and have already hit the flimsy wood once, twice, three times before I finally understand what I'm doing, what I've been doing since I woke up from the memory of another door I broke through realizing I could never save the people I intended, not Candace, not Vivian, and certainly not you, and having, maybe, the answer to a question I've been failing to address since long before I met you, since I saw other eyes that looked like mine: I am creating terror.

I let the chair leg—pathetic, brutal weapon—fall to the carpet. In contrast to everything else, relinquishing it makes no sound whatsoever. The silence falls over me like a blanket. A line of paint flakes drifts from the door like ash. I stand there, the mansion towering above, around, below me, bracing myself. I turn the knob—which rattles on both levels—wait a beat, and pull the door open.

Gunfire shatters the forced quiet, ear-splittingly loud, spraying the concrete wall next to the stairs and lighting the gloom in streaks. I jump backward and hit the table. The barrage doesn't stop after the first burst, not like the last time, but continues, drowning out the falling shells. I pick out that its bursts come three rounds at a time, barely separated, issued by something large and automatic. The smell of acrid burning lead and pulverized cement drifts up from the sub-basement. I'm back in the open doorway when, abruptly, the gunfire ends.

My ears are still ringing, but I'm able to hear again before whoever's down there, with all that echo. Beneath the ringing, again, the staggered, panicked breathing of someone who has been found.

It is my turn to speak. My shadow looming at the top of the stairs, multiple versions of the scenario unwind in my head: in one of them, I turn and run, once again—I run from the mansion completely, disappear, risking that they will follow, that I will spend the next indefinite period of my life in fear of pursuit. In another, I walk down into the sub-basement, confident that I'll be mowed down where I stand, that this can end, here and now, with my body on the stairs. Or, I call out something, announce myself not as an enemy but as another survivor—if that is what we are—reveal that, when all is said is done, I'm not cavalry. I stand there and deliberate, projected in different directions. The future sprawls like a lawn. I breathe in, at last, and open my mouth.

A final burst of three rounds cuts through the breathing, but not against the concrete wall, oddly soft, and then I hear something wet, turning freshly apart.

I am running down the stairs and screaming, "I'M NOT GONNA HURT YOU!" before the shells hit the ground.

*

The sub-basement is pitch dark. I hit the wall at the base of the steps and fumble for a lightswitch, my breathing smothering everything, the air hot and thick with the smell of mixed metallics. My hand finds a string above me. A lightbulb sends unanimous light across the narrow space. My eyes squeeze shut, and then I blink rapidly against the tears as my pupils adjust.

When I register the room, I cry out and trip backward over nothing. Opposite the wooden stairs, maybe twelve feet away, a body uniformed in black lies slumped against the wall, resting between an ancient washing machine and an enormous boiler. Most of the head is gone; the wall behind it and one side of the washer are soaked in dark red gore. Blood runs down the concrete with a soft hiss, its heat escaping, the body still pumping up and out. An assault rifle is propped between the two bent knees, clenched in white, vise-like fingers, angled backward, toward where the face was.

I plant my forearms against the wall and retch—aware, suddenly, that this is my response to everything, to just expel it— but this time nothing comes up, I cannot find relief here, my stomach has finally been totally emptied. A new, petrified sweat envelops my body, a different odor, and once again, I begin to shake, starting in my jaw and moving through to my fingertips, my knees: I did this. I did this. I will wake up a thousand nights from now, and still I will have done this. A pit opens inside of me, and out comes everything: the distinct memory of being dragged out of a swimming pool, screaming from every direction, wrestled to the ground with someone already laid out beside me like a failed competitor, suspended in a place before you're certain that everything has changed forever—before you realize that the loser isn't breathing, that there's hair caught between your fingers—an indication that I will never forget anything again, that my memory is crystal clear and always has been, always will be.

I collapse at the base of the stairs, letting the air dry and clear while the body settles into permanence. Around me, there's evidence that he had been living down here: empty cans, boxes, and foil wrappers discarded in the corners, food that he must have taken from upstairs; the typical smells of old waste. His boots sit before the washer, the laces loosened and tongues pulled forward, airing out. I focus on each object concretely by itself—the blood-spattered washer, the monstrous boiler, the bare lightbulb in the ceiling, an empty soup can, the mess of heavy iron pipes on the far wall—absorbing their significance independently, focusing on the make, the color, the texture, the provenance, the range of filth and decay and age, so that their raw physical data fills my mind completely, and I try to consider it all (how old the can of soup was based on the design of its label, the font, how long it had been stored here), and then I shift from one object to the next, as little space between them as possible. Still, through the cracks, the realization, the fact of the body rushes through in waves, a clock in me desperately rewinding. My throat knots, and again releases nothing.

I force myself to stand before I've plotted my exact course. In one motion, I pull the body forward by its clammy, socked feet, away from the gore and toward the center of the room. The upper half collapses to the floor among the spent shells, a sound I know from the crash site in the forest but which I don't expect to echo like it does. I roll down my sleeves and hold one arm over my mouth and nose, taking in the smell of mothballs. He's outfitted in the same bulletproof vest and black uniform as the bodies in the clearing. The gun is empty—he used the last three rounds on himself, gauged the end, when I would storm him—as is the ammo belt, as if he'd seen combat before he arrived here. The black fabric mask and gloves sit on a corner of the washing machine. There are pieces of the head that I distinctly recognize, hair—I turn away, obscure my vision as much as possible, but I don't throw up again.

I pry his fingers off the empty rifle, using the gloves between his skin and my own. I unsheathe the knife and throw both weapons over by the boiler—I don't even want to touch them. I hold my breath and hoist the top of the body toward me, keeping my head back, fumbling with the straps of the bulletproof vest. There is no resistance at all, and it peels away cold with recent sweat. Blood rings the collar. Emerging from one sleeve, I see that he has tattoos on one of his arms down to the wrist, a pattern that looks like flower petals. My mind hovers, briefly, on a name I never knew.

*

Another night, I awaken in complete, sudden awareness with the feeling that someone is standing over the bed. I'm out of bed almost instantly, my senses fully alert—the experience is similar to the morning in college I learned about the train accident in a text from a friend, realizing how quickly my body can shift from unconscious to full-action.

You don't stir—even in your sleep, your arm is stretched above your head to the wall behind the pillow. I can't remember how many times you knocked before passing out. There's no one else in the room, but still, in front of me there's a flicker in the texture of the door, someone ahead of time manipulating it, drawing me forward.

I open the door into the balcony hallway. As I exit in the dark, I notice the same rifts in the air, the same immaterial flutters of motion. One occurs down the hallway to my right, in front of the door to the bedroom where Vivian sleeps; another, more pronounced in the moonlight of the foyer, radiates from a point just above the stairs in front of me. I take the stairs. I run my right hand down the banister—it gives me a strange sense of validity, almost, that I have gained enough power here to treat the house casually, as if I've always lived in it, always been accustomed to its luxuries. As if I am following nothing, being led by nothing.

The stairs seem to spill directly into the smaller dining room (though I know I've taken at least one right turn to get there), and from here, the only logical path is to enter the kitchen, to kneel and open the cabinet beneath the sink, to draw forth the knife I know to be chambered there. The blade shrieks quietly against the metal piping.

To my right, again, a warping of the air in the door to the dining room, of potentiation. I step through it—I feel nothing—and then turn back, testing its physical bounds. The kitchen looks just the same; I am still holding the knife. I walk away from the potentiation and exit the kitchen the opposite way, again feeling the rush of control (despite knowing faintly that both paths lead to the same place, to the foyer). Flushed with this sense of moral victory, I cease to notice the permutations in the air, and the next thing I know, I'm halfway up the stairs. I catch myself and my stomach turns; behind me, twelve steps that I don't remember at all, this gap immediately in my past, already widening, and I don't remember if I entered the foyer through the dining room or the kitchen.

I burst down the stairs, almost tripping—when my bare feet smack the tile foyer, the sound echoes, and I'm suddenly sweltering. I use my momentum to barrel forward to the front door, before my body can recover enough to drag me back to the stairs, before the mechanics kick back in. I crash hard into the door with my full weight. I feel it resonate throughout me, a shivering flash of pain, the knife ringing in my hand. I bounce sloppily off, and at the same time I feel a pulling back in the direction of the stairs. As I detach, I grab the handle with my free hand and yank, so that the door comes flying open with me attached to it, revealing the moonlit steps outside. The door clatters on its hinges and then starts to swing back, while I hang desperately on and simultaneously fling myself forward. I let go just before the door slams, and am catapulted onto the terrace. I take quick, frantic steps down the stairs, as if I'm running down a hill and trying to stop. I reach out for the railing. At its end, I swing myself again, to the right, and then crash hopelessly into the front of the house, pulled ever backward, knife arm raised straight above my head like a maniac.

I force myself along the front of the house, trying fruitlessly to drag myself away, while a stronger force twists me toward it, magnetically, bashing my body over and over into the stone foundation as if to pull me back inside, to rip me through the wall. I continue raising and lowering the knife, as if perpetually re-setting into attack stance, and tears stream down my face because I've lost control of everything except the propulsion of my body forward, this one set of motions, because everything else seeks to put me in conflict with the house and those inside it. I think that when I reach the corner, I'll be able to propel myself out, into the lawn, and then momentum will take me, I will be subsumed into the hectic forces of the rest of the grounds. When it comes, I push off and feel briefly untethered, but the movement comes out wrong, like I've tried to swerve off a fixed track, my guts correct the opposite way with a vicious twist in my stomach, and before I know it I'm moving down the perpendicular, southern side of the house in the same manner—like there was never any other choice for me to make, like this path had been carved for years, the trenches were too deep to climb out of—my arm jutting in and out, stabbing repeatedly at nothing but brick, trapped in the broken, looped animation of a cartoon murderer.

I'm led to the back of the house, swiveled again like a toy, and then follow alongside the hedge, stabbing the wall. My actions repeat, my surroundings become abstract in the dark: a vague, changing landscape through which I'm negotiating, hacking at encroaching shapes in a feeble attempt to make them lessen, to reach the end of this circuit. My arm aches as the knife clatters and grates against the foundation of the house, striking and rebounding, striking and rebounding. Anyone asleep inside must be long awake, one floor up, and in the moment I do not care about waking them up, I know the goal, far beyond me, as deep within me as a basement, the goal is to bring them directly into my path. They should all come running. My opposite hand—the one not holding the knife—digs uselessly into my pants pocket, as if I'll find something there to kill the other, as if I ever had control of what I found beneath my fingers. I will myself to draw the knife from the wall, to redirect it into my chest, my neck, anywhere, but the physical manifestation of this thought feels impossible, like an idea someone else had. The hedges dig into my side as I'm thrashed continuously into the house, now parallel to the bedroom hallway on the second floor, the distance closing between us, a red streamer hanging from a window. To my left, there's a sudden flash of movement at ground level—I notice it there, like a sudden light. My arm surges from the brick—to follow it.

In the dark before me, interrupting its course, I find a body low in the bushes.

I stab it past death, a final act of relief, my mind flickering over the after-images of Vivian—you—Candace—on the floor in a room of mirrors, like something pulled up from a nightmare, like everything is just replacement, naked and simple, one for the other.

And, just like that, I'm free. I rise quivering to my feet. The action and release is so definite, so obvious that I feel completely uncontrollable—years have passed and we're back to this. I'm crying uselessly, still, or water is coming off my face as I stumble listlessly into the grounds, my feet uncertain, the knife hanging stupidly, thickly, dripping at my side like a part of my sick biology, as if I've just fucked someone. The sun is creeping toward the horizon. I wipe the knife in the grass, gesturally, not trying hard enough to mask the results (I am changing my suit for his).

And still I make my long meandering way back to the other side of the mansion, its front door hanging open as if to confirm every suspicion about the awful things you might find inside. I find the handle loose as I push the door shut behind me. Still, I stash the knife in the kitchen, under the sink, the same place that I hid it in the mansion before this one. I run the upstairs shower, rub more water over my arms and legs, my burning elbows and wrists. Still, I return to our stolen bedroom and climb back into bed on my aching side, knowing, of course, that your eyes are open and have been indefinitely. And I slide myself into the little pocket of gut-colored covers that I left, the train rushing in my head, and wait to awaken again.

The world contracts. A face slides into another without my noticing. I choose their names; I see what I want to see. I put on the uniform.

The tracks. Everything is an echo of something else. You have always been on the tracks.

IV.
FOYER

BOUND IN BLACK, I CLIMB BACK TO THE SURFACE. As the person before me entered, I climb out through the windows of the library, into the rolling greens beyond. I tear across the lawn in my new skin. On the southwest corner of the property, cradled by the forest, I locate an unlocked gate. I break the treeline again, the sun rising directly in my tracks. I hold your shoe to my chest. The trees move from my path; the forest shrinks or collapses, or I finally notice its true dimensions, the way that from far enough away or with quick enough movements, anything reveals itself in broader strokes: I see the border of the forest pushing out to the northeast, thinning in the south, and the whole of it seems so navigable and straightforward—I realize that there are streetnames in there, there were cars that traveled through it by instinct; it was home to somebody. I feel like I've reached a critical point, a summit where I can look out and survey the bounds of the world I'm living in, granted the geographic certainty that comes with knowing exactly where I stand.

The boots seem to offer an unfair advantage to my running, a kind of militaristic edge in their support and acceleration, a ruthless efficiency, and before long I intersect with the same elevated track where, further north, I'd found your shoe. The tracks are much closer to the coast than I thought, embarrassingly close, and for a second the scope of my entire journey from track to track seems laughable, child-sized. I had never strayed far afield. A few hundred yards down, I find a metal staircase attached to the overpass. I clamber to the top and emerge, all at once, on the rails.

I turn to my left, to the south: the track ahead disappears into a low layer of fog, oozing through the trees. I walk forward in the boots borrowed from the new body, evening my breath, the terrain generating one foot at a time beyond my vision, fulfilling and discrete: I imagine complex loops and circuits of track shrouded in the fog ahead, amorphous in possibility, reassembling before me piece by piece as the future is written. I run again, I test the speed of their generation, as if by moving fast enough I could beat it. The mansions lie at my back like some fantastical, absurd luxury I'd conjured while I died back in the city.

It's comforting to have a distinct path to follow, and before I know it, I'm moving automatically, without consideration of my destination, without thinking about direction or spatial orientation, liberated of all thought. Eventually, the burning in my legs is subsumed into the mechanics of running, and I stop feeling that, too, leaving only the mild propulsive thrust of the boots, the physical pattern beneath it. I'm sweating freely, and that also feels productive, like further evidence indicating progress. There's no telling how much track lies before or behind me. My elevation subtly changes, and at intervals the overpass under my feet switches out with gravel; the forest gently rises and falls beside me as I cut through it. In time, the fog lifts, and the sky goes pale with day full-on. The horizon line draws farther out. The first station I pass—a platform on one side and a railing on the other, an aluminum sign marking another desolate region of the north, a parking lot at ground level, empty as everything else—I acknowledge without slowing down. For the two minutes or so that I'm within its vicinity, my breath returns to me, dimly rebounded off the concrete. The track curves gently, and later, another track swoops in to join it. I see landscape now on both sides, far-off winding roads, motionless little towns, a river. Some distance later, I pass another crappy, abandoned station. I slow occasionally, and then I speed up again.

The progress is thrilling: I feel like I'll never have to stop, that this will take me straight on into eternity. At times, I detect the company of something else keeping pace with me, a twinned presence mimicking my movements, loping along beside me at knee-level, but there's nothing there.

Then in one step, gravel underfoot, it appears ahead: a train on the tracks, staring me down. My pace falters, my human body catches up—I realize how winded I am, how totally exhausted. I remember abruptly the kids on the tracks in Richmond years ago; I try to summon the moment they'd realized the train was coming toward them—frantically reassembling the seconds preceding this one, the steps they'd walked unknowing, the distance from the center of the tracks to the trench at either side, the input from their other senses (sound, heat, smell of smoke)—wondering how I could possibly have missed it until now, how I could be deliberating at all, as if there was a real choice to make. My life suddenly appears to me as a distinct weight, something I can either grab in my fist or throw away. I make my decision (and what if they had made the same decision?): I don't divert, I run straight for the train, and as we advance toward each other I feel a lightness wash over me, the abandoning of this weight, a physical relief that I have made a decision, and also abandoned all decisions. I remember leaving my dorm room in Richmond at some unspecified point in the past, closing the door and slipping something into my jacket pocket, and walking down the hallway with this same feeling, and into the night. My legs move like there's someone else controlling them; peripherally, I notice the station platform stretching alongside the train, but I don't draw the connection. The presence beside me feels closer than ever, racing with me, opening its snarling jaws. My boots beat along the ties, rhythmic and far away, like the soundtrack to an old movie, assembled long after the footage was shot, where in the finished scene the ambient noise is strangely absent, the footsteps recorded on an otherwise empty soundstage, echoing weirdly. And of course the train isn't moving, of course it never has, of course I am running for what I always have been, for a house where no one lives, for the unpeopled end. As I near the platform, my arms leave my sides, I open them as if for embrace.

A gunshot roars out ahead of me from the direction of the train, exploding in the gravel by my left leg. I yelp—or something yelps—and my foot sweeps out from beneath me, but I barely have time to lose my balance or react at all when a colossal force punches me in the chest out of nowhere. I hear the second gunshot as my neck ratchets back, the wind kicked out of me, and your shoe goes flying. I hit the tracks flat on my back in a swept-up plume of gravel. There's a second of stunned immobility before the pain arrives in a long wave, cycloning around a single point in my chest, pushing up beneath the vest, molding instantly around the bullet just above my heart, blood vessels bursting beneath the skin. A moment of darkness passes, a silence, and then I gasp like a man saved from drowning, sucking air into my lungs, body seizing and gulping. The pain is constricting, paralyzing me from the waist up, my arms wide as the muscles clench in anticipation of a blow that has already come.

The sky is a blank white. My left leg twitches spastically, flinching away from the wound it didn't take. My mind is racing, urging me to run, to shield myself from whoever shot me, to keep running toward them, but my body feels pinned down by the piece of smoldering lead in my chest. I keep urging movements to my hand, which seems yards away, just out of range of my influence. I will the sensation along the useless limb, reaching as if for a distant point. Minutely at first, pins and needles begin in the joints of my fingers and gradually spill down my arm, then into the rest of my body, like stutters of electricity lighting up a large, empty space. I carefully rotate my left foot, testing its agency.

Without demonstrably moving, I assert my hands on the gravel to either side of me, readying my arms for a push. I breathe out once, slowly, then in slowly, and then out again. At the same time that I let the breath go, I push off the ground, angling the top of my body to one side to make a smaller target. I simultaneously bend my knees, and slide one leg backward in the gravel to use as an anchor. I'm standing for a second, and then I stumble again, just as a third shot bursts past me, loud enough to buckle me again. I go briefly to the ground and sort of bounce back, deliriously grabbing the shoe from beside the tracks, regaining my center of gravity, trying to orient my eyesight on anything, and finally I take in the figure standing on the edge of the concrete platform some forty feet away, an oversized pistol pointed toward me with both hands: it's you.

I scream "STOP!" into the air and throw up my hands without ever really reaching true balance. I trip again, lurch forward, my vision pitching down and then bobbing up. It could almost be comedy. "Josephine, it's me! Don't! Don't shoot!"

I hear something clatter to the ground, a body after it. My thought—as I go down too, again, balance lost—my fleeting thought, which I lose as soon as I have it, is that your hair looks different from the way I remember it, unaccountably different.

*

I make it the rest of the way to the station proper by turns on my hands and knees, the train looming like a decommissioned missile. Above, as on a pedestal, you're seated on the concrete with your knees pulled to your chest (one foot shoeless and battered, the sock threadbare) and your head buried in your lap, dressed in the same clothes you'd left the third mansion wearing. The pistol lies a foot away. I haven't seen enough to know if they all look this similar.

I climb up onto the platform and lay the mangled sneaker beside you like an offering. It's a different color than when I found it, the material has absorbed so much of my stress. I roll onto my back to sit up. There's an almost perfect hole in the vest where the bullet entered, and my chest aches beneath. I pick out the crumpled little cylinder, still hot, and it skips out of my fingers. I think: *This is fatal.*

You raise your face from between your legs. It's still colored with fear, smudged with dirt. The wound from the kitchen counter has scabbed your cheek. "I didn't realize it was you." You reshape the shoe and gingerly slide your foot back into it, as if it's sustained some injury. I sense a widening gulf of knowledge and information between us, of the time since we separated; with each passing second, the chance that we will ever exchange these experiences decreases. "I didn't realize."

I move closer and wrap my arms around you, knees included, my own legs folded out to the side. It's wrong—given everything that's happened between us, it's completely the wrong gesture, assumes space that hasn't been earned back—but I can't think of what else to do, how else to justify being here. I realize that I have a beard again.

You don't react to them at all, the arms. I don't recognize them either. The empty straps and holsters on my leg, the double-laced black combat boots, all part of the same performance. I open my mouth and almost ask something about pleather, but the thought suddenly seems inconceivably stupid. My gloved hands clasp and unclasp in front of your legs, touching no skin, and then they let go.

I look to the train: the doors are open in every car, static, like it's always been sitting here abandoned, passed in and out of and between like trees in a forest. The sight registers as familiar, the same way the treeline did when I realized I was lost, a déjà vu feeling that I've been here before. This is the platform where we left, where we broke north. This is the train we walked out of.

My body alights with sudden opportunity. I reach into my back pocket for the roll of money I've kept there, that I've transferred from suit to suit. I hold it out without much ceremony—it's a thick roll, slowly uncurling—saying, "Look what I found."

You take it as we stand. Light sifts through the windows of the train and out the open doors like a ruin. "What's this?"

"It's money," I say.

You fan the stack out in your hands. "Are you kidding me?"

I look again. I realize that the bills have inconsistent, erratic borders, each a slightly different rectangle than the rest, and they're a cheap pastel shade of green, the numbers in cartoonish font, like something traded by children. You tear one of the hundreds in half and let the two pieces flutter away.

"It's fake," I say.

"Goddamn."

You throw the stack into the air. It catches the sunlight in predictable ways, dumbly translucent, a prop in someone's roleplay. You turn and enter the train like you're walking into another room. The money settles around my feet or else blows away onto the tracks.

I stare out in the direction I came from. I imagine the terror you must have felt when you shot me down, the sight of another body barreling toward you down the tracks. I take this moment from the platform, from your perspective, looking out. You must have seen me coming from miles away, long before I noticed the train. I see myself advancing while you stood paralyzed on the platform, unsure of whether or not you should run—where was there to go, really, but back the way we'd come, back to the mansions—the fear mounting exponentially, watching until my figure became unfailingly, threateningly clear on the horizon, disguised in uniform. And then, at the critical moment, you'd reached out your hands, and the gun had appeared. You pulled the trigger once, because that's where your fingers were, that's what was in your hands. Nerves dragged the shot amiss. You leveled your arms and fired again. A moment of gut relief, at the sureness of the second shot, and of my fall. And then I rose again, like nothing is supposed to. I nudge the pistol with the toe of my boot. Up close, it's obvious: the make, the model, the grip, all of it is exactly the same, recycled from another region, another time, fired at last, the would-be victim now standing above it, immortal. The gun grates against the concrete. I kick it as hard as I can off the platform. I don't hear it hit the ground.

I follow you onto the train. You're not in the first car, so I walk down the aisle and cross the divider into the second. Here, too, the seats are all empty, the fabric ratty and picked over. I cross through to the third.

When I enter the fourth car and you're not there, I start to panic. I think that you've disappeared again, or, worse, that you were never here in the first place, that I've created the whole scene in some kind of perverse hallucination, the phantom shooter, like Candace or August or Vivian, erased out of my world.

I find you in the sixth car, in an aisle seat halfway down, staring ahead. I see the top of your head first, facing away, contrary to the way we arrived. I look to the right, out the door across from you—it's the same car where we exited. Beyond, the staircase leads down to the parking lot, to the northern road, to the mansions.

You press your knees to the side so I can take the inside seat by the window. The empty gun holster, the narrow sheath in the pants that's meant to hold a knife brush against you as I pass. I sit heavily in the seat. I peel the gloves off and stuff them beside me. I want to ask about Vivian, if you found any trace of her, of your brother, just anything; but if you had, there's no way you would be here, there's no way you would have come back.

You look ahead and swallow once, trembling slightly. I notice the other cuts on your face, above your eyebrow and, under your chin, three short slashes in parallel. Your hair is coming in uneven, the collar separating from the rest of your shirt. Your arms cross in your lap at the wrists. Minute, old white scars etch upward. A lump forces its way up through my chest, into my throat. I turn to the smudged window. I wonder if the fingerprints are mine, how long you've been on this platform, if you were waiting for me, if we could proceed by saying nothing and find a livable pattern in the silence.

"How did you lose your shoe?" This is all I'm able to get out, without looking at you.

"It—"

The interior lights stutter on. I whirl around in my seat as if to find the cause, your answer lost. You look up at the ceiling, eyes shimmering. The car doors slide closed, then open briefly like there's something blocking the gap, and then close again. The collision resounds through the empty car—I can't fully comprehend what's happening around me, what all of this signifies. For a moment after the doors close, there's no motion, the air full of anticipation like a held-in breath. Then, a continuous, monotonous whirring beneath everything is present where it wasn't before. There's a clank, a minute shift backward (my stomach goes forward), and then the train is moving ahead, the breath released. The train is pulling out of the station, back the way it came. The train is moving.

My throat constricts, and my jaw starts to ache with something fighting to get out. My knees shake up and down, uncontrollably. I turn from the window back to you and my mouth sort of falls open in a weak, startled gasp. I crane my head to look behind us, to see if other passengers have appeared. The vest pinches my chest. The car remains empty but for us. The train slowly gathers speed, moving in its constant diagonal line. I think: If I hadn't boarded the train, it would never have moved.

The world would have stayed as it was. To the south, the city waits, at this moment both emptied and populated. Somewhere distant, Vivian runs through the woods from one mansion to the next, or she awakens in her bedroom three states away. Candace stands before a mirror and applies concealer to an old scar. Your mother's night shift ends. A set of parents mourn before an empty coffin. The world dwindles and swells around us—one by one, it grows and reduces in size, while I fight it back toward zero. It had never been catered to us; it had been served to me. I recall our conversation after Casey's death, my silent refusal of any attempt to escape, to put anything to rest, the naked room around us, and I realize what I've been taking from you since before we even met, which seems finally to have reached its absolute: everyone else. I imagine myself stepping forward out of the wallpaper, revealing in my silhouette the background patterns, the shifting, conspiring textures that have always hemmed you in. Immediately around us, the air of the train car becomes thick with possibility, like the way I awoke in the second-floor bedroom in the deep of the night, overflowing with intention. I look over and your face warps, as if through smoke.

On the side of my left leg, pressed against the wall of the train car, I notice a slight weight has materialized, a rigidness. My eyes water. I bite my lip, turning back to the window. I don't make any sound, don't breathe in, because that would make it obvious.

I stand up as carefully as I can and turn toward you. I say something about trying to find the conductor; it's clearly bullshit, but you turn to let me pass. My right knee touches your leg.

I walk down the aisle between seats with almost a limp, as if my leg's been paralyzed or bound in a cast, an old wound returned. I stumble walking in the opposite direction as the train is moving, I'm suddenly not used to more than one thing in motion at once. I put one hand out to balance on the seatback, trying to keep my pace natural.

I slide open the door at the end of the car, emerging outside, the wind at either side. I look through the little window in the door behind me, at your scalp; you haven't moved from the seat. I decide to go another car ahead. I open the door and stride quickly through the next one—not even thinking about my leg now, really, but lost in the momentum of purposeful movement. I open the door at the end, and close it behind me.

I'm standing in the divider between cars. There's a waist-high railing to either side of me. Beneath my feet, the tracks churn by in a blur; beyond the railing, the landscape rolls past, familiar in its shapes. All around me, the train rattles and thunders. The wind buffets my hair.

I undo one latch on the shoulder of the vest, and peel the thing away from my chest, revealing the dark shirt taken from the last mansion plastered flat to my body, into every crevice, white lines of salt wrapping strata of dried sweat. I unbutton it from the top down, the wind insistent. Cold air wraps around my upper half, taking the moisture. When I undo the final button the shirt flies open. Just above my left breast there's an enormous welt, dark red at the top, purple and sickly yellow at the base. The pain is mostly gone, but when I test it with my finger, it returns acutely, localized but intense.

One hand planted on the railing, I reach down my left side and draw the knife from its sheath on my leg. If it's the same knife—the kitchen knife from the mansions, the combat knife from the dead commando or the man in the city, a gun—it doesn't matter. I angle it inward. The train roars, but this is the sound they've always made.

I jam the knife under my ribs as deep as it will go.

It catches on some bony part of me as it enters. The feeling vibrates up into my jaw. I experience a moment strangely absent of pain, as if my mind is calibrating its reaction, and then, I feel like I'm being split in two. As soon as it's in, I pull the knife out, two fingers pressing the skin together around the wound. I drop the knife over the railing into the fleeting world without looking too closely. It goes shooting away into the past.

Before I even register the sight of blood, of anything, I pull one side of the shirt tight across my chest, then double the other half over it. I press the vest as hard as I can into my body with one arm and use the other to re-fasten it at the shoulder, tightening the straps as much as they'll go. I step quickly back into the train and start walking through the car. I hear the door slam behind me. I walk briskly so as not to feel anything moving beneath my clothes; besides the sensation of my upper half gradually lightening, slowly separating and lifting off, I don't detect any change.

I open the door to our car. I take eight steps to the row where you're still sitting. I stand next to you and clear my throat. "Excuse me."

You push your legs to the side, and I shuffle in—the empty sheath grazes your knee again as I go by. I'm keeping my movements short, my body parts close together, warmth on warmth, thinking to myself: *I'm doing so well*, despite the fact that I'm probably as white as a sheet.

I fall into the seat; it probably reads too much like relief, though you don't make any acknowledgment of it. My limbs are shaking slightly, all of them now, but combined with the vibration from the train, it's not really noticeable. Though I have the vest pulled as tight as possible, I feel, once seated, the motion of something down my stomach, toward the places where my body is creased. I've ceased to be able to discern hot or cold.

I turn to look at you. You're staring dead ahead, purposefully not at me, I think, but your jaw is set, pushed forward slightly, and within there I can see a muscle quivering, your front teeth and canines grinding against each other. This minute movement, reflected down your body, into your neck, pulled in and defined in anger, your arms folded and rigid, your thighs tensed. There was another option I'd failed to consider, and that was to simply disappear, to not come back.

I rotate my head to look out the window. The rest of me, I'd rather not unseat. Beneath my layers, the sensation is transforming from the tingling of motion into decisive wetness. I say, my eyes looking out, "That's—" but nothing else. The rest of the sentence sinks into me and disappears.

"I know what you've done," you say.

I flop my head back to face you. It's operating more or less on its own at this point. My gaze falls to your feet, one sneaker still marvelously intact, the other with frayed laces, broken and disintegrating from too much man-handling and sweat. From the corner of my eye, I notice the crotch of my dark pants is much darker, soaked through. I prop up the phrases *You've done, You did* inside my head, but can't make the effort to address them. On my own dusty, filthy boot, I see something glimmering, trickling out in a line.

My vision dips again, and then rises once more. You're in front of me now in the seat with both hands out, blinking furiously, pushing at my chest as hard as you can, giving in to the impulse that enough pressure can stop any bleeding.

My head lolls once more to the window, leaving your face elsewhere. I watch the landscape ebbing by, the same as when we arrived: outside, in opposition, the trees bend inward, while within, a steady pulse beats out.

AFTERWORD
Vandalia, Ohio

I'M ADDING A NEW SECTION TO THE SLEEVE, THE least dangerous and most rebellious thing I can do. As a backdrop to the hum of the tattoo machine, the Beach Boys are playing, one of the early-'70s albums not immediately identifiable as the Beach Boys, without overt Brian. The shop is a converted two-story house on a quiet street off 40, just north of Dayton. The floor is satisfying, creaky wood; the walls are hung with arcana and framed photos of Chad's wife and two daughters.

"Do you ever hear from any of those Richmond kids?" I ask, two hours in. It's a broad question—he's been in this county his entire life—but there's a specific answer I'm looking for.

"Not a whole lot," Chad says, without looking up. "I just see what's online, mostly. A few years back I used to tattoo a whole group of those kids on a pretty steady rotation. But now most of the Richmond punks have either gone off to school somewhere, left town, or, you know, can't afford it anymore."

He tells me about Rats, who I'd met a few times but existed mostly as a figure in the background, one of the repeat-faces, and his girlfriend Kelly, and where they are now—someone's in engineering—but I don't really care about Rats or his girlfriend. I watch the birthmark on my right arm disappear in a wash of blues. I wait for him to finish, to exhaust the list, and then I ask, "What about Allie Moore?"

He juts out his chin. "Punk rock Allie?"

"Yeah—we came in here together my first time. She got some kind of Edward Gorey image on her back?" I remember the image exactly, of course, had helped her select it from an omnibus of Gorey's artwork, chosen not only for its thematic appeal—the subject, a young girl, is faced away from the viewer—but for the complexity of its technique, the lines thin and densely packed. "We were really close for a few years," I say, "and then she just kind of vanished. It's been probably two years since I had any kind of real contact with her."

"Yeah, her. She had a baby," Chad says, nodding. He adjusts his foot on the pedal. "She was one of those *huge* pregnant chicks. You'd see photos of her at punk shows with her belly out to here, standing in the front like *raaaaah!*" The needles leave my skin and he makes a metal gesture with both arms.

"Seriously? Allie? Allie Moore?" It's a moment of almost primal dissociation, in which the world as I think I understand it shifts, takes on a different character. I try to reconcile the disparate, slight pieces of information about her that I've picked up over the last two years with what he's saying, but my mind seems to stutter in the process, like you never really know anyone. A child seems like a trap, a stereotype you fall into, nothing she'd ever plan or allow near her life.

"Yep, pretty sure." His focus is back on the arm.

"I can't even imagine that."

"She's cutting hair now," he says. "I guess her father or grandfather owned a shop, so she's working there."

A vision, hazy around the edges, begins to slide into focus, a picture of her as a working mother, standing behind a salon chair, foiling layers of harshly treated hair, estimating bangs and cutting with a straight blade, the air thick with a nearly visible haze of aerosols and whatever other gently toxic chemicals, her face in stark resolution beneath hot white light. I can't help but think: *This is what happens to people who never get out.*

"She's right around here, too," Chad says, "like two streets over. She's not in Richmond anymore. I'm pretty sure—let me check my phone, I'm terrible with names." He sets down the machine, wipes my arm with a wet paper towel, and peels off his black gloves, heels the trashcan open and throws them out. He goes to the counter. "Punk rock girls with weird hair—man, I know three hundred chicks like that, most of them named Allie."

"We can wait," I say, now desperate, both to retain this image and to shatter it, "I don't want to break your flow or anything."

"No no, I'm curious now too." He picks up his phone and scrolls through it across the room, thumbs moving. My mind, as always, swells with new meanings and associations, disappearances and unexpected returns, a network of lives unfurling, connected at arbitrary points. I pull into the parking lot of a strip mall after dark. The shop is closed, but the fluorescent lights are still on, and there's just one person inside.

"Nope," Chad says from afar, shaking his head. "Sorry, wrong Allie."

Related to no one else, in its isolation, the moment just passes, means nothing.

ACKNOWLEDGMENTS

Thanks to John Bennett "Blackjack" Baren: I didn't know about this nickname until after the fact, and I still don't know if it's real or not.

Thanks to my family: my parents, grandparents, and my brothers Eli, Michael, and Jack.

Thanks to Alyssa Bluhm, Joey Holloway, Jac Jemc, Ben Kopel, Eric Kranz, Graham Nissen, Tyler Pry, Jeanne Thornton, Two Cakes, Ross Wagenhofer, Brandi Wells, and Chad Wells.

Thanks to Two Dollar Radio: Eric, Eliza, Brett, and the rest of the crew.

Excerpts from earlier versions of *Palaces* were first published in *Forklift, OH* and *Everyday Genius*: I'm grateful to the editors of these publications.

—SAJ
April 2013–November 2017, NYC

Two Dollar Radio
Books too loud to Ignore

ALSO AVAILABLE
Here are some other titles you might want to dig into.

THEY CAN'T KILL US UNTIL THEY KILL US ESSAYS BY HANIF ABDURRAQIB

← "Funny, painful, precise, desperate, and loving throughout. Not a day has sounded the same since I read him."
—Greil Marcus, *Village Voice*

IN THESE ESSAYS Abdurraqib uses music and culture as a lens through which to view our world, so that we might better understand ourselves, and in so doing proves himself a bellwether for our times.

SQUARE WAVE NOVEL BY MARK DE SILVA

← "Compelling and horrifying." —*Chicago Tribune*

A GRAND NOVEL OF ideas and compelling crime mystery, about security states past and present, weather modification science, micro-tonal music, and imperial influences.

HOW TO GET INTO THE TWIN PALMS
NOVEL BY KAROLINA WACLAWIAK

← "Reinvents the immigration story." —*New York Times Book Review*

ANYA IS A YOUNG WOMAN living in a Russian neighborhood in L.A., torn between her parents' Polish heritage and trying to assimilate in the U.S. She decides instead to try and assimilate in her Russian community, embodied by the nightclub, the Twin Palms.

MIRA CORPORA NOVEL BY JEFF JACKSON

⇥ *Los Angeles Times* Book Prize Finalist

← "A piercing howl of a book." —*Slate*

A COMING OF AGE story for people who hate coming of age stories, featuring a colony of outcast children, teenage oracles, amusement parks haunted by gibbons, and mysterious cassette tapes.

Thank you for supporting independent culture!
Feel good about yourself.

Books to read

WHITE DIALOGUES STORIES BENNETT SIMS

← "Anyone who admires such pyrotechnics of language will find 21st-century echoes of Edgar Allan Poe in Sims' portraits of paranoia and delusion, with their zodiacal narrowing and the maddening tungsten spin of their narratives."
—*New York Times Book Review*

IN THESE ELEVEN STORIES, Sims moves from slow-burn psychological horror to playful comedy, bringing us into the minds of people who are haunted by their environments, obsessions, and doubts.

FOUND AUDIO NOVEL BY N.J. CAMPBELL

← "[A] mysterious work of metafiction... dizzying, arresting and defiantly bold." —*Chicago Tribune*

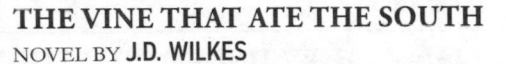

← "This strange little book, full of momentum, intrigue, and weighty ideas to mull over, is a bona fide literary page-turner." —*Publishers Weekly*, "Best Summer Books, 2017"

THE VINE THAT ATE THE SOUTH
NOVEL BY J.D. WILKES

← "Undeniably one of the smartest, most original Southern Gothic novels to come along in years." —NPR

WITH THE ENERGY AND UNIQUE VISION that established him as a celebrated musician, Wilkes here is an accomplished storyteller on a Homeric voyage that strikes at the heart of American mythology.

THE DROP EDGE OF YONDER
NOVEL BY RUDOLPH WURLITZER

← "One of the most interesting voices in American fiction."
—*Rolling Stone*

WURLITZER'S FIRST NOVEL in nearly 25 years is an epic adventure that explores the truth and temptations of the American myth, revealing one of America's most transcendant writers at the top of his form.

Did high school English ruin you? Do you like movies that make you cry? Are you looking for a strong female voice? Zombies? We've got you covered with the Two Dollar Radio Flowchart. By answering a series of questions, find your new favorite book today! ⇢ TWODOLLARRADIO.COM/PAGES/FLOWCHART